A DAY OF RECKONING

CD CLARK

AMAZON KINDLE DIRECT PUBLISHING

ISBN-13: 9798369665404

Cover design by: Joe Plenio
PIXBAY
Printed in the United States of America

MAP OF BAJA CALIFORNIA SUR, MEXICO
~TOURMAPS.COM~

BAJA CALIFORNIA

BAJA COAT OF ARMS
~WIKIMEDIA~

A very special thank you to those who inspired me to write this novel.
I dedicate A Day of Reckoning to those who have
ever suffered at the hands of another

And ne'er a word said she;
But, oh, the things I learned from her
When Sorrow walked with me
            Robert Browning Hamilton~ Along the Road

Lewis C. Henry
Best Quotations for All Occasions
Doubleday & Company
Fourth Printing February 1961
Premier Books, Fawcett World Library

CHAPTER ONE

Crime scene tape bounced and flapped in the cold, gray dawn, but Carla Simpson paid little attention to it. Her gaze was riveted to the blue Toyota Corolla now strapped down on a tow truck's flat bed. She could see clumps of grass hanging from its bumper and under carriage. The flashing yellow strobe from the tow truck lay as flat as the rain-soaked morning. Her skin tingled all over her body and a heaviness she hadn't experienced in many years crushed her soul. Her hands shook, so she grasped the steering wheel. Her eyes followed the long trail of black skid marks on the pavement where they started a few feet before the stop sign and across the intersection then into the field of tall grass. Carla shook her head, her eyes watered. She felt dizzy.

"You were only a mile away from home!" She shouted through the rivulets of water streaming down her windshield. Six hours earlier Carla had spoken to her daughter. Now she was dead.

Ten hours earlier......

"Jerk!" Katie Jensen tossed her cell phone on the kitchen counter. Her green eyes flashed and nostrils flaring, she took in a deep breath then exhaled. "I don't know why I even try to talk to him."

Carla stole a glance at her sister Abbey. Katie smirked, "I know, I know, he's not supposed to be calling." Her shoulders sagged. She looked at her mother. "I just wanted things to work out. I wanted a family." She turned to stare out the tiny kitchen window. A small smile flashed on her pretty face as she watched her two children playing on the porch.

"What did he say?"

She turned to face her mother and aunt. Her jaw muscles tightened. She took in another deep breath and exhaled. "He thinks Marcos isn't his. Anyone can take one look at that boy and see he's a tiny Juan!" She pushed away from the sink and started to fold a pile of shirts heaped up on the couch then tossed them into a laundry basket where they lay in another jumbled heap. "I never had the time to cheat. He's the one who cheated, not me!"

Carla shook her head; she understood the girl's sorrow, and stood up. She walked over to her daughter and put her arms around her. "Don't let him get to you sweetie, he's pulling at straws."

Just then Katie's two sons, Scotty and Marcos came in from playing in the yard and were coated with red Arkansas dirt. Marcos started to throw his arms around Carla's legs, but she stopped him. "Hold on there a second buddy. Look at your clothes! How did you get so dirty?"

Marcos stared up at his grandmother and grinned. His brown eyes twinkled; cheeks flushed from running, and responded in his toughest four-year old voice. "Real men get dirt on them. I'm gonna be a soccer star and Spiderman! Poppy said I could be both!"

Carla laughed then hugged her grandson dirt and all. "Sweetheart, you can be whatever you want, as long as it's for the good; you have my blessing." She kissed his grimy forehead then gave him a gentle swat on the behind. "Get on then Pele."

"Who's Pele?" Scotty asked as he grabbed the remote control, and flopped down on the couch.

"Okay you two, get washed up, supper will be ready soon." Katie corralled Marcos toward the bathroom. "Scotty! Get off that couch!"

He turned around to his mother. He resembled Katie more than his younger brother. He had her thick dirty blond curly hair, large green eyes fringed with thick, dark lashes. Whereas Marcos somewhat resembled his father; blue-black, wavy hair, nose and dimpled cheeks, but his soft brown eyes had a twinkle from an inner light. They were also tall for their ages, a trait they got from Katie and their grandmother. Juan was short, not quite 5'8"and dark brown eyes. This was Juan's argument of as to why he thought she cheated on him. In the seven years Carla had known Juan he was quick to point fingers; lay the blame on someone else instead of owing up to his mistakes.

"Both of you into the tub." Scotty started to protest, but Katie held up a hand. "No dessert or TV if you don't do what I say!"

Abbey Clarke, Carla's older sister stared after her niece. "How about we go outside and smoke?" She stood up and fished out a pack of vanilla flavored cigars from her purse. They stood on the porch watching the sun crest the stand of trees by the kid's playground. Vanilla and cigar aromas drifted into the early evening air. "So," Abbey flicked ashes and watched them fall to the ground. "How many times has he called today?"

Carla couldn't understand why her sister liked the tiny cigars. She tried one a few years back and couldn't handle the taste. "Three that I know of." Carla's voice was low. "Katie said he keeps threatening to take the boys away from her. He's been waiting for her at the school."

Abbey frowned. "Is there not someone there who can be there with her? "

"Oh sure. Other teachers; parents picking up their kids. Most of them know what's going on; they watch out for her." Carla inhaled on her cigarette then flicked ashes. "She shouldn't have to have twenty-four-hour protection and security guards too. "

"He's stalking her." Abbey snuffed out her smoke. "You know that don't you?"

"Of course I do Abbey." Carla scoffed and walked down to the edge of the yard and tossed the cigarette butt into the street. "Speaking of the devil, here he comes." Carla stood by the road, hands on her hips, watching for the vehicle. The unmistakable thump of bass guitar from the vehicle's speakers was heard long before the truck turned onto the street of the older run-down neighborhood. Carla smirked when Juan Pedraza's teal-green Chevy Blazer turned the corner and slowed to a crawl. Both Carla and Juan stared at each other, neither one giving up as he pulled into the driveway.

"Where's Katie?"

Carla's stare never wavered; all she could think of was wanting to pound the living daylights out of her daughter's former live-in boyfriend.

When Katie found out Juan slept with his ex-wife, she made him leave. At first Carla recommended that Katie try and work things out. Sure, it would be hard. She had told her daughter. But Juan was a good father; he doted a lot of attention on his sons. Katie told her mother his excuse for cheating because she was withdrawn after having their youngest son. Her doctor told her it was postpartum commonly known as "Baby Blues".

When Katie found out about the affair, Juan told her he was feeling neglected and shouldn't have gone to another woman for comfort. He'd made a mistake. She felt sorry for Juan sometimes because he had such a hard up bringing. Forgiving him of sleeping around was hard to do, but eventually she let him come back.

As time went on however, Carla noticed he started controlling what Katie did. It didn't matter what it was; whether going to the movies or buying clothes for the kids. He called and texted her often to keep track of her. When Katie asked Juan why he needed to keep track of her comings and goings, he rose up as if to strike her, grabbed her by the front of her shirt, and told her if she ever questioned him again, he'd have an answer for her. He wanted her paycheck the moment she got it, that usually meant he was at her workplace waiting on payday.

Then one day he shoved her into the bedroom door frame. She explained to her mother she fell and hit her nose on the framework of a door which gave her a black eye. Carla had her doubts, but didn't say anything.

A week later, Katie was at her mother's house when Juan came over and told her to get back home. If she didn't, he would find another woman to take care of his needs. She told him to go ahead and in front of Carla he tried to hit Katie. It was then Carla threatened to call the police. Two days later, he slapped Katie in front of the boys. Carla hoped that it would stop when Katie finally filed a restraining order and moved in with her. Being the victim of domestic abuse herself, Carla knew the signs, and his actions spoke volumes.

Over the week since the incident, Carla surmised Juan was a monster, and since he was in her driveway, she wanted him to understand she meant business when it came to hurting Katie or her grandsons.

Juan parked the blazer next to Abbey's F-150, close enough that if he got out, the door would hit the side panel of her truck. "You better not even think about opening that door, pendjo." Abbey stepped down from the porch, never taking her eyes off of him.

"Poppy!" Abbey whipped around and saw Marcos standing in the doorway. He turned his freshly scrubbed face up to her. "I poppy comin' in?"

"No buddy, Poppy has to leave." She scooped him up in her arms.

Carla took another step toward the Blazer. "She doesn't want to see you Juan, you need to go."

"I came to see my kids."

Carla never took her eyes off of Juan. "Go. If you don't, I'm calling the police again. There is a restraining order against you Juan." She stood with her arms crossed over her chest and moved closer to his vehicle.

Juan remained motionless for a moment longer. His eyes glittered with cold hate.

She'd had enough. "You wanna mess with me?" She hissed through clenched teeth. "Try it and see if I'm kidding around Juan. I'll make sure you never set foot on my property again if you try to pull something stupid, comprende?" It was too late to worry about the child hearing the conversation. Carla was sure Marcos had heard worse. "Now, leave."

Then, he smirked. "Okay, C-Madre'. You tell Katie I want to see the boys."

The women kept their posts, Marcos still in Abbey's arms. "I want Poppy." He pulled away from Abbey in an attempt to break his great-aunt's grasp. "I want down." Abbey turned and set the boy on the weathered wooden planks of the porch. "Whew, never knew a four-year old could be that heavy." She massaged her arms and made a grimacing face at her nephew.

"Go inside Marcos." Carla continued to stare at Juan, her eyes bright and hard, her heart trip hammering. All she could think of was kicking him in the groin with her size ten foot.

"Why?" He asked as he watched Carla take another step toward the Blazer.

"Inside little man, now." Carla didn't take her eyes off of Juan when she growled at her grandson. He began crying and protesting he wanted to see his father.

Carla took a step toward the Chevy. "You should have left ten seconds ago." She stooped down and picked up a baseball bat lying in the grass next to her feet.

Juan started the vehicle when he saw Carla heading toward him with the bat over her shoulder.

"What's wrong with you crazy old lady?!" He sent a shower of gravel into the yard, pelting Carla.

When he sped passed her, Carla heard a stream of words she figured to be

Spanish profanity. "I know what you said!"

She turned and stormed up to the house.

Abbey ran up to her sister. "It's gone on long enough Carla, you said there's a restraining order against him?"

"Yes, but he's gone now. I don't think he'll be coming back over here."

"Yeah, maybe for a couple of days, then he'll be calling or pulling up in the drive again. I think you should call the cops, let them know he's harassing Katie."

"I know, I know, but I don't think I should be the one to call them. Katie has to do it." Hands shaking, Carla pulled out her cigarettes and lit one. The first puff calmed her down enough she started laughing.

"What's so funny?" Abbey tilted her head at her sister.

"Did you see the look on his face when I picked up that bat?"

Abbey chuckled, "No, but I saw it when you slung the bat over your shoulder and started toward his Blazer!" She widened her eyes and arched her eyebrows and made an "o" shape with her mouth. She grew serious, and gave Carla a hug. "Katie should talk to the police. Please talk to her."

"I will Abbs. She'll think I'm trying to tell her what to do."

Abbey placed her hands on her younger sister's shoulders and stared into her blue eyes. "You're doing it for love."

After Abbey left Carla went inside to talk to Katie, but when she found her daughter snuggled next to Marcos she turned from the room and decided to take a shower. It would help relieve some of the tension of the day. With her hair covered in shampoo Carla heard Katie open the door to the bathroom "I'm leaving now mom, both boys are out for the night."

She quickly rinsed off her face and poked her head around the curtain. "Katie, be careful."

Katie grinned at her mother "I'll be all right mom. Paul is a perfect gentleman."

Carla stuck her face under the shower to rinse off the shampoo now running into her eyes. "Hand me a towel please."

She dried her face and handed it back to Katie. "That's not what I meant. Juan was here today; you were bathing the boys."

Katie let out a groan. "What did he want this time?"

Carla rinsed off the rest of the shampoo and shut off the water. "See Marcos and Scotty. I told him no. He's not supposed to be over here, you have the restraining order against him. I think it might be a good idea for you to call the police and at least let them know he was over here."

"I will tomorrow. I've got to meet Paul in Eureka Springs in an hour."

"You promise to call?" She pulled back the curtain again and stuck her hand out for the towel Katie was still holding.

"Yes, I promise mom. Gotta go, love you."

"Have fun, tell Paul I said hello and don't be such a gentleman."

"Mom!" Katie whispered, and then laughed as she closed the door.

CHAPTER TWO

"*M*y *dearest children." Carla wrote. "This is the fifteenth notebook of my journal I have been keeping for you. I hope someday you will get to read them.*" She shifted in her chair, scooting it closer to her desk. It was not getting easier as Abbey said it would. She hoped that with each entry into the journal the pain would ease; the throat swelling and the ever-faithful knotted stomach would stop. "*Lawrence and Charli, you are young adults now. How I wish I could have attended your high school graduation! I am so very proud of you two, my precious babies.*

Roger, my youngest, you will go through the same thing next year! So hard to believe you are a teenager! It is my greatest wish to see your beautiful faces, smother you in fifteen years of stored kisses and hugs."

Carla took a deep, shuddering breath, and adjusted the clip holding her long auburn hair in a bun at the base of her neck. She pulled back from the desk, deciding she would check on her grandchildren. She stood in the doorway, watching them sleep. Only Scotty's mop of dirty blonde hair could be seen sticking out from under his blanket. Marcos had his bed covers shoved against the wall. He lay on his back, his tiny arms thrown back over his head and his short legs spread apart, one of them hanging over the edge of the mattress. Scotty's soft snoring made her feel warm and happy.

Her house shoe covered feet whispered across the carpet as she gently kissed Marcos on his forehead. Although, it would do no good, she pulled the cover back over him. He's just like his mother, Carla smiled down at the child; remembering when Katie was his age, her hair, then, blond-white, and hard to control curls. Now twenty-five, Katie had thick, honey-colored locks she kept up in a pony tail most of the time. A child's sticky fingers spelled disaster if they became entangled in her hair. Carla sighed, smiling at the memories.

Carla was thankful she lived on the outskirts of town. It was quiet and the streets were tree lined with White Oaks that were over a hundred years old. Many of her neighbors had ancestors that moved to Green Valley in the late 1800s. She got along with those who lived by her and it wasn't uncommon to have barbeques with them in the summer months.

She could hear the hum of the refrigerator and the tic-tic-ticking of the water heater. They were familiar, comforting sounds. She went into the kitchen; the floorboards creaked as she walked to the coffee pot and poured a cup of lukewarm coffee. It was another procrastinating tactic to keep from writing in the journal. Had it really been fifteen years since she last saw her other children?

The twins were four then, and Roger three. She remembered the day she came home from work to find Katie sitting on the porch step trying to tell her mother between racking sobs how her stepfather took her brothers and sister; his truck loaded down with trash bags and boxes full of their belongings. He left Katie without even unlocking the door so she could go inside. By the end of the day Carla found out he also emptied the bank account and filed for full custody of their three children claiming Carla was unstable and unfit as a mother.

Hugh never said a word that he was unhappy, he just badgered her and Katie about their weight. He was quick to criticize them about many things; housekeeping, the laundry, the groceries; anything to verbally bring her or Katie down. In time she felt he got a lot of enjoyment belittling them because he didn't hesitate to say things around other people. It got to where Katie's grades were failing. She kept to herself and when Carla went to talk to the school counselor about her daughter, she realized Hugh was the one making Katie fall into depression. She decided that as a family they would start going on walks and eating better. They both lost weight but it did not seem to satisfy her husband.

At one time Carla loved her life with Hugh. He was a few inches taller than her and his dark brown eyes and dark brown hair that fell over his forehead drew her to him. He had been so nice and sweet, full of flirtatious words and made her feel special. They were a happy family; she did everything she could to make the home a cheerful one, yet when their youngest child, Roger, came along that's when the marriage went downhill.

Abbey told her to bide her time, it would all fall on his head one day. It might take a long time she cautioned her distraught sister over the phone. Abbey assured Carla that when it happened, she would have the kids looking for her. Abbey advised her move to Green Valley and live with her for the time being and to start a journal; it was good therapy. "Better to write down those feelings instead of keeping them bottled up inside so they end up rotting your soul." Carla did as she suggested. At first, the words were bitter; harsh thoughts poured themselves onto the pages as tears smeared the ink.

Years later, it wasn't getting any easier. Her hopes of ever seeing her children hadn't faded, but she was tired of writing; tired of waiting. She stepped outside and as she started to sit in a lawn chair, it fell apart with a loud clattering as parts of the aluminum framework hit the porch floor. Carla winced, and stepped back inside to listen in case one of the kids woke up from the crash. After a few minutes she was satisfied they were still sleeping. She left the door cracked so she could hear if one of the boys woke up then lit a cigarette, watching the smoke curl from the end and drifting away in the warm southern breeze. Tired of waiting, tired of hoping. Her only saving grace were her grandchildren and her daughter.

Inside, she heard the living room clock strike one. She wasn't concerned about Katie being out so late, she was twenty-five after all. It was the phone call her daughter made a half hour earlier that had red flag warnings. Coming home from her date, she called her mother to let her know she was going to stop by Juan's sister Demi, who called Katie as she was on her way to her date. Juan left some money for the boys.

"At this time of the night?" Carla had asked. "That can't wait until tomorrow? Why couldn't he have done that earlier when he was here?" Carla couldn't suppress a smile when Katie said Juan was a little intimidated by her mother and aunt. Katie promised she would only be there long enough to get the money and then she would come home.

At three o'clock, Carla woke up, her head resting on top of her arms which had fallen asleep. Her back sore from being bent over in her chair. The journal still lay open, untouched. She pushed away from the desk and decided to go to bed. Shaking her arms to get the pins and needles sensation to ebb, she peeked into Katie's room. Her bed was untouched, her room unoccupied. She closed the door, careful not to let the door knob click too loud. Scotty was a light sleeper could sometimes wake at the slightest sound. Too late; she heard the rustle of bed covers and a tiny voice call for momma. Carla went into the boy's room, careful not to step on the toys scattered about. She knelt down by her grandson's bed, not an easy feat for a woman of her size. "Go back to sleep, little man." She whispered, stroking Scotty's hair.

"Where's mommy?" Scotty asked his voice sleepy and muffled by his pillow.

"She's with Paul, honey." Carla made him slide over so she could crawl in beside him. She hated lying to the child but she felt it was for the better. All it would do she reasoned was keep the boy awake if the truth were told.

Katie's new "man friend" Paul Ames, called earlier in the evening wanting to take her to a late dinner in Eureka Springs. Carla was glad her daughter found someone new. When she first met Juan, he was lean and athletic, but had gained a lot of weight in the seven years he and Katie were together. He thought he was a player, a stud. She hated the huge baggy jeans with the pockets coming to the back of the knees, underwear hanging out and the white "wife-beater" undershirts Juan preferred to wear so his tattoos were visible. She wondered how anyone who wore those awful baggy jeans could even walk. She especially hated his gold plated; diamond studded "grille". She thought he could have spent what it cost on that to buy his children new clothes.

But Paul was tall, well built, well mannered, and well dressed. Scotty and Marcos liked being with him, they would come in from spending the day with him and Katie, full of the wonderful things they experienced, whether it was kite flying, looking for arrowheads, or eating at Taco Bell. Katie told her it made Juan mad if they spoke about Paul, but Carla loved it.

"We'll snuggle bug and wait for her, ok?" She whispered and wrapped her arms around his small body. "When you get up, mommy will make you pancakes for breakfast, but we need to go to sleep." He wanted her to rub his back, a tactic she used on him and his brother to get them to fall asleep. It had worked for Katie and her siblings as well. Within minutes both of them were sound asleep.

Carla slipped quietly out of the twin bed, intent on heading to her own. She noticed the digital read out of the alarm clock on her nightstand. Seven o'clock. She sat down on the edge of her bed, debating to check in on Katie, and whether or not to change from sweat pants and tee shirt to a night gown. She flopped onto the bed and climbed under the covers. She lay there, listening to the sounds of the house and nineteen minutes later, she threw the covers back and climbed out. Something wasn't right. Deep down inside, she had a bad feeling. She walked to Katie's room and her heart sank when she saw the bed still made and no sign that her daughter had been there.

CHAPTER THREE

An hour later, Carla took Scotty and Marcos to her sister's house. She held fast to her emotions, not wanting the boys to see her red swollen eyes because her daughter, their mother, was found by a man walking his dog.

When she answered the door and saw Police Chief Al Bristol, standing on her front porch, she knew Katie was dead. She barely heard Bristol tell her how the dog walker had seen the little vehicle in the tall grass and upon closer inspection he noticed how the person in the car was slumped over the steering wheel; he decided to check and see if everything was okay before moving on.

Her thoughts were like scrambling eggs, she had to find a way to tell Scotty and Marcos their mother was gone and never coming back.

Carla wanted to snatch the Police Chief by the neck and choke him, beat his chest and rip out his eyes right there on the doorstep. How dare he tell her to come to the morgue to identify her daughter's body!

Carla's grip on the steering wheel whitened her knuckles, her back rigid, and blinking far more than necessary to hold back her tears. She didn't want to drive by the crime scene, but it was the only way to the highway. She would have to drive by and see where Katie died. She knew as sure as the rain fell from clouds in the sky, her daughter fell victim to a violent, senseless death.

"Ma'am?" Carla swiveled her head to face a police officer. Judging from the cop's reaction to her face she knew her mascara was not as waterproof as it claimed. With a shaking hand she grasped for a tissue and wiped the large black smudges under her eyes. She rolled the window down, only realizing then she was stopped in the road. "I'm-" she groped for another tissue. "I'm the mother of the woman who was found here this morning." Her words felt thick and sticky on her tongue.

"I'm sorry for your loss, but I'm gonna have to ask you to move along. I hate to be this way-"

"No, no." She waved at him then blew her nose, stuffing the tissue in her jacket pocket.

"I'm just trying to make some sense of it is all, and I can't. I didn't mean to hold up traffic."

"It was blocked off, until a few minutes ago, that's how I came up on you, removing the roadblocks."

Carla started to roll up the window when the officer spoke, his voice sympathetic. "If it's any consolation, I lost my son three years ago to a senseless act; he was in the wrong place at the wrong time. I understand how you feel." He pulled out a card from under his rain coat. She took the card, but was unable to see it through the tears forming fresh in her eyes, and stuck it in the change tray. "Call these folks, they can help."

"Thank you." She croaked and gave the officer a weak smile before rolling up the window then drove to the county morgue.

Carla stood at the window waiting for the attendant to bring in Katie. She prayed it was a mistake; it was someone else's car at the old golf driving range. Many thoughts raced through her mind; how was she going to pay for a funeral? How would she tell her grandsons? Why didn't she make Katie call the police when she spoke to her the previous night? It wasn't supposed to happen this way! Carla rubbed her eyes to stop the tears then shook her head and took a deep breath. *Okay, I have to keep my wits.*

She rubbed her hands over her arms, forcing some kind of sensation to break the numbing cocoon she occupied.

The door to the viewing room opened and the attendant came in pulling a sheet covered gurney. Carefully, he positioned it to give her a clear view of the body. He pulled the cover back from the face. She saw the tiny bullet hole in her daughter's forehead; her skin pale, and waxy. Carla felt her legs turn to wet noodles, then the world went black.

◆ ◆ ◆

She opened her eyes to find herself staring at the ceiling; somewhere she heard a soft beeping. There were a sea of faces looking over her. Their mouths were moving, but she couldn't understand them. She felt herself being lifted and placed in a chair.

"Mrs. Simpson? Are you alright? Mrs. Simpson?"

She ran her hands over her head, her hair was coming out of the bun, without even thinking, she took it down and it nearly touched the floor. I need a haircut.

"Mrs. Simpson?" Chief Bristol was squatted by her chair holding a cup of coffee. "I took the liberty of adding cream and sugar."

Her hands shook, over and over she only thought of Katie, the night before, standing at the kitchen sink, happy and smiling, talking about having dinner with Paul.

Carla picked up the Styrofoam cup and managed to get it to her lips without spilling the hot contents into her lap.

"I know this is a hard time for you Mrs. Simpson, but I need to ask a few questions." He fished out a notepad and pen. "When was the last time you talked with your daughter?"

"Uh- around twelve-thirty this morning." She took another sip. "She had been on a date with Paul, her-" She caught herself, she couldn't bring herself to say "man friend", that was their private joke. "Her, uh- friend." She took a deep breath; *I need a cigarette.* "He was taking her to Eureka Springs for dinner. She called me around twelve-thirty to say she was going to see Juan's sister because he had money for her. I told her not to."

"Who is Paul?"

"Paul Ames, he works at the school as a teacher. That's how they met. This is his first year as a Pre School teacher. Katie was supposed to go for her certificate next fall. He was helping her with the exam."

Chief Bristol scribbled down the information. "You said she went to see Juan? Who is he?"

"Juan Pedraza, her ex-boyfriend. They have two children together. He tried to hit her in front of the boys, so Katie filed a restraining order against him last week."

"If she had a restraining order, why did she go to see Juan? Was he supposed to be at the sister's home?"

"He called and said he wanted to give her some money for the children. As to why he's at his sister's place, I only know that's where he's staying now. It was my understanding he wasn't going to be there. He came over earlier yesterday, trying to stir up sh-, uh trouble."

Chief Bristol stared at her for a few seconds.

"I know, I know." She waved a hand. "I should have called right then, but he didn't stick around when I told him I would if he didn't leave." She sipped the coffee and tried not to make a face, far too much sugar for her taste. "I know in my heart it's him, he did it, he killed my baby girl!" She started crying, huge sobs shook her body. "He's an illegal alien, you know that? So is most of his family."

"As of now, Mrs. Simpson, all we can get him on is violating the restraining order. Until everything has been processed, we won't know what we have. Where are the boys now?"

"At my sister's." On shaky legs Carla stood up. "I need to call her and make sure everything is alright." She searched for a phone in the bland, desolate room.

"You can go into the coroner's office and use his."

Carla followed Chief Bristol, her head still in a fuzzy wrap. He started to close the door so she could talk in private. "We'll get whoever did this Mrs. Simpson; I'll let you know if we have any news the second I know it. I promise."

Carla thanked him then picked up the receiver and punched in her sister's phone number.

Carla and Abbey stood outside the funeral home watching Scotty and Marcos play with a couple of children they knew from school whose parents had been friends with Katie. Paul stood next to them, his hands shoved into his pants pockets, his face vacant, and his eyes bloodshot. "I'll help you as much as you need Carla. Paul spoke, his voice cracked. "I love those boys, I loved Katie." A lone tear slowly made its way down his cheek. "I was even thinking about asking her to marry me. I knew she was the one. It took some time to find her, but Katie was my soul mate, we laughed at everything. She probably wouldn't have said yes just yet, but I would have waited. I wanted it to be right." He turned his face to the sky, and took in a deep breath.

Juan pulled into the entrance of the funeral home and parked. In a different vehicle, he was the passenger so when he rolled down the window Carla could see him looking into the side view mirror watching the boys run in the grass.

"I don't believe this." Carla said.

Both Abbey and Paul's jaw dropped open. The vehicle sat there for a couple of minutes, Carla hoped Scotty and Marcos wouldn't notice their father parked in the driveway. Juan smiled slowly at the trio; then she heard the engine of the Chevy Silverado growl. It backed out of the funeral home's drive and slowly crawled toward their direction. With the window still rolled down he blew a kiss to Carla and flipped off Paul. The unknown driver made the tires squawk as he cruised by them. When he got to the intersection, he did it again as he turned onto the highway.

CHAPTER FOUR

"*O*nce again, I turn to my journal. I'll die first before I stop writing now. It's been a year since Katie died. Scotty and Marcos don't ask me about their mommy as much as they used to. Sometimes at night, one of them may wake up wanting her. I tried to tell them that she's in heaven watching over them and that whenever they need her, all they have to do is close their eyes and think about her. There was one incident that absolutely tore me into pieces with Scotty. He told me he hated God. It was the first night without their mother. He wanted to know why God was mean. I had to think of something so I told him sometimes God needs extra special help in Heaven. He only wants those who can do the best job and solve the problem to be there with Him. God needed her help and one day they would get to see her again, but Scotty started crying again, wanting his mother.*

I let both of the boys sleep in my bed; I can't stand to sleep in this house knowing Katie will never come walking through the door.

Slowly, they are moving on, but here I am, stuck in grievance for the rest of my life.

WHERE IS MY DAY OF RECKONING?

My dearest children, now more than ever I wish to see you, just to make sure you are okay. As bad as this sounds, I hope you heard about your sister, Katie. Her story has been featured twice on a show that catches bad people.

I've told Marcos and Scotty about you three. They really don't understand what happened but they would like to meet you some day. Scotty will be turning six next month in July; he is excited about going to the "Big School", in September. He wants to play soccer, he's pretty good too so I've learned how the game is played so I can help him.

I told you about their father, Juan. I still think he killed her. The forensics evidence is stuck in limbo, and Juan is still a snake. I don't even think the police are looking for him because I see him everywhere. I think he's stalking us. He parks down the street from our home, at my sister's house, and sometimes on school property. I've talked to the police, they come, but he disappears before they get here. It's like someone gives him the heads up. Although I was given custody of Marcos and Scotty, Juan taunts me, trying to push buttons just to see what I'll do; he still finds ways to show up in our lives. I guess it wasn't important enough for him to show up for the hearing, but that's what I wanted anyway. A small victory for me. I wonder what your father would think of that."

Carla slowly closed the journal and checked her watch. She still had about three hours before going over to Abbey's for dinner. Abbey made Lasagna and Carla made homemade bread sticks and a salad. Made the night before, the salad consisted of Romaine lettuce, red cabbage, shaved carrots, cucumber and the little tomatoes the boys loved to pop in their mouths. In separate containers were dried cranberries, chunks of pecans and garlic flavored croutons, crushed bacon pieces as salad toppings.

She pulled out the bowl of refrigerator dough and let it set while preparing the cookie sheets. Next, she rolled out the bread dough, creating long threads then twisted two of them together, cutting them into six-inch lengths. Soon the house began emitting an aroma of home baked bread.

She was preparing a garlic butter spread when her cell phone rang.

"Carla!" Abbey was breathless. "Turn on the TV!"

"What's up?" She went to the cabinet above the oven and pulled out the remote for the small TV sitting at the end of the island in the kitchen. A television crew was at the sawmill where Juan and

several members of his family worked. There was at least a dozen or more Hispanic men outside the mill's main building lining up to get into vans provided by the State Police. "I don't see Juan."

"I didn't see him either, but I just turned it on. I heard some people talking about several raids on businesses around the area. They are calling it the biggest one so far!"

Carla couldn't help but smile. "Finally! I wonder what they will do with Juan?"

"I suppose I can do some snooping around. Surely, they would have to detain him because he's a suspect in Katie's murder." Carla could hear Abbey shuffling papers. "What time are you coming over?"

"What time are you getting home? I'm thinking I may stop and pick up some champagne to celebrate."

"Sounds good to me. Probably around five, I've got to get the month end reports turned in and still have a pile to go through."

"Okay, five it is. I've got breadsticks baking and boy they smell delicious!"

"Oooh, yummy! I'll see you then!"

Carla hung up the phone. It was too good to be true she thought. She felt bad for Juan's family members; most of them were good people, but they never offered any assistance. And not a single member of Juan's family came to Katie's funeral.

Katie had become good friends with some of the women in Juan's family; they taught her Spanish and how to cook Mexican food the right way.

When there was a get together it was always festive, children chasing each other or playing games, people smiling and laughing. Soft lighting from hanging paper lanterns fell on the dancers while a three-piece Mariachi band played lively Latino tunes. The men usually had a bonfire away from the activity, standing around it drinking and talking until they got enough nerve to grab someone to dance.

Most of them were hard workers, working long hours so they could save up and send money home to loved ones left behind. But she felt no remorse, they could blame Juan for it. They took his side; claiming Juan was a good man and would never harm her daughter.

Piled to one side of Carla were stacks of composition books. She had them arranged from the day she started writing in them, to the current one. There were so many! Then she realized that they had taken up a whole drawer, and decided they needed a place of their own. The day before, she took the boys with her to Wal-Mart to get groceries and spotted the perfect container in the house wares department. It was a simple royal blue suitcase with a gold metal band and a combination lock. Marcos asked her when she placed it in the shopping cart what it was for and she told him it was to hold something very special.

She sat on the floor next to the books, deciding if she should put them in the oldest first or the newest. She went with the oldest, and picked it up and opened it.

"At first, I thought about writing to each one of you individually, you deserve to know what happened. I have no doubt your father has fed you with all sorts of lies, but I can't do nothing but tell you my side.

I miss you Lawrence, Charli, and Roger so much!

Three months have gone by since the last time I saw you and it feels like three years. My heart and soul cry out for you kids every day. I mask the hurt, the pain gnaws away at me, but I dry my tears and put on a smile. Your aunt Abbey told me this would be the best way to keep you in my heart and a good way for me to face what has happened. I don't know why your father took you away. My guess would be that woman friend. Charli, a woman knows when something is wrong with the relationship. I knew he was acting strange, but to accuse me of being unstable while he is having sex with another woman then going behind my back and wiping out the checking account leaving me without a dime is just down right sick!

What I am about to tell and what you will read eventually, is how your father and I met, how you kids came into our lives and how we ended up in Louisiana, what lead up to the divorce, what happened through the divorce and courtroom. Why your father and I were constantly in court.

KNOW THIS, EVERYTHING, and I mean everything I write is as honest and raw as it will get. It will be up to you my darlings, my blood and flesh, my life; it will be up to you to decide what you make of it. My hands cramp up from time to time and so my penmanship may lag somewhat. I don't know how many of these little books I will fill up, I suppose when I feel the time to quit is how many there will be.

I have so much to tell you three. As of this writing, I am moving back to Green Valley where your aunt and Grandma Jensen live because your grandma is very ill. I feel guilty for moving out of the state, but what am I to do? I have no reliable transportation; jobs are scarce around here and I have to drive some distance in order to get decent work. I had to fight for what money I could get. Yes, I lost my job at the diner. They were closing it down since the new highway took the traffic away from town.

Katie, has a new puppy. I got it for her so she would have someone to play with. She misses her brothers and sister very much! I hope one day you will be able to see each other again. She still has nightmares and cries out in her sleep. I am hoping the pup will take her mind off of what is going on and put that beautiful smile back on her face. *We named the puppy Hope, because that is all we have left. I am told that as long as a person has hope, you can survive anything. I have one other thing close to my heart and that is your love. I strive to keep faith that one day we will get to be together, and I can hold you children close to me again.*

Katie keeps a lot of what happened bottled up and reflects back on the fun times with you three. She puts up a strong front to make me feel better, but I know she hurts as much as I do. Christmas is coming soon, less than a month away. When we get settled in Green Valley, I plan to take your grandma and Katie to visit your uncle Doug who lives in Branson, Missouri. You will have to visit that town someday, it has grown tremendously through the years and from what he tells me, it doesn't look like it's going to stop anytime soon.

I came across a picture of you, Lawrence, sitting in your high chair next your sister at your first birthday. You had chocolate cake smeared everywhere, your face, your high chair, and the floor. It made me cry because I have missed out on so much already!"

Carla's eyes welled up, fifteen years later, she still felt hollow and sad. Now that Katie was gone too, she didn't think she would ever be happy. She had her grandsons, they kept her going, kept her mind off of her daughter. She pulled another one at random and opened it.

"Your grandma Jensen had to spend some quality time in the hospital to get rid of a bout of pneumonia. She gets to have home health care for a while, until her doctor thinks she is ok. Every Sunday (for now) we are getting together once a month for supper at her house. You kids would have a field day with all the food! Everyone brings one or two dishes and spends time visiting, and eating! I think you all would like Doug's son Wayne. He is about your age Charli and Lawrence. Matthew and Teri's children are a few years younger, but they don't come around often. I'm glad to see them when they do. The girls are very well behaved and mannered. They always want to bake something, cookies most of the time and we have fun doing it."

She gently placed the journal in the box and pulled the next one off the pile.

"I'm guessing you are at school while I write this. Roger, I hope you are having fun in kindergarten and meeting new friends. It is very important to make good grades and go to college. I've set a little money aside for you children because I don't have an address to send it to. Your father had visitations cut. Letters were sent

back with "Return to Sender" stamped in red ink on the front. I know he gave me a false address. I've tried calling but, his phone number was changed and unlisted, I can't even talk to you kids!

I wanted to at least be there with pen and paper, what led to this long separation from my dear children. You have the right to know. Your dad was found in contempt of court when he tapped a phone conversation between us. He kept suggesting I seek help, hoping to get me mad enough to say something. And I did. I let him have it. I told him he had better watch his back because one day it's gonna get bitten. It won't be just a nibble I told him; it'll be a big ol' chunk torn from the bone. Well, he took it to his lawyer who took it to the judge and the judge found Hugh, your father in contempt of court for not telling me about taping our conversation.

I wish that could have been enough for the judge to see that your father was a snake. Then I found out about his newborn daughter, from a friend of mine. Born by my count six months after we divorced. Do you remember Tina? She had seen Hugh a few months after I left. In the car was Stacey, and her daughter plus a newborn baby. He was showing off the baby; I'm sure he knows Tina would call me and tell me about it. Very obvious he was having an affair with that woman."

Abbey called Carla one afternoon a few days after the raid. "I have some news. Juan wasn't in among the people at the sawmill. But I talked to someone who knows the owner. She said he told her Juan quit the day before and said he was going back to Mexico."

"That's wonderful news!"

There was a soft beep on the phone. "Abbey, let me call you back, someone else is trying to call." She pressed the talk button. "Hello?"

"Mrs. Simpson? This is Chief Bristol. We have evidence Juan Pedraza killed your daughter."

Carla pulled out a chair from the kitchen table and sank down. "Talk about impeccable timing. I just found out he's not in town anymore."

"Mrs. Simpson, that may be possible, but I'm not going to make any assumptions right now. I do want to assure you we are looking everywhere for him. I'd say he's not gone too far. If he loves his kids as much as you say he does;

chances are he'll be back."

"If he does, he'll wish he hadn't."

"If he shows up, call me. You don't need to do anything else. Or try to for that matter."

CHAPTER FIVE

"*I can't believe it's been two years since Katie died. My life is surrounded by my grandsons. They are growing so fast! Scotty is in second grade and Marcos is in first. They are good students and have lots of friends. Your sister's friend Paul was coming over and playing soccer with the boys now and then. He missed them and Scotty and Marcos missed him too. I thought it would help them in healing and it did. He's been there for every game they've played whether it's been at home or away. He and I were taking turns on driving to the away games. Sadly though, he has taken a position in another state and will be moving in a couple of months. The boys understand and I'm glad he was able to be a positive influence in their lives.*

I had hoped you would have tried to contact me by now, but I'm sure your lives are very busy. I am always thinking of you Charli, Roger, and Lawrence, never think for a moment I don't! I've come to a point in my life that the journals will soon stop. My life is so busy with Scotty and Marcos; I find I have barely a minute to myself!

I finally have a great job where Abbey works doing secretarial duties. I've set money aside to put a down payment on a newer car. This old rattle trap I have only works when it wants to. If I didn't know a little auto mechanics, I would probably be walking everywhere!"

Carla closed the notebook, noticing the date she started logging in it. Two and a half years ago. There were maybe a dozen pages left in it. She decided this was the last one, time to move on only because her grandsons were making her. She sighed and glanced at her watch. She had just enough time to change from her work clothes and drive over to Abbey's house. Tonight, was a big game for both boys whose team was in the running for the championship of their division, and fortunately a home game.

Carla and Abbey decided to take the boys out for pizza before the game, but for now she needed to get on the ball and go pick up the children. She changed into a pair of jeans that two years ago she would never have thought of even sticking a leg into. After Katie's death, Carla rarely ate for so long she lost almost seventy pounds before Abbey finally made her go to the support group the officer recommended.

Men looked at her now, and she enjoyed going shopping for clothes, she even cut her hair short for a mini makeover. It was hard for her to cut it at first, but she wanted to. She needed to do this for herself and more than anything; she wanted a fresh start. She told her hairdresser to make sure it went to Locks of Love foundation who used the hair from donors to make wigs for people going through chemotherapy.

Carla found she felt understood and comforted by being around others who went through losing a loved one in a senseless crime. There was even someone at the group session who lit a small spark inside. It was the officer who gave her the card on the day her daughter died. He was courteous, sympathetic, and had the greenest eyes she'd ever seen. They held compassion and at times, she could see the hurt he suffered in them too.

Neither one wanted a serious relationship just yet, but she felt something for him as time went by. They had a couple of dates, lunches in the park, very casual and fun. She liked the fact he understood her situation and had no wish to push her into anything. She found out his wife left him after their son died, leaving him to take care of their daughter, Haley who was still in diapers at the time. They enjoyed talking on the phone and the occasional afternoon cup of coffee at the diner near the school where they would sit and talk while she waited for Scotty and Marcos. She found out that Richard, or Officer Martin, was also the School Resource Officer. He even promised Carla he would make it to the game, since he had to be there for security and traffic control.

Carla zipped up her the hoodie she'd bought to support the school's soccer program. Quickly, she checked her face in the mirror noticing fine lines beginning to creep in around her eyes. With a few quick strokes from the hairbrush, she was satisfied with her appearance.

She called Abbey but got no response. She decided to stop at her sister's house first before getting her grandsons and talk her into using her car since it was reliable and had more room. Carla thought Abbey told her she would be home by three o'clock. She glanced at her watch, five minutes after three. School didn't let out until 3:30, so she wasn't too worried about being late to get the kids. Most of the time she tried to get there early so she wouldn't get stuck in the long line of others picking up their charges. Carla thought maybe Abbey hadn't made it home but would surely be there soon. She slung her purse over her shoulder, humming as she closed the door.

◆ ◆ ◆

They stood together at Abbey's open grave, staring at her simple coffin. She had made it clear several years ago she wanted a big party when she died. There were to be no tears, no grieving. Carla figured Abbey wasn't expecting to die a horrible death. There would not be a party. Carla wasn't in a partying mood. So was no one else. Abbey's death affected many people; she had many friends from what she saw at the funeral. Carla wondered if her sister knew her murderer. She suspected she did. Carla knew in her soul who it was too. The same person who took her grandsons from school that same awful afternoon. Juan.

She relived the scene over and over each night as she lay in her bed, in her now empty tomb of a house. When she tried to start her car, it wouldn't. Thinking the battery had a bad connection, she opened the hood to discover she had a missing distributor cap. Trying not to panic, Carla called her sister to come over and pick her up, but the phone was busy. She tried several more times then started running the mile to Abbey's house.

A quarter mile down the road she felt a pinching pain on her right side and slowed down to a fast walk. She shunned the hoodie and wrapped it around her waist. Carla took several deep breaths to slow her heart rate. She was deeply worried about her car getting sabotaged. More deep breaths. Maybe she was overthinking the worse, but it's not everyday someone yanks out the innards of your vehicle. She tried calling Abbey again. Still busy. Carla knew Abbey was not one to talk no longer than ten minutes on the phone and it had been nearly a half an hour since she tried calling her sister. Several minutes later the stitch in her side faded away, and Carla began to jog.

Even though her anxiety grew the closer she got to Abbey's home Carla slowed down when she heard a couple of Blue Jays squawking at a squirrel in a nearby tree. Then a small, yellow butterfly landed on a cluster of wild rose bushes growing in the ditch next to her. The mid-spring air was warm and humid, and the richness of the earth from the previous night's rain shower filled her with a calming effect; melting her fears at least for the moment. Carla decided that maybe she was over reacting when she reached her sister's street. The sabotage could be someone wacked out on drugs and wreaking havoc. Green Valley was becoming more populated with several new industries building in the area. That meant more people moving from other places and bringing with them more issues growing towns have to deal with.

That happy feeling was whisked away when she walked up onto Abbey's porch, the door wide open, and TV blaring; a daytime talk show was on. Abbey hated those things. It wasn't unusual for the door to be standing open since she had a screen door. Abbey was frugal and kept the air conditioning at a minimum through the warmer months. When she walked into Abbey's home and found her big sister lying face up in the bathroom, her pale blue eyes staring at the ceiling but not seeing anything, Carla had sunk to the floor. She tried to scream but it stuck in her throat. She could see the pool of blood spreading away from Abbey's body, the red splatter of blood on the walls resulting from a bullet hole in her sister's chest.

Each time, Carla woke up; gasping for air. She'd sit straight up, listening for anything unusual. Most of the time her labored breathing and choking sobs were the only thing out of the ordinary, but then, for her it wasn't so ordinary. Juan and Hugh had done everything possible to make sure her life was shattered. For her happiness nothing but a gauzy dream. Crushed every time she thought it was in sight. She wanted to get eye to eye with both of them and let them know she would not go down without a fight.

"We have to go find Juan." Doug spoke up, bringing Carla from inside her gloomy thoughts.

"What?"

"We have to find him. If we wait for the law to step up, it'll be years, maybe never. Who knows what he's done with Scotty and Marcos?" Doug's eyes glistened. "I want justice for Katie, for Abbey." He turned away and wiped his eyes in an angry swipe.

"That isn't going to solve anything, but, if it did, I'd be there helping you out." She walked over to him and put her arm around his sagging shoulders and hugged him tight. "This isn't the Wild West."

Matthew walked over and gave Doug a light punch on the arm. "I get it. It makes complete sense but, we could end up in a lot of trouble and not just with the law."

"I'm calling that t.v. show again, the one about missing and exploited children, to see if they will repost Katie's story and ask for help finding the boys. Carla turned away from Abbey's grave. "If we don't hear anything within a month, then we'll start our own search."

Katie's story reappeared on t.v. for the third time in two years. This time Josh Grahmann, the host, came and talked to Carla and Chief Bristol. Mr. Grahmann sat with them at the Green Valley Police Station while the camera focused on them. Carla told her story about Juan's abusive nature toward her daughter Katie. She tried to keep the tears at bay, but with Abbey's death still fresh in her heart and the disappearance of her grandsons she couldn't hold them back any longer. Grahmann told them to cut the filming until she was able to regain composure. When she told him she was alright, he walked over to the couch and sat next to her. "Mrs. Simpson, this is the very reason I do this show, for people like you who have lost loved ones in violent crimes."

"Why do you think I asked for you Mr. Grahmann? Because you do understand. I want justice for my daughter. I know Juan Pedraza killed her, I know he killed my sister or had her killed, and I know he took my grandsons. He doesn't have custody of them because he's an illegal alien and so it's kidnapping. He's a murderer and a thug. Chances are he's back in Mexico, and where? It's anyone's guess." Carla wiped her eyes and stared straight into the camera lens.

"I welcomed that man into my family, fed him and treated him like a son. When he started abusing Katie, I asked him why he thought he had to act like an asshole. He said he was the man and it's necessary to keep her and all women in line, that was the man's job."

She turned back to Grahmann. Carla dried her eyes with a tissue, her face became set, her jaw line rigid, her lips pressed so tight against each other they were almost white. Her voice shook. "Know what I told him? He was nothing but a dirt bag, scum and other things. He needed castrated." Carla's bottom lip trembled. Then she swallowed and took in a breath. Once again, she faced the camera.

"Juan Gonzales-Pedraza I hope you are watching. You will get caught. I want my grandsons back safe and sound. If harm comes to them, you can be rest assured far worse things await you in Hell." She continued to stare into the camera lens, unblinking and shaking, ready to cry again.

Mr. Grahmann placed a hand on her shoulder. "We will get Pedraza, Mrs. Simpson." He turned to Chief Bristol, "Chief, you know for a fact that Juan Pedraza was the one who murdered Katie Jensen from DNA evidence found at the crime scene. Have there been any leads on the missing boys?" A picture of Scotty and Marcos came on screen. It was both of them sitting on the front steps of their house taken a couple of weeks before they were kidnapped. They were in their soccer uniforms, Marcos holding a soccer ball in his lap. Their happy, carefree smiles made Carla turn her head away from the monitor.

"Yes, sir. DNA evidence found around the vic- I mean, Miss Jensen contained enough markers to match Mr. Pedraza's. We couldn't find his DNA on record, so we used cheek swabs from his sons and cheek swabs from a brother of Mr. Pedraza's we had in custody at the time. As for Ms. Clarke's murderer, evidence is still being processed, so at this time we do not have any leads. I suspect her murder and the abductions of Scotty and Marcos Jensen-Pedraza are linked. However, that's pure speculation on my part."

The story aired once more, and no hits, no leads. By the end of June, it was apparent Carla and her brothers were going hunting for a killer.

CHAPTER SIX

"Do either one of you have any money set back?" Carla asked her brothers as they sat around the table in her kitchen.

Doug shrugged. "I've got some, but you know most of it goes to Beth for child support. The most I can pitch in is a thousand." He searched for the steno notebook he kept with him since they decided to locate Juan. "I found out he has family in La Paz, Mexico."

Carla flicked the ashes from her cigarette into the ashtray in front of her. She had been close to a year without smoking, but here she was again, puffing away. It helped the anxiety, and gave her something to do. "Where in Mexico is La Paz?"

"On the Baja Peninsula."

"How'd you find that out?"

"Oh, a little investigating, and a little interrogation of a family member. One of Abbey's friends told me this guy had made it back into the country. So, I followed the guy and caught him outside Wal-Mart and we took a little ride. At first, I hoped for cooperation, but he didn't want to say anything. Fortunately, I know enough Spanish to tell him I would take him to the nearest detention center and he would be deported again. He said Juan's parents and an uncle live in La Paz. His family is poor the relative told me. They sell native crafts to tourists in a little booth on the beach. I also found out Juan used to be in the top echelon of a gang called Hell's Devils, and hangs out in Cabo San Lucas a lot. I asked him if he talked to Juan lately, he told me no, but I got the feeling he was lying. I convinced him to fess up."

Carla stared hard at Doug. "You hit him?" She shook her head, "what makes you think he won't go-" She stopped and smirked. "Guess talking to the cops wouldn't work for him. You didn't have to hit him though."

"Yes, you are right I didn't have to hit him and I didn't." He grinned at Carla and reached behind his back and pulled out a Rutger 9mm. "I just introduced him to Gina."

Matthew snorted. "You named your gun?"

Carla gently pushed Matthew off to the side. "What the hell Doug?"

"I'm legal. Conceal and carry." He kissed the weapon and slipped it back inside his holster hidden under his jacket.

Carla smirked, "Although I don't like them, given the circumstances, I guess it was a necessary action. What'd he say?"

"He talked to Juan the day he took the boys; he saw them sitting in the truck. Juan told him they were going to go eat and then to the game." Doug stood up and got a bottle of water from the refrigerator, he motioned toward the fridge, "Anyone?"

Carla gasped. "Why didn't he say anything?"

Doug sat back down in his chair and twisted the cap off the water. "Probably didn't want to get involved. Besides Juan could have lied to him too."

Carla turned toward Matthew.

"What about you? How much money can you throw in?"

"I don't know, I'll have to talk to Terri, she's the banker."

"We might as well forget you getting any money for this. We are driving by the way; I am not getting on an airplane. It's a long shot, but we could find them before we cross the border into Mexico." It was obvious she would have to foot most of the bill. Carla had a tidy sum of money saved up for her other children. As much as she hated to, she felt she had no other choice but to use some of that money to finance the trip. "Since it's a high possibility that Terri isn't going to help, we take your Kia."

"Well, I don't know, I'll have to talk to-"

"If you don't want to do this, say so Matt. I really thought you were all in for this trip."

"It's not that, she's not working now. She's been diagnosed with Bi-Polar disorder and trying to get it in check has been a costly expense for us. In case you forgot, she's Diabetic and has Fibromyalgia. It's been rough on us lately and we're waiting to get her disability going, it's been approved, but now we're waiting for some paperwork to come through. Plus, I have to use that car for work! I don't even know if I can take off longer than a couple of weeks Carla."

Carla tried to warn Matt about Terri when they first met. The woman was a flurry of drama filled problems. She would have him by his gonads, get him into situations better left alone, and Carla was right. Terri even went so far as to involve her once when Matt left Terri and needed a place to stay. Terri came over that night yelling from the car and squealing her tires when she'd drive off. After the second time of hearing the chaos Carla told Matt he needed to make Terri leave. When Carla picked up the phone and threaten to call the police; Matt got into the car with Terri and left.

She wasn't a bit surprised when he started making excuses. "Yes or no Matt. If you are serious, you'll work this out with Terri and your boss. Tell him the truth, I don't care. Tell your wife to go to take a hike, jump off a cliff, I don't care. If you don't want to go, then leave."

"I didn't say-"

"That's your problem Matt, you never do say! Terri says it for you! I guess you forgot the time you left her? You know, when she had that affair?" Doug drank from his bottle of water. "You came crying to us about how she did this and did that and you were fed up. You told us she tried to keep you from leaving by climbing on the car completely naked, remember? When that didn't work, she came after you with a baseball bat, still naked!"

Doug sat at the table and shook a cigarette from Carla's pack. "I wanted to help you out so I let you stay at the house, had you a good job lined out and even a little cutie pie from work interested in you. What'd you do? Whine and cry about how you missed your wife and ended up calling her to come and get you. You've been hen pecked so much I bet you can't even go to the bathroom without getting permission!" Doug's blue eyes glittered, he took a drink of water, staring at Matthew, waiting for a response.

Matthew stood up and slammed the kitchen chair against the table. He glowered at Doug and Carla; his jaw clenched. "She's bi-polar! I have kids to feed and clothe! Don't you get it?" He laughed and shook his head slowly. "You have no idea what it's like Doug." Matthew glared at his siblings. "You know what? I don't have to take this crap from either of you. I'm out, you two have at it. I hope you find them." He stormed through the kitchen and slammed the front door hard enough to cause photographs hanging on the opposite wall to shake.

"That went pleasantly. I didn't even get a chance to ask for a joint!" Doug sighed and finished his drink. "I wish you had a beer somewhere in here." He said grabbing another bottle of water.

"You don't need to be smoking that crap, and if you have intentions of bringing any with you on this trip, don't. And drinking and driving will get you in trouble too." She stood up and went to the living room window staring outside at the sun filled yard. "How is your ride Doug?"

"Well, it's got over one hundred thousand miles and the clutch needs work. For what we're about to do that car isn't going to be reliable sis."

She thought about using Abbey's vehicle but couldn't bring herself to get inside of it without thinking about her sister. Carla pulled out the phone book off of the counter and started leafing through the yellow pages. "I guess we rent a car."

CHAPTER SEVEN

Carla couldn't help it. She opened the suitcase and picked a journal at random.

"I remember coming home one night from work. The company had shuttle buses that kept me from driving the long drive to LaFayette. Anyway, I walked up to the gate in the front yard, the front door wide open, all the lights on, and the stereo blasting full volume. Thankfully you kids were sleeping except for Katie, she was frightened and holed up in her room she shared with you three. I asked her what was going on. She said that Hugh was drunk and started calling her names and made her take you three into the bedroom. She said she cracked the door open because she heard voices. There were two men she didn't know there and a woman sitting in the living room drinking.

I went searching for your father but I didn't have to go too far as he was passed out on the floor in front of the couch in the living room. I turned off the stereo, to this day I hate Cheap Trick. There were beer bottles everywhere, and an empty bottle of whiskey lying next to him.

I left him there passed out on that nasty old carpet. I did put a pillow under his head which was hard to do. I managed to get it under him after dropping his head a couple of times because it kept rolling around while I tried to slide the pillow underneath. I guess sometime around five that morning, I heard him rummaging around in the kitchen, kicking the beer bottles around. I got up and went to make sure he was okay and of course he was still pretty drunk, but had enough of his senses to start chewing me out for leaving him on the floor. I told him I tried to wake him up. I also told him if he's going to get that drunk, he better make sure he makes it to bed. If he passes out in the front yard, I'll leave him there too and without a pillow. That was the first time he hit me. It was a glancing blow, but it still hurt. It left a nice bruise on my chin.

I think I need to tell you how your uncle Harry lost his job, it's part of the puzzle. He used to drive the shuttle bus I took to work. I was glad he drove the bus at the time because I didn't know anyone who rode on it. For a while I sat near the front so I could talk to him. He complained to me sometimes about his neighbors, he felt they were taking things from him. Then he began to accuse your father of stealing money from him. I tried to assure him that his brother would never do such a thing. Of course, Harry thought differently. He told me that there were times in the past Hugh had screwed him over. I kept trying to reassure him that he couldn't be that person, but in a way, I did wonder if his accusations were valid. I never let on that I had my own suspicions. But I thought it best to just stay neutral, it was between him and Hugh.

One day, he went way out of character. I got on the bus as usual and sat next to a woman I had made friends with since we rode together. We were laughing about something she said when Harry got up from his seat and walked back to where I sat. I started to ask him what was wrong, but when I saw his eyes; they were dead; distant like he was drunk or stoned. Then I started to feel that he was mad at me. I was right. He took another step toward me. I stepped out into the walkway of the bus and met him face to face. He got right in front of my face and cussed me out. He made accusations that your father and I killed his dog, spit was flying from his mouth and getting louder. I told him he was delirious and needed help. I looked him square in the eyes and told him if he did not get back to his seat that when we got to work, I would report him and he would lose his job. He was clenching his fist and then started toward me again, like he wanted to hit me. I wasn't scared of him, at that point, I wanted him to hit me.

I was past fed up listening to him for months. All I ever heard was him complain and moan about his troubles. He just stood there for a few more seconds then turned around and drove us to work. When I went to get back into my seat, three men who rode on the bus were standing, waiting to help me out if Harry did hit me. When we arrived at work (fifteen minutes later than usual), nearly every one of the people on the bus went to the office and reported him anyway.

The next thing I knew I was pulled off the line and told to go to the office and tell my side of the story. Questions were asked and they were answered. I was asked if I thought Harry should continue to drive the bus. That was when I found out there had been other people who had reported him before this incident. I told them that if *he was causing that much of a problem that maybe he should be relieved of his duty. I offered to take the position until they found someone suitable. At first break, Harry came and apologized for acting the way he did... His excuse was he found out he had stomach cancer. I admit, I was angry with him, I didn't know why he made those accusations. I told him I was sorry about that, but it wasn't an excuse. If I had behaved the way he did, in front of all those people he would have been the first one in the office demanding I be fired. Besides, he wasn't supposed to be around me at work until the situation on the bus was resolved.*

Well, later that night, I was called into the office again. This time I was asked why I started a fight with Harry at break. That made me really upset with him so I told the H.R. Manager to ask the Shift Manager and anyone else who was in the break room at the time. I had not even raised my voice when he came to talk to me. I don't know who said we were arguing, but they got it all wrong. To make this short, he lost the driving job. He didn't know the Shift Manager was standing in the break room at that time so he ended up losing his production job too. They made him take a urine test and he had meth in his system.

I told your father about the whole thing, of course he was mad and wanted to fight Harry, I told him it wasn't worth it. He knew about the meth, it had been a problem for Harry many years, but he didn't know Harry had Cancer. The next week your grandpa and grandma Simpson came down for a visit so they said, but they were fishing for answers because they kept asking about Harry and why he lost his job.

Your grandpa said Harry told him I was jealous of his girlfriend who was twenty-two. No way in the world I wanted him. Of course, after hearing the accusation your father thought I had a thing for Harry. The whole time I was married to your father, I never had a desire to be with anyone else. We had several fights about that. I think he was trying to find a way out then and looking for excuses.

Marriage is sacred to me. My parents and grandparents raised me with morals and values of devotion and commitment. I don't think you know this, of course you will now, but your grandpa Simpson cheated on your grandmother, but they worked it out and stayed together. Your father cheated on me three times. Twice before we got married and then once when I was pregnant with you, Lawrence and Charli.

I should have seen the next one coming I suppose. But I wanted it to work, just like I was raised to do. Your Aunt Abbey was married twice, but the first one nearly beat her to death and the second one nearly robbed her blind. I guess that was enough for her, she's sworn off men for going on three years. I suppose that's the best solution for some people.

We got everything straightened out eventually with your uncle Harry, it was a good thing because six months later he passed away. It was pretty hard on your father. I don't know if he felt guilty or what, but he didn't talk much about it."

A ringing interrupted Carla's thought. The phone sounded like death calling anymore. It felt like things were going in the wrong direction. She hadn't heard from Richard in four days, might as well add that onto the pile of woes. Carla sighed and pushed herself up from the couch and walked over to the desk where her phone sat.

"Hello?" Better not be some stupid sales-

"Hey, Carla, uh- it's me, Hugh."

She stood there numb, stuck to the spot, unable to feel anything for a few seconds. "Hello Hugh." The words choked in her throat.

"I wanted to say how sorry I was, I mean, about Katie, her children and Abbey."

"How'd you get my number?"

"I called Matthew. I begged him to let me call you. I know you probably won't believe me, but if you need anything, let me know."

"Need anything?" She guffawed. "From you?" Carla broke out of her trance, here he was the source of fifteen years of pent-up frustration, bitterness, and contempt. "You son-of-a-bitch."

"Look, I know you think I'm evil incarnate, but at the time, I felt what I had to do for the protection of our children."

"Where are they at? I want to talk to them."

"They're at camp."

"What kind of camp, Hugh? Lawrence and Charli graduated this year."

"They had to be held back a year because of all the, you know, issues at the time. We moved to Dallas. I'm a Supervisor at American Airlines."

"I hate flying. Tell me, where are my children? They are old enough to make decisions on their own."

"They are happy kids. Lawrence has plans to get into Chemical Engineering and Charli wants to be either a lawyer or a teacher. They really are at camp, a summer camp they go to every year with their church. Roger has a girlfriend and plays baseball. He's looking at different colleges with scholarships. Things are fine with them Carla."

"I think you're lying. I want to talk to them Hugh. I want to see them, why haven't they called? You're a low enough slime ball to have lied and told them I died."

"I didn't tell them anything, as far as I know, they don't know where you are."

"Of course, you ass!" She screamed at him over the phone. "They don't know because you haven't told them and I haven't seen them! You low, slimy assed snake!" She started pacing the floor. "I have evidence, lots and lots of it."

"You don't have anything Carla, you're bluffing."

"Oh no I'm not."

"I have to go. I just wanted to make this quick, send condolences."

"You ruined my life, Hugh." Carla's voice shook. "If Katie hadn't been with me during that time, there is no telling what might have happened. You destroyed my spirit, but I came up from the ashes mister!"

"See? There you are screaming at me like a loon on crack. This is why I did what I did, you're still off the rocker Carla."

"What, you recording this conversation too?" She wished she could pull him through the phone line and strangle him with whatever was close. Beat him, strangle him, it didn't matter, she hated that man and forgiving him was out of the question.

He tsk-tsked her. "Carla, Carla, Carla, so insecure. I hope the rest of your life works out." There was a click then the dial tone.

Once again tears flowed hot, "I'll find you, first stop is Dallas with the journals! SEE HOW YOU LIKE THAT YOU BASTARD!" She jammed her hands into her purse searching for her cigarettes and lighter. She snatched up her phone from her desk and went outside and sat down. Her hands shook so bad she dropped the cigarette once and then couldn't light it. She didn't know if it was adrenaline or shock from Hugh's phone call, but she couldn't sit still, the longer she thought about it the more agitated she became.

Pacing back and forth across the porch Carla pulled up Doug's number. A

41

recorded message told her to leave a message. "It's me, you'll never guess who called me just now. We head to Dallas first. I think the sooner the better. Call me back. Love you, bye."

She hung up the phone. Her pacing slowed and she sat back down. *Matthew, I think I'll call him too.* She dialed his number which also told her to leave a message. "I have a bone to pick with you Matthew Jensen, call me back." She mashed the phone icon to disconnect.

She went inside and collected a few things to take with her to the library, she had some research to do on two different matters. A road map and information about California Baja Sur. Had this been an actual vacation it would have been very exciting. Even though searching for her kidnapped grandchildren was a serious task with huge consequences, she thought the trip might be the thing that could set her free at last. Her hopes renewed about reuniting with her children and handing the journals over to them was going to be nothing short of a miracle should she find them. But Carla had hope.

First, she stopped at the bank and bought three traveler's checks for five thousand apiece. Five thousand transferred into her checking account and the other fifteen would go to the kids. She decided the five thousand would be enough to start and if she needed more then she could have more money transferred from her savings to her bank account. She had one credit card she decided to take, hoping she wouldn't need it.

Carla searched different sites on one of the library's computers regarding illegal aliens and violent crimes committed against U.S. citizens. According to one site, Cato At Liberty, many studies were done and by 2019 it showed more native-born Americans were likely to be incarcerated than illegal aliens. She read on.

"We do not attempt to count the number of immigrant ex-felons, criminally inadmissible aliens who entered unlawfully, or other non-incarcerated foreigners. The ACS counts the incarcerated population by their nativity and naturalization status, but local and state governments do not record whether the prisoner is an illegal immigrant. As a result, we have to use common statistical methods to identify illegal immigrant prisoners by excluding incarcerated respondents who have characteristics that they are unlikely to have. In other words, we can identify likely illegal immigrants by looking at prisoners with individual characteristics

that are highly correlated with being an illegal immigrant. Those characteristics are that the immigrant must have entered the country after 1982 (the cut-off date for the 1986 Reagan amnesty), cannot have been in the military, cannot be receiving Social Security or Railroad Retirement Income, cannot have been covered by Veteran Affairs or Indian Health Services, was not a citizen of the United States, is not living in a household where somebody received Food Stamps (unless the individual has a child living with them as the child may be eligible if they are a U.S. citizen), and was not of Puerto Rican or Cuban origin if classified as a Hispanic."

She found another article that gave her a little reassurance, but more than likely would take years to find Juan since she figured he had many connections who could hide him and the children.

"While some new procedures are now required, the Mexican government has never been more willing to help capture and return fugitives hiding in their country back to the U.S. for prosecution.

The international bridges to Mexico are literally blocks away from some neighborhoods, and the belief that freedom is just beyond those borders is too great a temptation for many criminals.

More commonly fugitives have to be rigorously pursued deep into Mexico

Department of Justice (DOJ), Office of International Affairs (OIA), U.S. Marshals Service, and Federal Bureau of Investigation (FBI); it has also established a solid working relationship with Mexican prosecutors in the various PGR (the Mexican equivalent of the Attorney General) offices throughout the country and in Mexico City, and with the Mexican Consulate's Office in El Paso. The good news is that any DA's office can also look to any of these agencies for help in locating, arresting, and extraditing fugitives who are hiding in Mexico.

Extradition treaty with Mexico

In May 1978, the United States signed an extradition treaty with Mexico, which went into effect on January 25, 1980.1 The treaty's appendix lists the extraditable offenses; in addition, Article 2 of the treaty states that willful crimes that fall within any of the clauses of the crimes listed in the appendix are also extraditable. An intentional crime punishable by at least one year in jail may also be extraditable.

Article 3 of the treaty sets out the evidence required to successfully obtain an extradition. This article states that the extradition shall be granted only if the evidence is sufficient, according to the laws of the requested party, for committing the defendant to trial.

Provisional arrest warrant

To request a PAW, the Department of Justice requires a certified copy of a capias, certified copy of the indictment, and draft of the extradition package. This last requirement, the draft of the extradition package, previously was not required in seeking a provisional arrest warrant. But these days, DOJ likes to have a draft of the extradition package to expedite the process.

DOJ will review all of the affidavits and documents submitted in the package; therefore, the draft must contain all of the necessary affidavits (unsigned—more on why later), and all the other required documents and evidence. DOJ will review the package carefully, and once it is satisfied that there is enough evidence to move forward, officials there will request the PAW.

Armed with a PAW, the Mexican Federal Police will arrest the fugitive in Mexico. Once this occurs, the clock begins to run on the requirement that the formal extradition package be delivered to the Mexican authorities within 60 days of the fugitive's arrest, or the fugitive will be released."

That last paragraph made her realize it was the most probable scenario in most cases. It sounded like there was a lot of procedures in order to bring extradition to fruition. Why she thought that; Carla wasn't sure, but the government sometimes was as slow as pine sap in the winter. Unless it was a high profile case, Carla surmised most cases probably never saw prosecution and the fugitive was released.

The only positive outcome on that was the statute of limitations on murder never ran out. That didn't matter, she was going to find her grandsons no matter what it took and bring them back home with her. She kept on surfing the web, looking for answers. She wondered if she would get any help from the Mexican government. Just like asking strangers for help in searching for her own children, asking couldn't hurt her chances for finding Scotty and Marcos. If she told the Mexican Authorities the charges pending in the States, she just might have a chance.

She looked up Mexican government and although extremely boring she read the *"Political Ladder of the Mexican Government"* to see who could help her the most. It didn't look promising. She wrote down the addresses and phone numbers of government offices. She could call those in the morning. She made a list of questions to ask, hoping someone would be able to answer them.

Carla loved the satellite-based program that lets the user virtually travel around the world without leaving the chair. She thought the idea of cameras used to see from road view three hundred and sixty degrees was about the coolest thing and wished the cameras could be installed on every street, road, highway and dirt roads. All she had to do was type in a city then enter, the virtual earth would set coordinates and begin its search all the while closing in on the location. A person could add features like hotels, gas stations, supermarkets, almost anything.

She followed Mexican Federal Highway 1 all the way down to La Paz. She used the mouse's wheel to zoom in closer until the image blurred. She adjusted the distance and studied the map of the city. Somewhere she thought, in one of those buildings is where Scotty and Marcos probably were being held. She reached out to touch the screen of the computer and closed her eyes. "Hang on babies, I'm on my way and I will find you. "

CHAPTER EIGHT

"*When I was pregnant with you twins, your father and I worked at a food processing plant in Fayetteville, Arkansas. One night, I went to tell Hugh my department was getting off of work two hours early. He wasn't at his work station, but I caught the top of his head near the front of the department so I went toward that direction. When I got there, I stopped cold in my tracks, your father had a huge fillet knife and was heading for some guy with the intentions of stabbing him. I knew who the man was because he gave us both a hard time on breaks. I had to shout above the noise of machinery, but he heard me. When he saw me looking at him and the knife in his hand, he put it behind his back. As if I hadn't already seen it by then. Unfortunately, one of the supervisors saw the whole thing and fired your father right on the spot. Sorry kids, but your father is an idiot.*

Not too long after that incident he wanted to talk to me about his new friend, Stacey, a woman he met at his new job as a maintenance man for a refrigeration storage facility. He wanted to make sure I would not be worried about him riding to work with a female who wasn't his wife. It cost him one hundred-fifty dollars a week to drive the F-150. If he had riders then it would be less cost for him. I thought it was a great idea, I had no problem with that especially since other people were riding with them. It was close to an hour drive from our house. Based on your father's "behavior" from the past, even a half hour was too long for him to spend alone with any woman other than me, his mom, and sister. Against my gut instinct I told him I had no problem with it. I'm no fool, but I had to give him a chance.

One Saturday morning I got a phone call from your father needing me to pick him up from work; something was wrong with his truck and would wait for me in the breakroom. When I walked in there not only was he there but a woman with dark hair and a tattoo of a rose on her upper arm sat next to him. He introduced me to Stacey his co-worker.

I felt extremely uncomfortable about that whole thing and how odd it was that he did that. So, I got to drive her home as well. I can't tell you how uncomfortable that felt. We had polite conversation but the chatter between them, was like having a conversation between close friends, laughing at inside jokes only they knew. I'd ask about the joke and all I got was "You wouldn't get it, had to be there at the time." I think I knew then something was going on between those two.

The following weekend I didn't have to work and got the opportunity to stay home with you kids. I wanted to make cookies that day but I needed some flour. I don't know if you would remember, but we also watched movies and ate popcorn. Anyway, I sent Katie to the store to get the things we needed for cookies when I heard a honk in front of the house. It was your father with Stacey sitting in the passenger seat with a kid. I wondered why he wasn't home when I got up, but it was obvious he wasn't at work. Hugh wanted me to meet Rebecca, Stacey's daughter who was a couple of years older than you, Lawrence and Charli. Cute little girl, I felt sorry for her, she didn't look like she was having a fun time. I asked her if she wanted to stay and help us make cookies, but Hugh interrupted and answered for her by saying he was taking them home and would be right back.

When he returned, I told him I needed to speak with him in private so you kids couldn't hear us. When we got inside, I wanted to know what was going on. Why wasn't he here at home with his family? What business did he have running around with Stacey and her daughter? I thought it was wrong and showed a huge lack of respect. Married men or women for that matter just didn't run around town with people of the opposite sex.

He said she called while I was still asleep that her car wouldn't start and needed a jump, when that didn't work, they went to the parts store to get a new battery. All I could think of was the last three times he cheated on me and the hurt it caused. I didn't buy it, but I let it go. I wanted him to see I trusted him and give him the opportunity to know I was taking the step of faith in that direction.

A card fell out of the journal and Carla picked it up. *It's A Party!*, it announced with a dancing bear holding bright colored balloons. She opened it up and it was an invitation to Lawrence and Charli's fourth birthday party, the last one she got to share with them. Carefully, she stuck it back in the journal and returned it to the suitcase. The journals would be taking the trip as far as Dallas. She took it into the living room and began a pile of things she would take. How long would they be searching for Scotty and Marcos?

She decided a week's worth of clothing, socks, underwear, for each day, at least seven pair of each, with two extra of each, just in case should be enough. Three pair of jeans, three pair of shorts, tee shirts, two blouses, long sleeved, four sleeveless blouses and a sweatshirt and a light jacket. Shoes.

She went to her closet and stared down at the three pair she had, in addition to her house slippers, two pair of tennis shoes and a pair of flipflops were all that made up that part of her wardrobe. In a box at the back of the closet were her dress shoes, a pair of black, low-heeled pumps. She hadn't put them on in nearly two years. They were the ones she wore to Katie's funeral. Carla set them on the floor and pushed them back into the back of the closet.

She stared at the pile of items she planned to take; clothing, toiletries and cosmetics. In addition, she kept a folder containing research information on everything they may need to know. Her plan was to read the materials each night they stopped to rest, concerning the next phase of the trip. Her newest purchase, Dell XPS 15 laptop computer, came equipped with satellite wi-fi, 13.3" screen; plenty big for her. And easy to store. It was a necessary expense. She also got a satellite phone that was compatible with her smart phone.

 She wasn't up to date on the latest gadgetry and technology, but when she got off the phone with a customer representative, she felt better equipped to use the device. These items she decided would go to her kids when all was said and done.

She knew in her bones they would find them. It was like they were in her head; waiting for her to come to them. Carla thought it might be a good idea to write out a will on a flash drive and give it to them. She didn't have a lawyer, but if Charli had plans to become one, Carla wanted her to take care of the finalities should she die. Documents she felt she needed, birth certificate, shots/vaccination records, driver's license, social security card and passport, all contained in an accordion file folder. Traveler's checks and the only credit card she owned stayed close to her in her purse. All she needed to do was find someone to watch the place.

Carla debated about putting Abbey's house on the market. Her finances were in fair shape, but with the sale of the home, she could take care of her sister's final debts. If anything was left, she would donate it to the local animal shelter in Abbey's name. It struck Carla a little ironic how all these years, how casual their discussions of what they wanted in final wishes suddenly seemed important.

Carla knew without a doubt Abbey would approve. For the time being she decided she would wait until everything was resolved before searching for a real estate agent. Whoever she got to watch her home could keep an eye on Abbey's too. She stepped outside to smoke when the phone rang with Doug's number flashing on the television screen.

"Hey,"

"You'll never guess who called me today." Carla inhaled, letting the smoke fill her lungs then exhaled watching the smoke float out into the front yard. The air was heavy and still, a far cry from that morning when blue, sunny skies and fresh dew on the grass dominated the scene.

"Santa Claus, come Carla, I don't have a clue." Doug replied.

"Hugh." She let the name drop like a huge slab of stone from a cliff.

"No way!" Doug gasped. "How'd he get the number?"

"Matt."

"Are you serious? Why?"

"Maybe he thought it would make us, or me rather change my mind about finding Juan. I don't know why. I haven't talked to Matt since he stomped out of here. I called him already. I had to leave a message, so I'm waiting for him to call me back. My guess is that he won't."

"I haven't talked to him either. I hate that too. Want me to call him?" Doug asked.

"If you feel like it, but I still want to talk to him. I don't want him mad at me or you." Carla heard a distant rumble of thunder. She finished the cigarette and went inside and switched to the Weather Channel. It was airing a commercial about Terminix Pest Control. "I think there's a storm moving in Doug."

"It's supposed to get pretty hairy tonight."

"Great."

"Why? What's wrong?"

"I hate storms."

"Aww, come on. They're cool to watch."

"Yeah, when I'm not underneath them it's great, wonderful and beautiful."

Another rumble of thunder. Good, it was further away. The local weather segment came on showing a line of showers and angry red blotches on the radar screen, above and to the south of her. Behind that system looked clear. Maybe it'll pass by without too much incident. She went to the kitchen and opened the refrigerator. "Are you ready to leave?"

"I'll be ready, got your passport?"

"Yep. I guess you can either meet me at the car lot, or drive over here. Better yet park it at Abbey's that way it looks like someone is there. I bought some of those timer switches for my place and hers. You know anyone trustworthy enough to do some house sitting?"

"What about Matt?"

"Him, yeah, I'd trust maybe. It's his wife I have problems with."

"What about Dusty?"

"Katie's friend? She moved six months ago to Portland, Maine. Got married."

"Frank?"

"Who's Frank?"

"That guy Katie was dating."

"You mean Paul. He moved away a couple of months ago." She pulled out a t.v. dinner from the freezer and put it on the counter. "I may know someone after all." She forgot about Richard, he's a cop. She thought and wrote his name down on the note pad she kept on the counter. He could just patrol both places and it wouldn't be an inconvenience for him at all. "Have you told Wayne about the trip?"

"Yeah, he wants to go, but I told him it was a very important trip and next time he could go."

"Did you promise him that?"

"Sure. I'll take him to Cancun on his eighteenth birthday, six years from now."

"Huh." *That will be the day Beth lets you take Wayne to Cancun.* "I've got another call coming in, probably Matt, if he knows what's good for him." She told Doug goodbye and pressed the phone icon. It was a telemarketer wanting to sell her timeshare at a Mexican Resort. How ironic. She hung up the phone while the woman at the other end of the phone began her sales pitch.

◆ ◆ ◆

Carla sat up in bed. There it was, the tornado siren; rotating, sending out the urgent message bad weather was on the way. She fumbled for the remote and turned on the TV in her bedroom. At the bottom of the screen in a red banner scrolled a list of counties under a severe thunderstorm warning, and Benton County, the one next to hers was in it. Carroll County was under the storm warning until 3:15 am. The radar screen showed a massive red and purple blob heading her way, the banner continued to read out the history of the storm, damaging winds exceeding 70 miles an hour and hail the size of golf balls had been reported. She switched to a Springfield, Missouri station where the meteorologist stood in front of the screen discussing the severity of storms in the area. He zoomed on the one located near her. Now, a tornado warning was issued for the county of Benton and western Carroll.

He informed viewers the tornado was Doppler radar indicated, no confirmed reports as of yet. He took his cursor and tracked the storm; it was heading in Carla's direction. She threw off the covers and went into the living room. Lightning flashed across the sky; angry, jagged bolts arced the bottoms of clouds, sending an occasional bolt to the ground. She could see clouds boiling, and large tatters of low flying clouds raced across the sky. The siren sounded off again. "Aw, not now!" She ran back into the bedroom, on the banner continued to roll this time adding a tornado was spotted on the ground between Huntsville and Berryville, heading northeast at ten miles an hour.

She snatched up pillows and took them to the bathroom, it was the only interior room she had and the only safe place she had to go. Next, she took the boxes of journals and her purse, it was all she cared to save. Carla went back into the living room and noticed lights from a vehicle pulling into the driveway, a patrol car. She opened the door and stepped outside. The wind whipped about tossing lawn chairs and discarded trash. She could hear her neighbor's wind chimes clanging against each other like falling silverware from a drawer.

"Richard!" His name whipped from her mouth by a strong wind gust.

"What are you doing here?"

"I came to see if you were alright!" He tried to shout over the angry swishing of tree branches on the south side of the property. Richard ran up the porch steps, his patrol hat covered in a plastic shower cap, and yellow rain slicker. "There's a tornado on the ground about five miles from here. I wanted to make sure you had a safe place to go." He stared into the sky, she watched him as he studied the clouds and lightning strikes.

"I am so sorry- I wanted to call you, I should have called you, been by your side."

"It's okay, really." She took in a deep breath, wincing when lightning struck in a nearby pasture. "Right now, I'm worried about this storm. It isn't your obligation to keep me company. We are acquaintances, friends on a casual basis. I'm dealing with it." She glanced back at the piled luggage.

"Taking a trip, I see." Richard nodded at the couch.

"I was actually going to call you tomorrow, but, "she chuckled. "I guess I don't have to now. Can you stay?"

"Only for a couple minutes, let me call in." He ran to his vehicle. Carla could see him talking into the microphone of the car radio. Slowly, big fat rain drops started to fall, but the intensity of the rain increased in a matter of seconds. Another bolt of lightning lit up Carla's front yard. She watched as he shut off the car and took his mobile radio from the charger, and hooking it onto his belt and dodging nickel sized hail now bouncing off the hood of their cars.

"The tornado is gone for now, but it doesn't mean it won't drop back down. I can't stay long." He stayed outside the door. "I mean, not that I wouldn't like to."

Carla continued to stare at the sky. "I need a favor."

"Sure, what's up Carla?"

"I need to get away."

"That's not a bad idea. It helped me out." Richard stared at her then directed his gaze to the sky. "Look, Carla, please hear me out for a second. The reason I didn't come over is I didn't think I could handle seeing you go through the pain and suffering. I feel horrible for being that way. I didn't need to be an influence. I thought if I didn't come around and that you needed to deal with it the way you see fit, I kind of feel like it's my fault Scotty and Marcos were kidnapped. I was waiting for you then the call came your sister was found dead. By the time I got there you had already gone, I guess to the school to get the boys. One of the other officers told me she drove you down there and they were gone. We kept missing each other. I'm not a very good friend. I'm grateful you didn't tell me to leave when I came up here."

"I need someone to watch my house and Abbey's while I'm gone." She couldn't bear to tell him that it had hurt. She knew it would make him feel worse and she needed his help.

"Mind if I ask where you're going?"

"I'm not sure. I'm getting in the car and just driving for a little bit, see where I end up."

"So how long will that last?" He glanced inside one more time. "You seem to have a lot of stuff to be taking for only a week hiatus. You doing this by yourself?"

"Well, uh, no. My brother is going with me."

"Call it my keen cop sense, but something tells me you have a destination in mind." He held up his hand, "but, I won't ask questions."

"Just drive by on your watch, nothing extra special, you're a cop, you can even get out and check out the premises.

"Mail and newspapers? What about your lawn? It's June, the grass still grows."

"Got mower?"

"Carla, please, I hope you aren't thinking of going after Juan, you've got an obsessed look."

"How do you mean? I'm merely taking a drive, letting loose for once."

"Your eyes Carla. They're too bright, too hard. I can see it. Your jaw is set too firm and there's a hardness around your mouth. I know body language, and I don't think I like what yours is saying."

"I'd just appreciate it if you could do me that favor."

The wind suddenly fell silent, the air became heavy as pressure dropped. Carla and Richard walked out to the front yard and stared at the sky, scanning the clouds for a funnel. Carla had an advantage point from where her home sat, facing south toward the town of Green Valley. A flash of lightning lit up the southern end of town revealing a huge wall cloud. Another flash followed.

Richard snatched the walkie-talkie from his belt and radioed the station with the news of the wall cloud, again the siren sounded, one long uninterrupted blast.

"You need to get inside Carla, those things can drop out of nowhere. The air is too calm, too quiet." He spoke in a hushed tone, as if the storm would hear and reek more havoc.

She could feel stirrings of air, then a loud noise broke the silence. "Look!" Carla pointed at the south west side of town. A swirling, pointed finger poked out from the wall cloud, it's tip elongating trying to contact the ground.

"Got a funnel! Got a funnel! Southwest of Green Valley!" Richard shouted into the mike of his radio. Static riddled confirmations from other law enforcement officials and emergency personnel blared back at them. The next flash showed it still in the sky, the tip was gone but the funnel cloud continued to linger.

"Is it heading this way?" Carla noticed the lights winking out across town. Hers, thankfully were still on, the television had the red banner scrolling across the bottom of the screen, sure enough a tornado was heading northeast and she was in its path. Enthralled with the tornado, they watched the funnel cloud pass over the top of Carla's house.

Stupid as it may seem, she couldn't help but follow Richard as he walked toward the road to get a better view of the cloud. It raced off to the northeast, at last rain started falling and the wind picked up intensity. Richard jogged back to Carla and stood in front of her on the porch. "I have to go. I'll watch your and Abbey's place, it's the least I can do. If anyone asks, you are living with your brother until you decide what you want to do, or something to that nature. I don't want to know what you are up to, but, let me know when you get back, okay?" He took a step closer. "Just take it easy and stay safe. I want to see you again. Maybe go on a real date, if you want to. Dinner and a movie?"

Carla reached up and hugged him tight. He slipped his arms around her and hugged her back. Carla wanted to kiss him; she hadn't felt a man's arms around her in many years. For a few crazy, impulsive moments she wanted to take him to her room. She pulled away from him and stepped inside. "You better go. I'll think about that date." She stood tip toed and kissed him on the cheek. "I'll be careful Richard. You will be the first one I call when I get back.

Deal?"

"Yeah, okay." He started down the stairs then turned back to her. "Be careful Carla." He turned away and went to his squad car. She watched him as he backed down the driveway and pulled into the street.

Carla had no sooner lay her head on her pillow after the threat of the storm passed when there was a frantic knocking at her door. She opened it and there stood Richard. He grabbed her and held her close. She pulled away from him and took his hand, leading him inside the house and closed the door.

◆ ◆ ◆

She rose up from the tangled sheets of her bed, almost noon. Then she realized she was naked and remembered Richard sweeping in and carrying her to her bedroom. She forgot how making love felt. Neither one had said a word through the whole thing. At daylight he got up from Carla's bed, picking up his clothes as he made his way to the bathroom.

She felt a little guilty that she had had sex and was not married to Richard. But why? Why would she feel like this? Did she love him? Did she want to be with him? The last relationship she had ten years ago, only lasted a couple of months. Fearful of what could happen if she let her heart out of the cage, she kept it in. She wasn't ready for the commitment, but Richard showed that he too was alone and needed her.

They had talked at length many times about relationships. She knew he tried in a way to keep her from leaving. Even though neither one spoke about it, now was not the time for feelings to fog her mind. She must have fallen back to sleep because she didn't hear Richard leave. She found her robe and slippers and went into the bathroom. On the mirror was a note.

My Dearest Carla: you are an incredible woman and I hope you find what you are looking for. Never in my life have I felt so much passion and tenderness. It's been so long since I wanted to stay with anyone and only get out of bed to eat (maybe). Be careful Carla, I want to give us a chance, so that means you will have to come back. You have my phone number so anytime you need to talk, please call me. No matter where you are.

Richard

CHAPTER NINE

The evening before she was to leave, Carla picked up the rental, a 2019 maroon colored Jeep Wagoneer. Complete with GPS, fog lights and four-wheel drive on the fly. Since Carla had never owned a vehicle under ten years old, she thought it was a little too fancy for where they were going. She worried about thieves taking off with it. She expressed her concerns to the dealer, telling him she was going on a research project in Mexico. He told her the four-wheel drive would come in handy and offered her an insurance policy for an extra one hundred and twenty dollars that carried full coverage on the Jeep and a hundred thousand dollars in life insurance.

◆ ◆ ◆

She stuffed the last of her belongings into the back then closed the hatch. She was ready but Doug was still in Branson, something about a snag at work. Doug assured Carla he was on his way.

"I have to stop by Beth's and say good-bye to my son. He isn't happy about having to stay home." Carla heard the rustle of paper through the phone.

"I'm sorry too. I really wish it was a vacation."

"Beth thanks you though, she said he wouldn't stop talking about going with his dad and aunt."

"You didn't tell him he could, did you? "

"No."

"Doug."

"I got it worked out, okay? He understands besides I told him there'd be times we would have to use an outside toilet or a ditch if we couldn't find woods to take a crap. I made it sound as unattractive as I could."

Carla sighed then chuckled at the idea of her brother trying to dissuade Wayne. Dear God. "So how long are you going to be?"

"Within the hour, I'm walking out the door."

"Are you packed?"

"Won't take me but a few minutes, ten tops."

"I'll see you in an hour and a half." She liked her new cell phone now she was getting used to it.

She went back inside and picked up the new journal from the kitchen table. This set would not be addressed to her children, but a documentation of the trip. She took it and a pen and went outside to sit so she could smoke and think of how to start the log. She stared at the small town of Green Valley, nestled in between a set of mountain ranges. The Boston Mountains to the south and the Forest Range to the north.

They weren't mountains like those of the Rockies or Cascades. The Ozarks were low hills, rounded as millions of years of erosion, and weather wore them down. Human intervention of blasting roads and making pastures for livestock made it hard to picture settlers and Native Americans traversing over them. She could hear cicadas, crickets, and frogs in the humid summer morning. She thought that she would probably miss that wonderful mixture of noises and was surprised she had tears in her eyes.

Carla opened her new composition book.

"I am of sound mind but crazy for even thinking I will be able to find my grandsons. The chances are slim. I have to find them; I cannot let another family member be taken away from me. The pain is so deep in my heart and soul; it hurts to the very core of my being. I must do this. I fear if I stand idle and wait for law enforcement and government agencies to act, it could take months or years. I have been afraid and unsure of many things. But if I let my insecurities rule me, I may never see Scotty and Marcos again.

I am going to find my grandsons; I have nothing else to live for but them. I don't know if my children will want to see me, but in the end, they will know the truth. They will know their mother loved them and still loves them very much.

This series of journals will be for me to document what I find out about the children's whereabouts and how I can get Juan extradited, prosecuted for Katie's death, and kidnapping Scotty and Marcos. By all rights I have legal guardianship over my grandsons because their mother is dead and their father is an illegal alien and murderer."

She looked up from the notebook when the sound of tires crunching on the gravel in her driveway broke her thoughts. There were two people in the vehicle; Matthew and Terri. Matt as she called him was a good person, he'd do anything to help someone in need. Of all her siblings, Matt and Carla favored each other the most. Abbey had curly red hair, Doug was blond headed, but like herself, Matt had straight, course auburn hair. They all had the same color eyes, icy blue. She stood up and stretched, wondering what they wanted. She still wanted to chew him out for giving Hugh her phone number, but that could come after she found out why they were here on the morning she was leaving for Dallas. They pulled up next to the rental and got out. Terri walked around the Jeep and whistled, its shrill nearly piercing Carla's eardrum.

"Wow, Carla, this is really nice!"

"It's not mine." Carla watched her sister-in-law peek inside and acting like the Jeep was the greatest vehicle to ever come around. "I've rented it for the trip."

"Yeah, I heard about that. Do you think it's a good idea to go searching without any idea where they are? I mean, Carla, that is a long way." Terri walked up the porch steps and sat next to her. "Honey, I know things have been really hard for you, and that we, or rather I, haven't been as supportive as I should. If the shoe were on the other foot, you would have come with pistols blazing and cannons roaring. I've done nothing to help."

"You have your own things to contend with Terri, so don't worry about anything. Are you two here to send me off?" Carla stood up to put the journal into the case containing her new laptop. "You want some coffee?"

"Sure, but Carla, please sit down for just a minute." Terri motioned for her to come back to her chair. "I, uh, we, talked about this trip. At first, when he told me about this crazy plan," Terri's fingers made small circles near her head. "I honestly thought you had gone completely mad. I didn't want Matthew going, because there was no telling how long you planned to be gone."

"He doesn't have to go, Terri. Doug doesn't have to either. And," she added. "Originally, I had no intentions to find my grandchildren either, Doug did suggest searching for Scotty and Marcos. The longer I thought about it, the more likely it seemed we would probably find them quicker than the authorities. I have to do something; I can't sit on my thumbs and wait! I feel every day that slips by is another day further from finding them. So, Matt," Carla turned to him. "if you feel obligated, I don't want you to come along. If you go because you feel it's necessary and are truly helping me out, fine."

Matthew walked up to his sister and hugged her. "It's not an obligation." He pulled back and held her by the shoulders, staring straight into Carla's eyes. "We've thought about this from every angle, She's the one who thought I should come with you and Doug. Like it or not, we are family, and we need to stick together." He pulled Carla back when she started crying. "No matter what we find, what the outcome is, we are family and we need each other."

Suddenly Carla felt tired, worn to a stub like a pencil gone through the sharpener too many times. She tried to control the tears but they felt so good, like a cleansing. She wanted her brother to go, he was bigger than Doug and actually between the two he was the smartest. Maybe not with his marriage, but at least he stuck it out. She actually had a lot of respect for him because of that. To Carla that was love unconditional, nothing could break that bond he and his wife Terri shared. She stepped back and hugged Terri. "I want you to know Terri, I am grateful for the both of you. I know it's going to be hard without Matt being there, but I promise to take good care of him."

"Oh Carla!" Terri hugged her sister-in-law back. Her cheeks flushed and her dark brown eyes sparkled. "That means so much to me but I'm going too!"

CHAPTER TEN

Carla glanced over at Matthew then back to Terri, "Oh." *Great.* "Well, you do speak Spanish and an extra pair of eyes wouldn't hurt. You are welcome to come along, but both of you know this right from the get go; no drama." She bore right into Terri's eyes, "If there is, let it be known now I will, and I mean, I will, dump your butt right on the spot. We have a long way to go, I'm close to a breaking point and I don't think either one of you want to test that."

"I know we have our differences Carla, but I'm here to help. I'm really good at reading maps, ask Matthew." Terri nodded toward her husband.

"That's true, she's got some kind of built in GPS mechanism. Plus, she's been teaching me Spanish. 'D`onde est`an los ba~nos? '

Terri chuckled. "Leave it to you to want a bathroom!"

Carla relaxed a little then chuckled. She turned to Terri, "When we moved to Montana, every state we went through, he had to be the first one to pee. It was the same on vacations too. Dad at first thought it was funny, then he wanted to be the first one, Matt always beat him." Carla and Matthew laughed recalling the memory. She wiped a tear away. "Oh, here's Doug." The three of them turned as they watched him pull into the driveway and park next to the rental.

He climbed out of his pick up, "I see we have a sending off party." He grinned but it faded when Matthew told him both he and Terri were going. "Well, the more, the merrier I guess." He walked to the other side of the truck and pulled out his luggage. Carla could tell he was not happy about the arrangement, but she found herself defending Terri.

He whispered as he jammed a gym bag into a space by the wheel well. "What makes you think this is going to be a good idea?" He picked up another bag, their father's old army duffle bag and crammed it on top of the other one.

"I don't, but I warned her. Besides, she knows Spanish better than any of us. I don't know if you thought about that part, but it skipped my mind, kinda busy you know." She dusted her jeans after climbing in and out of the back of the wagon. That was the downside to living in the country. Dust seemed to get into every niche. She watched Matthew and Terry sitting on the porch steps looking at them, talking to each other.

"I know, I'm sorry. If they start arguing-" Doug whispered.

"Her sincerity seems genuine."

"Yeah, but if you remember when mom passed?" He squinted his eyes searching for the memory. "What? A week later? She kicked Matt out because he stayed too long over at Abbey's."

"I know, I know. She may be helpful with navigation and reading maps kind of thing, she's an extra driver, we have a lot of miles to cover, and, she's willing to help out. They told me they can pay their way. She said her mother loaned them some money and is watching their kids."

Carla and Doug walked to the front of the vehicle. Facing his brother and Terri, Doug folded his arms across his chest and leaned against the Jeep. "Okay, you win. Get your things and put it in the back Matt." He stared straight into both of their eyes. "I'm backing Carla's rules, first time you cause any drama," he jerked his thumb toward the road. "you are out."

"It's a done deal. We already had this discussion once." Matthew stood up and fished his keys from his pocket. "I don't have to listen to this. We came to help, if it's going to be you two making the calls the whole time, we'll just go home."

Doug caught him by the arm. "I'm sorry man. I'm wound up, had to go to work because of some kind of engine design question by one of the investors of the project. Terri, I'm sorry. I know you mean well." He walked over to her and hugged her. "Start with a clean slate?"

Terri hugged him back and flashed him a huge toothy grin. "Sure. I promise to be good." She dug out a bottle of pills. "I'm on even keel a little better these days. They keep me safe and sane." She chuckled.

"Matt, let me help you with the stuff." Doug offered.

Carla stepped in front of her brothers. "One more thing." She stared at the three of them, her eyes stone cold. "No weed."

"What? No weed?" Terri spun around; her round face filled with concern.

Carla sighed, "If you get us busted, it means we will lose the car and win a stay in jail." she pointed her finger at Doug and Matthew, "You know how I feel about weed. I'd rather you didn't bring any."

The three stared at Carla. "Okay." Teri walked to the back of the house, Matt and Doug followed.

Carla continued to double check things in the Jeep then went into the house and make sure everything was secured. She pulled back a curtain and watched as her brothers and sister-in-law puffed on a joint. She sighed and went to the living room scanning it to make sure she had everything. She wanted more than anything to stay home. She wanted things like they used to be. But reality spelled it out loud and clear; she didn't want to be a casualty; a sad statistic. There was no time for second thoughts. She pulled the door shut and locked it.

Carla was the first to start the trip. They rode in silence for a while, watching the familiar scenery slip by. Lush green hills bursting with growth from the abundant late spring rains, and an array of wildflowers such as Queen Anne's Lace, brown eyed Susan, and corn flowers filled ditches and filtered into wooded areas. For the thousandth time she wondered if she was doing the right thing as they slipped into the Bobby Hopper Tunnel near the outskirts of Fort Smith, Arkansas. The answer was always the same, yes, she was. She said a silent prayer as they crossed into Oklahoma, for them, Scotty, Marcos, and her children in Dallas. She prayed for safety, and a positive outcome.

They stopped at the Oklahoma Welcome Center, to take a break and stretched their legs. They sat at one of the covered picnic tables drinking sodas and water. "This place is pretty nice." Terri commented as she plopped down on the bench next to Matthew. She pulled out a joint. "Just a couple of puffs." She told Carla. "We're far enough away from the restrooms and parking area, and nobody is here anyway." She stuck it between her lips and lit the twisted end, puffing until it a red glow caught. Pungent smoke drifted toward Carla and she waved it away from her face.

"I didn't want you bringing weed." Her face turned red. She stared at the three of them. Their eyes red from coughing. "It had better be the last of it and just so you know, that stuff stinks." She got up from the table and put her empty Diet Pepsi can in a recycling bin.

"I never asked, how much cash did you bring?" Carla asked Doug extracting a cigarette and lit it.

"I managed to get a thousand, Beth pitched in two bills." He took the joint from Matthew.

"There's something to be said for Beth doing that. She still loves you I think."

"Yeah, Wayne wishes we would get back together, but it ain't happening." He passed the joint to Carla, not thinking. She stared at it for a second. She never tried the stuff. "No, I pass"

She stood up. "Hurry up and finish that thing, we need to get back on the road, it's still a long way to Dallas."

Finally, it was Carla's turn to stare out the window. She sat in the front passenger seat listening to Matthew and Terri talk about Mexico. Terri lived there with her first husband, near El Paso, Texas. She said there was so much dust and scrub brush that when they moved to her mother's place in Green Valley, she forgot how green the grass and trees were compared to the desert landscape of Mexico. There were clothes lines everywhere and chickens running loose in the front yards of old adobe homes; even in the upper scale neighborhood of the town. At the time, people rarely drove vehicles. Bicycles and burrows filled the streets near bustling open markets loaded down with the vendor's wares. Everything from bolts of cloth to bushels of prickly pear lobes and strung up chili peppers laced in decorative fashion in some booths. Pots and pans were popular items as well as cassette recorders. "That was almost twenty-two years ago, you were considered pretty rich if you had a cassette player." She told them.

Carla opened her journal, thinking about what she wanted to write down. After staring out the window for a few minutes longer, she took the top off the ink pen and began to write.

"We are about sixty miles from McAlester, Oklahoma. We will probably stop to

eat there and take a break. Right now, Doug is driving, and will take us into Dallas, he's been there many times when he drove eighteen wheelers for a living and is familiar with the city's streets and the tangle of highways that intersect. I have never been to Dallas, in a way it's a little exciting. I haven't seen a large city since I left college at Memphis State University. That's something else I'm going to do. I just decided that right now. After all this is over, I'm going back to school and finish my degree. I regretted it for years that I did not get the chance to do that.

Well, now things have changed in my life and I have to stop regretting the choices I made in the past and learn from them. The one other thing besides losing my children to their father is losing my daughter to murder. I now know I should have acted on the warning signs of Jaun's abuse Juan. At first it was verbal. Nothing too harsh, it was just the way he said things to Katie, talking down to her as though she were a slave instead of his partner. If he wanted something and was closer to that object, he told her to get it. She waited on him hand and foot. One time she told me that the crease on one of his shirts wasn't ironed right and he threw the iron at her. Fortunately, it was plugged in, otherwise it could have caused serious damage to her face. She had just turned it off when he threw it.

It was more than one occasion that she and the boys stayed with me because he had locked her out and she didn't have an extra key because he felt she didn't need one. Still, she hung on to him. I didn't want to pry and cause a scene. I was raised that once married; you stay married. Of course, I do not believe in that aspect of a relationship any more. I am fortunate though Katie and Juan never married. Legally, he could have been the kid's custodial parent and I would have never seen them again. How ironic.

The night she came over with bruises on her arms and a swollen lip, I told her if she didn't leave him, he would kill her or possibly hurt the boys. I gave her an ultimatum, leave Juan, or I would call child's services. I had no choice, I feared for her and my grandbabies. I worried at night when they were at their home, wondering are those poor little guys huddled in a corner crying and begging their father not to hit them? Thank God, three days later with an escort from a deputy sheriff, we moved her things into a storage unit until a place was found. Funny, she never got the chance to do that."

Carla looked up, Doug was concentrating on the road, watching a small convoy of truckers and waiting for the opportunity to pass them. The landscape had changed considerably, from winding hilly roads of the Ozarks to long straight stretches of Oklahoma interstate. The sun winked across the water of Lake Eufaula; a large man-made lake named after the once tiny town that had grown considerably around it. Several boats could be seen gliding in the distance.

Carla wondered what those people's lives were like. As they drove further on, she noticed the landscape changed a little more. From oak and pine trees to huge clumps of sage and dry, cracked earth, two years in a row, she recalled Oklahoma had not seen their average rainfall totals and were on the edge of a drought. It wasn't too severe yet, but she got a small glimpse of what it must have been like back in the Dust Bowl of the nineteen thirties. At least, she thought, a tornado could be seen for miles out here.

They pulled into McAlester, Oklahoma a little after three in the afternoon. "I'm thinking a thick, juicy steak." Doug said. "And I know just the place."

"Do they have anything else?" Terri inquired. "I like steak, but I think I want shrimp."

Doug glanced in the rearview mirror and nodded at her. "I think they can accommodate each one of our taste preferences." He turned his attention to the road. He began to pick up speed, and moved into the passing lane. The convoy contained about five rigs, and Carla could feel the wind shake their vehicle as they passed by.

Even though they left Green Valley less than six hours ago; she felt a small pang of home sickness. She wondered what Richard was doing. He would probably be at the diner drinking his usual afternoon cup of coffee. She wondered what Lawrence would look like, how long would Charli's hair get before she lopped it off? How tall was Roger? Would they look like her? Would they recognize her?

Doug took George Nigh Expressway and pulled into Brangus Feed Lot Steakhouse. The lunch crowd was thinning. "This place is great, they have a beer garden out back, we can eat out there too. It's a little windy today though, probably not a good day to sit outside. They climbed out of the Wagoneer, their legs stiff from sitting for the past hour and a half. Carla found herself actually having a little fun. "I'm glad we all are together." She linked arms with Terri and Matthew. "Come on, let's run!" She tried to get them to join in.

Terri said she had to pee and was afraid she would wet herself. Matthew broke loose and took off, beating her to the door of the restaurant. They caught their breaths waiting for Doug and Terri. "I've got to quit smoking!" Carla gasped holding on to her knees.

They waited to be seated, glancing at the patrons eating and talking amongst themselves. It was light and airy, a wooden floor that supported many a customer, shone with a soft, warm glow. They chose one of the booths that lined the walls and sat down, waiting for their server. A large array offered tasty dishes for the lunch crowd, including burgers, and sandwiches from the grill. Terri was disappointed that shrimp was offered but only on dinner selections. They did have an all you can eat seafood menu but it was on Fridays. It was Monday.

Instead, she opted for one of the burgers with onion rings. Matthew and Doug settled for a thick Brangus burger, and Cajun fries. Carla went with a patty melt and onion rings served with more grilled onions and two different cheeses, American and Monterey jack melted on top of them. They decided on sweetened iced tea which were served in large mason jars.

While they waited for their food, Carla and Doug went to the beer garden to smoke. Carla was surprised at how cool it felt. Thick ivy vines draped over the open wooden trellises, creating lots of shady places. Large Caribbean ceiling fans with wide blades, gently circulated the air throughout the area.

"We need to find a place to stay for at least a week I figure." Carla said.

"We shouldn't have any trouble finding a hotel. Before we even get into Dallas itself, there are hundreds of them off the interstates. The only trouble we'll have is finding is Lawrence, Charli and Roger. I guess when we get to our rooms, we can start looking in the phone book."

"It's a start, more than what we had before."

Terri came out and told them the food was coming. They went back inside and sat down where a young Hispanic woman came towards them carrying a large tray over her head and a fold out stand.

Carla stared at the girl. "Excuse me," Carla thought it couldn't hurt to ask. "Can I ask, how old are you?"

"Nineteen."

"I know this is an odd question, but are you from around here?"

"Been here all my life. I'm going to Texas A&M this fall. Computer Science."

"By any chance," Here goes. "you wouldn't happen to know anyone named Lawrence or Charlie Simpson?"

"I know a Roger Simpson. He's my younger brother's bull riding buddy."

Carla felt an enormous lump swell up in her throat. That can't be. Bull riding? "Can you tell me-" she pulled out a worn photo of the children, taken about a year before her world crashed around her. "I know this is old, but does the younger one look familiar to you?" Carla's hand shook as she handed her the picture.

The waitress peered at it. "Add about fifteen years to that and yeah, I can see a resemblance." She handed the photo back to Carla.

"Do you think you could get a phone number, or where he is living?" Carla glanced at her brothers and Terri. None of them had even touched their food. They were listening to the conversation.

"I could call Sergio and see if he has Roger's number, I'm sure he does. I'll get back to you before you leave anyway, but I'll see what I can find out."

They watched her leave the table to fetch her next order.

"I can't believe what I just heard. What chance could there possibly be we get a hit on the first person asked?" Doug shook his head and took a drink of tea.

Carla stared after the girl. "I would have never thought that out of all places, in Oklahoma no less someone would know Roger. Does that mean they don't live in Dallas?"

"Maybe Roger left to be out here sis." Doug answered.

They ate the rest of their meal in silence. Carla thought about what she would say, what she would do when this time finally came. Now that it was so close, she didn't have a clue what she would do. True to her word, the waitress came back with a phone number and address.

"Sergio, my brother, said Roger and his siblings had some family in Arkansas. Are you them?"

"Yes, we are. Aunts and Uncles." Doug offered.

"He'll be happy to see you then. Sergio says he talks about them a lot, wondering how he could find them." Carla couldn't help but put her hand to her mouth when she gasped. She breathed in and collected herself. This was no time to get emotional.

"Thank you so much. Here," she pulled out a twenty-dollar bill, "for your help."

◆ ◆ ◆

They decided on a Days Inn motel in Garland, Texas, complete with a swimming pool, wi-fi and a gym. The trains rolling through at various times during the day wasn't expected, but no one complained. Carla and Doug had their own rooms and so did Matthew and Terri. They didn't expect to be next to each other, but they were on the same floor and in the same section of the motel. They all sat on the unused bed in Carla's room. She stared at the phone, unsure if she should try the number given to her by the waitress. "Here." She handed the piece of paper to Doug, "You call. If Hugh answers, he won't recognize your voice."

He took it and moved closer to the phone and began dialing. "Busy." He put the headset into the cradle. "Wait a few minutes and I'll try again."

Several minutes later, he tried the number again. "Still busy." He put the phone back up. "I'll try later."

"I think I'll check out the phone book and see if I can match the number." She began opening drawers and found it. "I bet this thing is a foot thick, feels like it weighs fifty pounds!" She heaved onto the bed. In the background, another train rolled by, shaking the picture of a Yucca cactus in front of a Spanish stucco home with adobe roof tiles.

"I hope I can sleep through that." Matthew said.

Terri yawned and stretched out across the bed "Right now, I'm tired enough, it wouldn't matter if two trains back-to-back rolled through. I'll sleep right through it all with no problems whatsoever."

Carla opened the phone book to the "S" and found Sims, her index finger tracing names until she came to "Simpson". "There must be at least three pages of nothing but Simpson." Slowly, she followed the list, none of the names she was searching for came up.

"Phone's ringing." Doug put his hand over the mouth piece. "Uh, yes, I'm looking for Roger Simpson."

"This is Roger."

"My name is Doug Jensen; I'm wondering if I could talk to you for a moment."

"I was told that there were some people asking about me and my family. Are you related to me?"

"Well, I'm not sure. If you don't mind, I need to ask you a couple of questions."

"Sure."

"What are your parent's name?"

Carla saw Doug's face fall. It wasn't her son.

Doug slowly hung up the phone. "I knew that was too easy."

Now what? Carla wanted to cry. In a matter of seconds, hope turned to sorrow. She stood up and went outside to smoke. The moon crawled up from the horizon, its bright light bounced off the tops of the vehicles in the parking lot. The wind was warm, but gusty. She lit up a cigarette and leaned against the building. Scraps of paper tumbled next to a wooden fence that separated the Days Inn from an Economy Lodge. On the street, cars and other vehicles could be heard driving to their destinations. Doug, Matthew and Terri came out and stood with her watching the moon rise. "We'll find them sis." Matthew put his arm over her shoulder and gave her a squeeze.

"I know." Tears started to pool in her eyes. "I had no idea it would be this, this-"

"Painful." Terri offered, who by now, was on the other side of Carla with her arm wrapped her waist.

Carla's voice cracked. "That about sums it up." She slipped away from the embraces and wiped her eyes. "Yep, that puts it right there in black and white." She sniffed, desperately needing a tissue. She went back into the room and pulled several out and blew her nose. She took a deep breath and sniffed again. "You know what? I think I need a drink."

CHAPTER ELEVEN

About a block and a half from the motel was a restaurant called Moe's. They walked in and liked the atmosphere immediately. A long string of tiny white lights draped around frame of the huge mirror behind the bar. More lights circled the windows and doors. Several small groups of people sat talking or playing pool. A Tom Petty song, American Girl, was playing on the juke box and a couple of girls were dancing to it. Although the back doors were wide open and the ceiling fans hanging from rafters were in use, thick smoke hung in the back where patrons played the pool tables. Carla walked up to the bar and ordered a beer. After they got their drinks, Matthew spotted an empty booth near the bandstand. He turned to the bartender and asked if they had anyone playing on Monday nights.

It turned out there was an acoustical three-piece called, Black Haired Possum that played Southern and Classic Rock every Sunday through Wednesday night from 9 pm to one in the morning. The bartender went on to explain the group was popular with the locals. Matthew thanked him and sat with the others. "Since we're here, might as well stay for the band." Matt took a long drink from the bottle then smacked his lips. "Boy that's a cold beer." He took another sip. "That's how beer is supposed to be, ice cold and fresh."

"You sound like a beer commercial." Doug chuckled and took a drink of his. "Anyone for a game of pool?"

Carla got up and dug out three quarters. "I'll give it a try."

"I thought you hated pool."

"I do." Carla's ex-husband was very proficient in billiards. He could predict the English on the ball and sink them in every time. When they started dating, Hugh showed her how to play pool. Many nights they spent in a local bar which hosted pool tournaments and practiced their shots. When a tournament came along, they participated and did well. They even won several big tournaments and were hometown celebrities. When she became pregnant with the twins Carla had to quit competing and was put on bed rest.

When the twins were born, they took up all of her time. Even with Katie's help she had babies to take care of and ended her days as a billiard competitor. Hugh on the other hand, continued to play on occasion which helped with finances. That was the third time Hugh cheated on her. He found another person to team up with in the tournaments. What he didn't tell her was the new partner was female. Only that the partner's name was Sam. Short for Samantha.

She walked over to a pool table and stuck the quarters into the coin slot and pushed the lever. Doug pulled out the triangular ball racking frame and began to put the balls in respective order, solid, stripe, solid, stripe, with the eight ball in the middle. "Okay, you break."

Carla concentrated on the cue ball then drew her arm back and connected the cue stick with the cue ball and gave it a huge whack. The colored balls rolled around the table, bouncing off of each other and the green felt covered rails. The orange solid ball rolled into Carla's far right corner pocket.

Doug offered his advice. "Go again, you're supposed to hit the solid-colored ones."

She glanced at him and widened her eyes.

"Oh, yeah, I forgot." He chuckled.

Carla tried another shot, but missed, sending the cue ball into a corner pocket. She went back to the table and took another drink of her beer, realizing that she needed another one and signaled a waitress.

When that game was over, Matthew and Doug played a round. Carla walked over to the juke box and read over the selections. *AC/DC, Styx, Eagles, Merle Haggard, Ricky Skaggs, Allison Kraus, The Beatles, Bob Seger and the Silver Bullet Band, Lynyrd Skynyrd, .38 Special, Lover Boy, and Kid Rock, Stone Temple Pilots,* and even a couple of Hip Hop artists like *Nelly,* and *50 Cent* thrown in for variety. She chose a couple of songs and went back to their table.

Several more customers had come in by the time Carla was ready to order a third beer. It was odd, she thought, she hadn't felt the effects of the two she already had. It was rare she drank; God knows she could have used drinking as an excuse to escape the pain of loss. But that wasn't her way of seeing an end to things.

Usually, a glass of wine with dinner on occasion or a Holiday drink like Hot Buttered Rum, maybe one or two beers, depending on the occasion was the extent. The third beer was half way gone when the band members of Black-Haired Possum came in with their equipment. Carla stared at the small knot of people gathered around them, smiling and shaking hands and hugging the regulars who were probably here every night. One of them, a tall, slim man broke free and walked to the stage to set his guitar down.

He wore faded denim jeans with rips in the knees and cowboy boots. He looked young, maybe eighteen at the most. Carla couldn't resist. She took her beer and walked over to him and introduced herself. The man stood up and shook her hand, introducing himself as Buddy the lead vocalist and guitarist.

"I wonder if I could ask you a question."

"Sure, fire away." Buddy said. He squatted down and opened his guitar case.

"Are you from around here?" She watched as he began to strum the instrument, listening for sour notes.

"Not too far, Sunnyvale, near the lake."

"I- uh, my brothers aren't from here. I know it's a long shot, but would you happen to know a Lawrence or Charli Simpson?"

"Sorry, can't say that I do." He continued to strum the guitar, turning its keys ever so slightly, his ear close to it. "You staying for the show?"

"Yeah, for a little while. We just came here to have a couple of drinks and play a little pool."

"I hope you like it. My girlfriend will have tee shirts and our CD for sale after the show. Every little bit helps."

They were good, Carla even got up and sang a song with them, she was on her fifth beer and feeling great. She hugged everybody who came by, she danced with strangers, she laughed so hard at times her stomach hurt. For a short time, she was just Carla, having a good time, not Carla, the woman searching for her day of reckoning.

◆ ◆ ◆

Carla woke up disoriented, her tongue felt like it was stuck to the roof of her mouth and her head felt extremely heavy. She stumbled to the sink and opened a sterilized plastic cup and got water from the faucet. She drank three more cups of water, then went to the bathroom. She hung her head as she finished urinating. *How many beers did I have?* Her business finished, she crawled back into bed and slept. She vowed to never drink again.

Her dreams were filled with scenarios of how she would meet her children grown into young adults. In her dreams there were hugs, kisses and tears. She tossed and turned, but by five o'clock she was up and dragging out the suitcase of journals. The tiny bed side light aided her as she pulled out several of them and began to read.

"April 11, the twins' birthday was the last time I got to be with you three. Now you are reaching your teen age years. It was a birthday party and an awkward one at that. There was a woman there from Child Services to watch over us; Katie and I were the only ones present. How fun. Thanks to your father, he accused me of choking you Lawrence because I caught you just in time before you fell off the couch and almost hit your head on the concrete floor. You went back with a couple of small bruises on your neck and he wanted all visitations cut off, but the judge at least allowed supervised visitations. Your father has managed to completely cut you kids off from me now. I haven't heard from or seen you in almost ten years."

Carla put the journal back in the suitcase and pulled out another volume.

"I know you had to be surprised by Katie's visit last Valentine's Day. She took you each a box of candy and Valentine's Day cards from all of us, your uncles, aunt Abbey, and Grandma. Katie wanted to see you three, so she and a friend drove to Louisiana. She said they were met at the door by a young woman who claimed to be Stacey's youngest sister. Katie told her she was looking for you kids and wanted to give them her gifts.

Georgette, the girl, said that no one was home but her, but then the door opened and a boy about your age Roger, came outside. Katie told me that Roger, when you saw her, you ran towards her and knew who she was right away! Georgette couldn't hold you back, way to go baby! Katie said you hugged her and begged to come back with her. Then she said Charli and Lawrence came out, but Georgette ordered them back inside.

Katie said she could see them staring out the window. She also asked if she could take some pictures so she could show their mother and was given a solid no, and that if she didn't leave, she would call the police. She also said at about that time your father and Stacey pulled in the driveway, demanding to know what was going on. She said your father threatened to call the police. He even told Katie there were warrants issued against her and me, and it was best if she left. She told him she would be back one of these days. He took your gifts and threw them in the trash can by their driveway and told her once more to leave.

It's Mother's Day and not a very good one. Katie, bless her little heart, had saved up some money and bought me a bouquet of flowers, thinking it would cheer me up. I was supposed to have you kids for the weekend, but your father and Stacey took you to his parents instead. I left your father's house with a note saying I thought it was very rude to not have let you come over on Mother's Day.

I didn't want Stacey to be around you children at all. She wasn't supposed to be until the divorce was final, but just like everything else that happened with this whole ordeal, it fell in your father's favor. He came over the next day, screaming and yelling, calling me every name in the book and that I had no right leaving a note or being at his home when he wasn't there.

I reminded him it was my weekend to have you kids and he said he couldn't care less about me getting to see you. He even accused me of breaking a glass of some kind and putting the broken pieces under his tires. I asked him how he thought I could do that when his car wasn't even there. Charli, he had you with him. You started crying and telling him you wanted to be with me. He told me he would have terroristic threatening charges brought up against me if he caught me by his house anymore. He threatened me by saying if I wanted to see you kids again to not try to manipulate things. Huh, me manipulate anything? How's that for calling the kettle black? He went as far as to say he would get Katie taken away from me too if I didn't leave well enough alone.

I was so proud of Katie just then. She told him exactly what she thought of him. Katie was only twelve then. She stood up to Hugh, and told him he had no right barging into their home, she was going to have him arrested for threatening them. He didn't want his parents to know he was divorcing me. He knew I would tell them just exactly what happened. Katie gave him both barrels, she told him she thought he was trash for making her feel bad about her weight, and constantly nagging me about mine. She thought he was scum of the earth for making her get up every *morning and doing exercises, taking care of the kids, cleaning the house and having no friends over or being able to go stay the night with friends. She told him how he hurt her feelings.*

Charli, I was holding you, trying to get you to stop crying, all the while Katie is telling your father he was a lousy step father, not to mention a horrible husband. She told him she hated him especially when he called me names like fat cow, or only whores wore make up. I've worn make up ever since I was eighteen. She told him he needed his butt kicked and one of these days she would have the honor of doing just that. He took a step towards Katie, and raised his fist, ready to strike her. She told him to go ahead and that he better knock her out. I had to step in then and told Katie to take you, Charli, back outside.

I told your father Katie had every right to tell him off and that was why I let her go on. He was the one in the wrong this time, barging in and making accusations when it was he who left, hiding behind his lies. I know he coached you kids, told you what to say to the judge, when it's completely clear who's to blame.

I thought it was a horrible thing he did to have Katie not be present if I got to see you kids. Let me back up.....He once again lied to his attorney and had a motion filed to keep you kids from your sister. In other words, if she was around, you three, she could be held in contempt of court and all visitations would cease. But that didn't matter because I never got to see you again anyway.

The following week I tried to call to find out what time your father was bringing you kids over. All I got was a message on there saying the phone number was no longer in service. I jumped into my car and drove over wondering what was going on and found he had moved. Nothing was left, not even a scrap of paper. All I found was a tiny little ring I got for you Charli when you wanted a piece of gum. I wear it on a necklace around my neck.

I know this is going to be hard to believe but a month later your father did call me and wanted to know if I knew anyone who could be hired to "take care of Stacey". I told him I had him recorded saying that. The next thing I know I'm getting served a subpoena to court and being accused of getting my friend's husband and her son to target him and sabotaging his vehicle. I told the judge I didn't know where he even lived, he violated the custody agreement and moved without notice, he was the one barging into my home and causing problems, he wanted to have his new wife eliminated. I never saw you three again.

CHAPTER TWELVE

Carla realized she had fallen asleep when a loud, urgent knocking woke her up. There were all of the journals spread about the bed, a couple of them fell to the floor. She stumbled to the door and looked through the peep hole. It was Doug, Matthew and Terri. She opened it, squinting her eyes against the bright sun.

The three of them were smiling from ear to ear, Terri started jumping up and down. "Guess what?"

"We found Charli."

Carla stood there taking a second to let it sink in. Charli?

"Actually, she found us." Matthew held up a box of coffee and several sacks of McDonald's breakfast. "She works at a gas station about two miles away from here. We let you sleep so we decided to go grab breakfast and put gas in the Jeep. Anyway, we went in and paid for the gas when a girl came up and asked Doug who he was and before he could even answer, she said his name!" Matthew set down the coffee and handed one of them to Carla.

She set it aside. "What did she say?"

"She wants to see you. I told her where we were staying and she's supposed to come over when she gets off work." Doug pulled out an Egg McMuffin and wolfed it down in three bites and pulled out another one.

"I asked her if she knew about Katie. She said she hadn't, but I told her that we could fill her in when she came over." Matthew offered Carla a hash brown and an Egg McMuffin of her own. She put them next to the coffee. "She wanted to get her brothers and bring them too, but I told her it was best this time to come by herself. She said they all lived together in an apartment not far away."

"What time did she say she would be here?" Carla's voice had that far away down a hole sound to it. Could this be the real thing this time?

"Sometime around noon. She wanted me to tell you she can't wait to see you." Doug sat next to Carla. "She looks just like you too. Straight copper brown hair and fiery blue eyes that say, 'I'll kick your butt'."

"She's tall like you and she said Roger is taller than her and Lawrence." Matthew took an orange juice from a sack and opened it up. "She's curious about the journals. I told her you had about twenty of them you wanted to give to them."

Carla stood up and ran her hands through her hair, forgetting that she had only cut it short less than a week ago. She still found herself checking to see if she needed to fix her hair. After twenty years of growing it, the habit was still there. She paced back and forth, stopping to take a sip of her coffee every now and then. "I've been waiting for this so long, what do I say?"

"This is so exciting!" Exclaimed Terri. "I remember those kids when they were just beginning to walk." She grinned, shaking her head slowly. "Which one of the twins was the first one to take their first steps?"

"Lawrence." Matthew piped up. "Remember on Christmas Eve? We were all over at Abbey's house eating Christmas dinner and while we were eating, he was playing on the floor and then the next thing I knew, there he was clinging to my pants leg one minute and off he went to you Carla."

Carla barely heard them talking. "What time is it?" She stared at the digital alarm clock on the end table between the two double beds. "Eleven thirty?" She gathered up her suitcase and pulled out a fresh sleeveless blouse and under clothes. "I need a shower."

"Your breakfast is getting cold."

"I'll eat later. I smell like I rolled on the floor of that bar."

No, you behaved." Doug smiled and chuckled. "You liked dancing with that one guy, Mr. I am good looking."

"All in fun. He seemed surprised I didn't ask him to stay the night though."

"He did act like he was super cool, too sexy for my shirt character."

"Narcissistic." Terri added.

Carla smiled and raised her eyebrow at her sister-in-law. "I'm keeping my mouth shut on that." She picked up her egg McMuffin and took a large bite then laid it down on its paper wrapper. She was almost to the door of the bathroom before she changed her mind and decided to eat. "That's really good. I didn't think I was hungry, but the stomach says otherwise."

Carla stood outside staring down into the parking lot. Each time a vehicle pulled into the lot, she strained to see if the person inside was Charli. Carla wondered what kind of car her daughter drove. Each one that came through Carla thought would be Charli. She must have stood out on the balcony for nearly fifteen minutes. It was almost twelve thirty. *Should be any minute now.* Carla thought and started to pull out another cigarette, the second one in less than ten minutes, then decided she didn't need it. She put her hands into her jean pockets and walked the length of the motel's upper balcony, continuing to watch the vehicles passing on the busy street. Ten more minutes slipped by when two vehicles pulled in together. One was a silver VW Beetle, and a Red Dodge Ram pickup truck. A young girl climbed out of the VW and two boys from the pickup. They stood near their vehicles staring up at the rooms when one of them pointed at Carla.

She ran along the balcony, watching them watching her. She waved and they waved back. They started for the same stairway Carla was coming down, trying not to fall and break her neck. She met them at the bottom and grabbed all three at once, trying hard not to cry. But it was no use, she let the tears flow and kissed their faces and the tears that they were shedding. Everyone talked at once, hugging and laughing, more kisses followed more tears. This was how it was supposed to be, Carla thought staring into the eyes of her grown children. Matthew and Doug came down the stairs and shook hands with the boys, then more hugs for Charli. Carla suggested they go to her room where they could talk. Everyone agreed and walked up the stairway.

Once they were seated in the room, Carla sat facing Lawrence, Charli, and Roger. "You all have changed so much! You are so beautiful Charli, and look at you two, my strong handsome sons!" Both of her sons were blonde, tall and lanky. They had the most beautiful smiles and rich, deep voices.

"I couldn't come over here without calling Lawrence and Roger." Charli said, looking at Doug and Matthew. "We have talked about this day for a long time. Never around daddy though, he didn't want us to even say your name."

Roger extended his long legs out in front of him. "Stacey left daddy about five years ago, for someone about ten years younger than him. At first, I was mad. She hurt dad, but at the same time I didn't have to do what she said anymore."

They spent the next hour talking about what was going on and what happened to their older half-sister. Carla showed them pictures of their nephews. Lawrence and Roger both wanted to go and help with the search, but Carla told them no. The best thing to do she told them was to not say anything about their visit and read the journals, they would explain a lot of things.

They could help out she told them by watching for the boys in their own area. Roger offered to build a website for Scotty and Marcos. When all was over with and she had her grandsons back with her, they would stop back in Dallas so they could meet their aunt and uncles. "You make what you want of those," Carla said as she handed them over to Lawrence. "I'm sure you'll have lots of questions to ask your father."

The three children stared at the suitcase holding fifteen years of anguish and sadness. "This is going to take a long time to read all of these."

"It took me a long time to write them."

"When do you all plan to leave? I'd like for us to go have lunch somewhere." Charli asked Matthew.

"You'd have to ask your mother. But as far as lunch is concerned, I'm ready. Egg McMuffins don't stay with a person too awful long, especially when you got a bottomless stomach like me."

"He eats all the time, but look at him!" Terri pointed to Matthew's flat stomach. "He hasn't gained or lost any weight in the past five years or so. I wish I could boast about that." She patted the small paunch on her stomach. "The beginning of the middle age spread."

"If you like Chinese food, I know a wonderful place about a half mile from here called Su Wong. They have the best Sweet and Sour Pork in the state. It's spread-out buffet style too." Charli said, as she put the blue suitcase in the back seat of her VW. "Mom, if you want, you can ride with me."

Mom. Carla hadn't heard those words in over two years. Marcos occasionally called her that, but coming from her only living daughter was like sweet pollen to a honey bee. They climbed into her car and the rest followed them to the restaurant.

Carla couldn't take her eyes off her daughter. She looked so much like Katie except she was slim and had her big feet. Charli was still in her work clothes from the gas station, her name tag still attached and, her hair in a ponytail. "I didn't want to waste anytime changing my clothes. I don't care what people think anyway." Charli looked ahead at the traffic light changing from green to yellow. She slowed down and came to a stop. "Daddy doesn't know we came to see you. I think it would make him mad. But he has a lot of explaining to do. Why didn't he tell us about Katie? Why couldn't he have told us he called you?"

"He told me you all were at some kind of bible camp."

"Mom, I haven't been to summer camp since I was twelve. I started a dog sitting business that following summer to save money up for college tuition."

"Well, it's a good thing I am here then. I wanted you to just find the money when you started reading the journals." Carla nodded at the suitcase sitting in the back seat. "Since you brought up the subject, the three colored envelopes have your names written on them. Inside the first journal, you'll find an envelope with a traveler's check written out to each of you. I set up a trust fund for you three many years ago. However, I have to use some of it for this trip, but I'll make sure it gets put back in the account." Carla glanced over at Charli. It was too surreal.

"Mom, I don't need this money. I want you to use it for finding Scotty and Marcos." She glanced in the rearview mirror when she heard someone honking.

"College tuition is not cheap so, please use it for that."

Here she was, just days ago agonizing on how she could possibly ever find her children. Now she was sitting with them at a Chinese restaurant talking, and eating Won Tons and Moo Goo Gai Pan like it was a normal thing to do on a Tuesday afternoon. As much as she hated it, she had another mission and needed to move on. When they finished the meal, they stood outside the eatery, hugging each other. Fighting back tears Carla hugged each of her children tight and apologized for the quick reunion. She didn't want to leave;

even though they were newly reunited. This time however, she didn't have to worry about them like she had all those years. They knew she loved them. Carla stood with her brothers and sister-in-law, watching the VW and the Dodge pull into traffic.

Carla took in a deep breath. The smile on her face felt foreign. "I couldn't have expected this to turn out any better than it did."

"Me either." Doug slipped an arm around Carla and hugged her. "Funny how things work out sometimes."

CHAPTER THIRTEEN

By nine o'clock the following morning they were back on the road. Matthew opted to drive with Terri sitting shotgun. They crossed over bypasses and through intersections while people went about their daily routines. They finally came to Interstate 20 and headed west to Tucson, Arizona.

They were twenty miles from Dallas when Terri had the idea of playing a little trivia to help pass the time. "I knew this game would come in handy!" She pulled out a small box of cards. "Okay, I'll start. Who wants the first question?"

"Shoot." Carla answered.

"Okay, are there volcanoes in Canada?"

"Uh, yes."

Terri flipped over the card, "got it right. Want another one?"

"Sure."

"What West Coast city was named for a Suquamish Indian Chief named Sealth?"

"That's easy. Seattle." Doug leaned over the front seat, "let's have another one."

"Do pearls melt in vinegar?"

"Huh, let's see, pearls are pretty hard, but they're organic. Vinegar cuts through a lot of build up like lime, so I'll say yes."

Terri flipped over the card and clapped her hands. "Good guess Doug."

"How many cherries are there in a slot machine cluster?"

"That's easy, three."

"Yep!"

"Which of Cheech and Chong once sang with Captain Shagnasty and His Lock Ness Pickles?"

"Well, since Cheech was the one to sing in Up in Smoke, my guess would be Cheech." Matthew answered.

"Oooh honey, you got it right!" Terri kissed him on the cheek.

"Let me ask you one." Doug picked up a small stack of the questions and shuffled through. "Okay, here's one. What four-legged animal is associated with the World Wildlife Federation?"

"Panda."

"Yep."

It did help eat up an hour before everyone got tired of playing. Carla pulled out her journal but it remained in her lap. She was so wrapped up in her thoughts she hadn't noticed the change in the terrain since leaving Dallas. She could see for miles on the open landscape. Cati replaced the tall graceful oak, elm, and maple trees. It was easy to imagine crossing sweeping prairie grasses and wildflowers when it rained, and dry, cracked earth during drought in a covered wagon. It would have been an awe inspiring moment to watch the buffalo by the hundreds grazing as they wandered about the plains.

In a motel room, near Tuson, Arizona, Carla sat on her bed reflecting the day. So much had changed so quick! She wondered if they were reading the journals. She hoped they would understand why she left Louisiana and why she had no choice.

The urgent desire to save Scotty and Marcos were now the only reason that kept her going. She hoped and prayed Juan wouldn't do anything to his sons. If he found out Carla was looking for him, it could certainly put the boys at risk. Their trip would almost have to be a covert operation of sorts. Play the tourists. Wear silly clothes, take pictures, buy handmade souvenirs, and drive the Baja Peninsula. Carla was scared, petrified actually. They were taking on something they had no business taking on. If one person came searching for one person, it probably wouldn't be too noticeable. But if a group of people who happen to be white skinned Americans, coming to Mexico, asking questions trouble was sure to follow.

Carla jumped when her cell phone rang. It rarely rang and most of the time she forgot about it. That was another thing, the phone company assured her they could keep her connected, she had her own spot on a satellite high in the sky. She looked at the number on the screen; Richard.

"Hey you." Carla couldn't hide the fact she was glad to hear from him. She had to admit she missed him.

"Hey yourself. I had to call, everything going ok?"

"Well, I guess I can tell you. I found the twins and Roger."

"Carla! That's terrific!"

She could feel him grinning from ear to ear, she wiped a tiny tear from her eye. "It is terrific, Richard, I played out that scene so many times and it wasn't exactly as I planned it."

"Why? What happened?"

"Oh, it was wonderful! We had a lot to talk about, and I gave them my journals."

"That's the perfect thing to do, they need to know the truth. I know you never really talked about your other children because it was plain to see how much pain it put you through when you did in our support group meetings. It's a giant step in the right direction."

"Yes, it is."

"So," Richard paused. "what direction are you going now? Need I ask?"

"Oh, just driving in the desert South West, thinking about visiting the Grand Canyon."

"Really?"

"Possible. Hey, how are things at home? My house is still standing?"

Richard laughed. "Just the front porch. I have the couch sitting on it."

"Oh, well, that's all that matters then." They both laughed. "How's Haley?"

"She's great, said to tell you hi and write her a postcard now and then."

"That I will do first thing in the morning. They have some really pretty ones in the hotel lobby."

"I have something else to tell you. Chief Bristol got some information about the case. Other than Homeland Security, I think we all know where you are going." Richard's voice dropped to a whisper. "There's a possibility that Juan is in Cabo San Lucas."

"How would they know that?"

"A rival gang in La Paz. His group hit some powerful people in the gang world there. Brought up some interesting names and Juan Gonzales- Pedraza came up in the mix. No information about the kids."

This was comforting for Carla in two ways, someone was else was searching for them, and one of those people would like to do nothing more than toss Juan to the sharks. "If the boys are with him Richard they are in grave danger."

"You'll probably have to talk to Homeland Security."

This gave her a wide-open channel to hone in on Juan and find her grandsons. "I'm going to the embassy in Mexico City then. Surely, they can do something."

"Well, I mean, I suppose since you are out that way. If you are just rambling around the country that wouldn't be out of your way huh?"

Carla chuckled softly.

There was an unusual long pause, she was beginning to think the call dropped connection.

"I miss you, Carla."

She hesitated. She wanted to tell him she missed him too, but she froze. "Before you know it, I'll be back. Hey, can I call you later? We're going to try to get an early start tomorrow since we will be in the desert, hot weather and all."

"Oh."

"Probably in a day or so" She liked the idea of having a life line. She felt the less he knew the better off for him. "I'll get Haley a post card out tomorrow, tell her that for me, okay?"

"Sure thing. Well, I gotta go. Haley has homework."

Carla laughed and wished him luck then disconnected the call. She climbed out of the bed and double checked her luggage to make sure everything was packed except what she would need the next morning. She made a mental note about finding a Laundromat. Three and a half days out and it would probably be a good idea to keep up with it and maybe even wear the same clothes a couple of days in a row. She needed to be frugal with her money, what she spent would have to go back into the kid's trust fund and the less the better.

She decided she was hungry and picked up the motel's directory and chose a pizza place. She ordered a large thick crust with everything on it and a thin crust with extra pepperoni and cheese. She picked up the ice bucket and walked down to the ice machine, stopping on the way back by Doug's room to let him know food was on the way. When Doug answered the door, thick pungent smoke followed him out. She pushed him inside the room and slammed the door. "You guys! You lied to me again! You can smell that a mile away!"

"Only when the door is opened." Matthew replied and pointed to the ice bucket. "What's in there?"

She tilted the bucket to show him the ice. "What do you think? I ordered pizza and came by to tell you it's on the way." She nodded to the joint being passed from Terri to Doug. "I thought you had finished that off already."

"This is the last of it." Doug offered her the joint and she waved it away.

Carla arched her eyebrow. "Oh?"

"Really, Honest." Terri grinned at her. "So, when is the pizza getting here? I could eat a horse right now."

Carla sneered at her. "I'm sure you could," She looked down at her watch, "ten minutes, give or take five." She pointed to the joint as Doug handed it to Terri. "Put that thing out, turn on the exhaust fan, and spray the room before you come over!" She stared at the trio briefly then opened the door closing it as fast as she could. Thank God they at least had the sense to keep the curtains closed she thought dryly.

She went to her room and set the container of ice in the sink and turned on the television. There was a dust storm wreaking havoc on I-40 near Kingman, Arizona, stopping traffic for nearly five miles with no sign of letting up until the next day; another one reported twenty-three miles east of El Paso on I-10. That one had traffic backed up a long way too.

Tragically, it involved an accident with six vehicles; two of those being semis. She was glad she wasn't stuck in either one of them. Other than a mention of a low-pressure system crossing Central America her attention to the news was minimal. She liked a little background noise because it helped her think and the room not be so quiet. It was a habit she picked up after her grandsons were gone. She heard a knock at the door and opened it up. There stood Lawrence, Charli and Roger.

CHAPTER FOURTEEN

"What do you think you're doing?"

"We followed you."

"You kids can't do this! What about your father?"

"He doesn't know."

Carla opened the door wider to let them in. She motioned for them to sit on the bed. "You are going to call him this instant."

"I'm pretty sure he's probably passed out right now in his chair. When we got home, we read some of the journals, enough to tell us he's been lying all along, so then we showed him the journals." Roger smirked. "Boy was he mad!"

Charli nodded her head in agreement. "Did he really drag you off of the couch because you fell asleep?" Charli stared at her mother.

"I'm afraid so. He could be a mean drunk sometimes." She opened the curtain looking out onto the parking lot.

Charli set her purse down on the dresser and turned to her mother. "Yeah, he threw some of your journals against the wall and left. Two hours later he showed up drunk and confessed he had the affair with Stacey and staged the whole thing about you threatening his life."

Carla couldn't help the twisted smirk. She knew it looked evil. It felt evil, but right then it was the greatest feeling in the world. "You still need to call him. He will try to blame me for kidnapping you."

"We're over legal age." Charli replied.

Just then the door opened and just like Carla, Doug, Matthew and Terri were surprised to see them as well. Carla filled them in on how they got here and Hugh's confession when there was another knock on the door.

"Welcome to Tucson!" Doug announced.

They all laughed.

"Good thing I ordered two large pizzas," she handed the delivery man the money owed plus a tip. She thanked him and closed the door. "There is Pepsi, Diet Pepsi, and Dr. Pepper. It was all they had." She turned to the kids, "Have you eaten? Help yourself if you're hungry." What in the world was she going to do with three teenagers? They had to go back. She couldn't let them risk their lives. "You can stay over tonight, but you have to go back home."

"We are here to help, mom. Katie was our sister, dad kept things from us and we finally get to see you after fifteen years! We are not going anywhere but with you."

"What about school Roger? You're starting your senior year; you need to graduate and go on to college son." She turned to her daughter. "Charli? You want to go to law school, Lawrence, you have dreams and ambitions too. I would much rather see you achieve your dreams than blow your money and worry your dad." She stared at them. "And me."

"We're staying mom. No more arguing, okay?"

"Call your father, get some sleep, then we'll talk."

They pulled into a Flying J truck stop. It had every traveler's needs- Groceries, clothing outlet, shower stalls and bathrooms. Next to the store a red neon sign said Murphy's Diner that boasted of its huge stacks of pancakes and large plates of hash-browns and eggs. Coffee drinkers sat on stools at the counter bar, talking about their loads of cargo or discussing other issues such as politics or the economy. Carla and her kids along with Matthew Doug and Terri walked inside the diner and found two booths together and sat down. They ordered coffees and sodas and studied the menu.

"What did your father say when he learned you all talked with your mom?" Terri asked taking a large swallow of iced tea.

"Oh, he wasn't very happy with us and he tried blaming mom for all of this, just like she said he would. He wanted us to get back home, he ranted and raved for nearly ten minutes before he finally gave in and told us to do what we wanted."

"Tell her what else he said." Lawrence said, rubbing his hands together when the plate of thick, fluffy pancakes was put in front of him.

"He told me that he was moving and wasn't going to say where. I told him go ahead, that we would find him, he was more than welcome to pack up everything and load it himself into that run down piece of junk pickup truck."

"So, this means you are going with us?" Matthew tore into a biscuit and drowned it in sausage gravy.

The three children looked at each other and Roger spoke up. "We want to help out as much as possible but we decided to go back home. We need to work things out with dad. I don't want any more secrets kept from us. He deserves what he gets, and he needs to own up. I hate to think of him sitting at home alone in his underwear drinking whiskey. Roger looked away from his siblings to his mother. "I haven't decided what to think about all of this anyway, it's still a little far out and weird."

"I know the feeling honey." Carla squeezed his hand. "I'm having a hard time just seeing you three sitting across from me!" She laughed and stared at them, hoping she wouldn't tear up again. "We have so much to talk about, but you need to work things out with your father, even if I think he's scum of the earth, he is still your dad. He raised you all of these years and from the looks of things he did okay." Carla she forced a grin then jabbed her fork into a runny yolk with her toast.

"Well, I think we need to talk about what's next." Doug took a sip of coffee and returned to his breakfast. "It's been a long time since I came this way and that was only once because Johnson Steel needed an extra driver on this route."

Carla opened a composition book with the directions written down. "We stay on I-10 until we come up on the I-8 West exit ramp. That takes us into Yuma, we continue on eight until we get into California and then we get on 94, we'll be close then. This route also connects us with Carretera Federal, or Mexican Federal Highway One. We can enter Mexico at Tecate, without a whole lot of hassle. Tijuana will be crowded, so will Mexicali. They also take different directions from what we want." She looked up from her notes, glad they were paying attention.

"The closest place to the border is in Campo, California. We may need to stay there tonight and start out fresh in the morning." Carla almost blurted out that it would be a good time to get rid of any pot they had left, but held her tongue. The last thing she needed was her children finding out their aunt and uncles smoked weed.

The group finished their breakfast and went to the cash register to pay for their meals. Carla picked up Lawrence, Charli and Roger's tab and went outside. Hugging each child tight, afraid she may not get another opportunity; she told them as she wiped tears from her eyes, "I am so thankful you all want to help out. Katie would be proud of you."

Matthew, Doug, and Terri came out behind them and bade their farewells, hugging each one of the kids. They stood together and watched them drive off in Charli's VW toward Dallas. "You think they'll go back?" Doug stood next to Carla waving at them as they sped into the distance.

"Yeah." Carla hugged herself and walked to the Jeep. The closer she got; she noticed something odd about the back end. "Oh no!" She shouted and ran to the vehicle, inspecting the bumper. A large crease crinkled the thick protective coating in toward the tire and the tail light cover was broken. "Great. Just friggin' great. Now I have to call the rental place and report it."

Doug ran his hand over the light cover. "It's cracked, and the bumper isn't too messed up, it won't rub the tire so all is not lost. It's hardly noticeable."

Carla got off the phone with the dealership and went back to the vehicle, surprised she had walked so far away. "Well, at least it's some good news. Mr. Kearny said not to worry, they would make a note of it and report it to the insurance company, but I have to get a police report."

Doug straighten up from stooping to inspect the damage. "It happens sis. It would have been nice if the person who did it could have at least left a note."

"Probably someone who doesn't have a license and had no business being out on the road." Matthew scoured the parking lot, searching for someone who could have seen the incident. He asked several people who walked by them if they had seen anyone near the vehicle, but unfortunately no one did.

◆ ◆ ◆

The sun climbed over the roof of the building. It wasn't even nine o'clock in the morning and she could see heat waves coming from the black top of the parking lot.

Carla was tired of waiting. She was becoming aggravated when a patrol car rolled into the lot and pulled in behind her Jeep. He inspected the damage and took pictures. When he finished with the inspection, he told her if she wanted a copy of the report she would have to come by the station in a couple of days.

"I don't suppose you could just fax my insurance company and the rental company a copy of the report?"

"Sorry ma'am. It's your responsibility." The officer's voice sounded programmed. She could tell he was completely bored and probably had a contempt for tourists. She couldn't tell him she was actually on the hunt for her grandchildren and that she was extremely worried about them; that she was fearing for their lives, that she wanted to throw Juan into a lake of fire after kicking the shit out of him. "I can't wait two days, sir. You see I'm on vacation and I-"

"If you want the report, you'll have to wait at least two days. I'm sorry, department policy." He tipped his hat and climbed back inside the squad car.

"I don't have two days, but I have a camera." Carla rummaged through her purse and pulled out her digital camera and took several photos of the Jeep. She went back inside the restaurant and requested a booth with a plug in and downloaded the images and sent them off to the car dealer and insurance company with a note indicating they could contact the Tucson Police Department for the report. She hoped it would work, but she didn't have the time to wait for a report. She thanked the Hostess and left the restaurant. "Pile in and let's go." They pulled into the traffic and got onto interstate eight, heading to Mexico.

In spite of the incident, she was happier than she'd been in a long time. Shortly, they ran into a construction zone, slowing traffic to a snail's pace. They sat in traffic waiting for a highway worker holding up a stop sign to turn it over and maybe move another twenty feet. Looking out the passenger side window, she spotted a prairie dog watching them. The rodent popped up like a furry jack-in-the-box, staring at passersby causing Carla to laugh. She watched a small, graceful cloud of desert dust skip across hills and shallow washouts over the Arizona landscape like a well-practiced dance routine. Just as quick as it started, the funnel died.

Slowing down Carla got to see the desert closer and marveled the striations in carved rock, arroyos clogged with tumbleweeds and cactus. The Santa Catalina mountains to the north of them had facinating shapes from violent upheavals in the Earth's crust as it evolved into the massive ridges punching through the arid land. As they drove further, the scenery became tedious. Everything was the color of sand, including the vegetation and wildlife. Even the horizon of the desert sky seemed to absorb the color. Terri asked if anyone wanted to play trivia again.

"Anything is better than watching out the window. It's so bland, and blah, just like I remembered." Terri pulled out a stack of cards. "Okay, how about each of us get to ask five questions? Should we keep score?"

"I can do that." Carla reached for her composition book. "A point for each question asked and up to twenty points. Sound fair?"

All agreed. "I'll guess a number between one and one hundred, and whoever is the closest goes first, next closest is second, and so on. Fair enough?" Again, they agreed. Carla gave it brief thought then told them to pick a number between one and fifty. Terri said 14, and Matthew called 38.

" It's 34. Matt, you were the closest, then Terri and I'll go last. Doug is driving so it might be hard for him to read cards and ask questions. Sound fair?"

All agreed.

"Okay here's an easy one." Matthew held up the card to read it better.

"I can see the answers, Matt." Carla laughed.

"What president is named in the opening theme for All in the Family?

"You knew what you were then...."Carla sang out.

"Girls were girls and men were men, ooh, ooh I know, Herbert Hoover!" Terri exclaimed and clapped her hands.

"First point on the board. Pick another one Matt."

"Got it. Does a squid's arms face forward or backward from its head?"

A couple of seconds drifted by. "Forward." Doug spoke up.

Matthew turned the card over. "Good guess. One for Doug."

"What kind of animals does a hippo phobic blacksmith fear?"

"What?"

Matthew repeated it again.

"Never heard of one. Hippo phobic blacksmith, animals, meaning more than one." Doug said. "I don't know, fear of shoeing hippos?" They all laughed at his answer.

"Nope. Anyone else want to give it a shot?" Matthew grinned at Terri.

"Let's see, hippos are called river horses. A blacksmith shoes horses, so horses, he's afraid of horses." Terri grinned and licked her index finger and made a tally mark in the air.

"You know all the answers." Doug snorted. "You have had all day to sit around and memorize all those questions."

"I have not!" Terri shot back.

"Hey, just a friendly game. Everybody ease up." Carla cautioned. "Come on, Matt next one."

"Okay, what country's two-dollar bill features six Eskimos, four kayaks, and two spears?"

"Russia." Carla answered quickly.

"Nope."

No one had an answer. "Okay five seconds up. It's Canada."

"Aww, I knew that!" Terri piped up.

"Why didn't you say so?" Doug asked.

"I wasn't really sure."

"Next."

"Uh, okay, here's one. Can fish smell?"

"No." Both Carla and Doug answered in unison.

"Ohh, no!" Matthew groaned. "Yes, they can smell!" He made a buzzing noise. "That ladies and gentleman, signals the end of the first round. We'll go to a commercial break and come back with more fun when we return!"

"Nice job with the radio voice, Matt." Doug glanced in the rearview mirror at his brother.

They pulled into a gas station in Gila Bend, Arizona, to stretch their legs and go to the bathroom. Carla and Terri went inside to pick up a few items while they waited for the women's room to become unoccupied.

Terri grinned and spoke out the side of her mouth. "It's a good thing I don't have to go that bad."

Carla shrugged her shoulders and paid for her purchases and took them to the Jeep. When she returned to the inside of the store, Terri was coming out of the restroom, drying her hands on her jeans. "No paper towels."

Carla walked into the toilet and sat down to relieve herself. The air was nice and cool and the bathroom actually smelled nice, some kind of flowery fragrance drifted in her nose. The owner of the store took great pains to keep the graffiti covered up, but the new coat already supported fresh signatures of so and so loving so and so forever. Somebody named Ruby had been in the same stall in June and was from New York.

She went to the sink to wash her hands and remembered the paper towel dispenser was empty. She opened the door to the ladies' room and went to the register, the attendant showed her the row where paper towels were and told her it was okay to take one into the bathroom. There were five people in line ready to take their purchases home and more coming in, so she went and picked a roll and put it in the dispenser since it didn't require a key. By the time that was all done, her hands were dry so she washed them again and pulled a couple of sheets from the roll and dried her hands. *I had to get them; I will use them.*

She walked outside and stared at the street heading into Gila Bend, Arizona. Far off into the distance she could see what looked like some kind of industrial plant. The mountains made a nice background. At least the employees had something to look at she thought.

The horizon stretched for untold miles, how anything could possibly survive in a desert anywhere in the world was beyond her. She noticed the air was different; dry and hot, forecasters predicted highs in the 110's with night time temps in the 90's. If she had to endure 90-degree night temperatures back home with the humidity factored in she would have to live in front of the air conditioner. It wasn't too bad though; a nice breeze blew in from the west off the Gila Bend Mountain Range in the distance.

Doug was leafing through some tourist brochures and smoking a cigarette at one of the covered picnic tables. Carla sat down next to him. "What's all this?" She picked up one. "Sweet Desert Shrimp Festival. Where do they get the shrimp from?"

"Here's this Painted Rock Petroglyph display that might be interesting or

The Gillespie Dam. I was thinking we could just take a little side trip and check out the town."

Carla thought it was unusual at first, then she realized they hadn't taken the time to slow down and look around them. They had to play tourist. It was part of the covert plan. "I know it's starting to become a bit dreary, but remember why we are out here and not playing full-time tourists. We will have time for that on the way back home."

He cleared his throat. "It's not that, there's a girl who used to live here. We hit it off really well, yes, we slept together, but when I woke up, she was already gone. Her name was Lilly. She used to work at the Space Age Restaurant, just down the strip a little way.

"That's been a long time ago."

"I know, there could be a chance she is still around. I just wanted to tell her hello. I was in the neighborhood and thought I'd drop in." He grinned.

"You think you'd remember what she looked like?" Carla had to admit it was intriguing to land in a town miles from home, and find out you know a person in it.

"I remember she had long, black hair and dark brown eyes and the sexiest voice."

"That could be anyone, Doug."

Doug shook his head, "Not so."

Carla stared at him for a few minutes, started to open her mouth and then thought better of it.

"What?" Matthew sat down beside them holding red and white checkered baskets full of French fries and corn dogs. "Who could be anyone?" Matthew asked as he balanced the baskets, slowly setting them down so the corn dogs wouldn't roll onto the table top. Terri also had a variety of fried goods, mushrooms, okra, and cheese sticks.

"Someone Doug met here once. You know, we could have gone somewhere to eat if you guys were hungry."

"Oh, this will work fine for now. You two help yourselves, we bought plenty for that reason."

"Okay, we'll eat now, and take a quick trip to that space place so you can find your swwweeet Lillllly." Carla teased.

Doug explained the encounter to Matthew and Terri. "Awww, that's so sweet!" Matthew crooned through a mouthful of corn dog.

"Maybe she'll be there and you can reunite, how romantic!" Terri gushed.

Carla thought she might gag. "Please, Terri."

"I love reading romance books; the hero sweeps the damsel off her feet and they ride into the sunset."

"Not real."

Terri popped the last of the mustard covered corn dog into her mouth and took a large drink from her Diet Pepsi. "That's why I like 'em. It gives me a chance to go somewhere else besides what reality has to offer."

"What's that supposed to mean?" Matthew set his second corn dog in its container and wiped his hands on a napkin.

"I'm just saying that it's like a 'Calgon take me away', kind of thing. I wasn't talking about us, babe."

Matthew didn't say anything, but grunted and stared at his wife. He scooted down away from her a few inches and turned to look out at the desert. A train whistle broke the silence as it barreled down the track. The ground shook as the five-engine train and its cargo of colored cars and railroad logos ambled past them. They held onto their drinks in fear of them bouncing onto the ground.

They sat in silence as weighted cargo cars creaked and groaned passed by. The clackity-clacking of its wheels and squealing of brakes had Carla hypnotized. She watched it lumber past, wondering where it was going; what was inside the cars. Did hobos still ride the rails? She wondered. She speculated they did, but most of them now days were nothing like Currier and Ives paintings, and most were probably illegal immigrants.

◆ ◆ ◆

"How cute, a spaceship restaurant and a motel too." Carla thought both places needed upgrading. Paint peeled off the walls of the restaurant and she couldn't remember the last time she saw so many yellow bug lights. "I think

I'll just stay out here." Carla told Doug as he started up to the window.

"This place used to have the best burgers; they were out of this world." Doug tilted his sunglasses down. "No pun intended. I'll be back."

Several minutes later, he came out with a woman walking next to him. He walked up to Carla, Matthew and Terri and introduced the woman as Lilly Sanchez, owner and proprietor of the Space Cowboy Grill and Motel. "I never expected to run into this beautiful lady!" Doug's face beamed. "How many years has it been since I came through here?"

Lilly held up five fingers. "Give or take." She walked to where Carla stood and shook her hand. "I saw you on TV. I'm sorry about your situation."

Carla nodded her thanks and sat back down in the shade. "I don't suppose you've seen anyone resembling the man who took my grandsons?" Carla fished out the photograph of the boys featured on the show and handed it to Lilly.

Lilly studied the photo for a moment then gave it back to Carla. "Unfortunately, no. I left Gila Bend about three years ago, and just recently came back. Both the restaurant and the motel were in disarray and I bought them dirt cheap.

I remember this place when I was a kid, tourists used to come because they thought the Roswell, New Mexico myth and this area had ties. Personally, I don't think it does, but then there were all of those experiments with the atom bomb not too far from here, so when someone asks about it, I tell them to leave it to their imagination." Lilly smiled showing her perfect, white teeth against her dark complexion.

"I hate to break up the reunion, but we need to get going. Still a long way to go before we stop for the night." Carla turned away from them. She walked to the edge of the road and stared westward. She wanted to get closer to the boys. Each day she was separated from Scotty and Marcos, the more she worried. Were they eating? Getting enough sleep? Were Marcos' allergies any worse? Did Scotty still have nightmares? She kept away from the worst-case scenarios, because it only made her anxiety soar and her imagination run rampant. Whenever the conversation tried to steer in that direction, she made them talk about something else.

She lit a cigarette and watched the occasional vehicle turn in from the interstate come in for gas and bathroom breaks. Halfway through the smoke, she turned toward the Jeep. Matthew and Terri were having an animated conversation which meant a flurry of hand gestures and storming away from each other. Carla swore under her breath. She knew a break down was coming. Things were going too smooth.

Carla had made herself perfectly clear before leaving Green Valley, she would leave them standing alongside the road. She entertained the possibility of staying the night, but once they entered Mexico, Carla did not want to waste any more time finding the boys.

In addition to desert temperatures, weather forecasters were keeping an eye out on a large cluster of storms coming off the northern coast of South America. Forecasters thought the storm would die out as they usually did because the water of the Pacific was cooler. However, thanks to El Nino it had been an unusually hot summer. There was a strong possibility of the storm may gather strength over the ocean and move north toward the Baja. Carla first heard about the possibility of the next named Pacific tropical storm, Nadia, earlier in the Texaco Food Mart.

She didn't like tropical storms or hurricanes either. She experienced Hurricane Rita in 2005 and was fortunate enough that most of the hurricane's strength died out before reaching them. They only got a glancing blow from the storm but, it was enough to cause great concern for her home and family.

She walked toward the Jeep where Matthew and Terri were sitting inside in the back seat. She could tell they weren't talking or sitting close to each other like they had been. She walked up on Terri's side and motioned for her to roll down the window.

"Everything okay in here?"

Terri's answer was clipped. "Fine."

"Good, we leave in ten minutes, and you're driving to Yuma."

"I'm not feeling good." Terri tried to turn her head further away from Carla.

"Too bad. Everyone else has had their turn." She walked to the other side of the jeep and opened the driver's side door. "Listen to me, both of you." Carla lowered her voice and kept it even. "We are stuck in small spaces for long periods of time. I understand that. We are going to have disputes and snap at each other from time to time. The trick is to resolve them quickly and get on with why we are out here." She poked a finger at Terri. "You promised to help and so far, you haven't done anything except keep the boredom away playing games." Carla's voice softened. "I want you to know, that has been the best medicine so you need to keep it up, but you offered to drive too."

She turned to Matthew. "She didn't mean what she said about getting away from reality so get over it already! Lord Jesus, please help me!" Carla looked upwards and raised her hands. She climbed inside, and started up the vehicle. She rolled up the window after cool air from the air conditioner chased out the one hundred-thirty-degree heat. "How can you two stand it in here?"

She turned in her seat so she could talk to the both of them. "You've been married over twenty years and you still argue about petty issues? I thought that by you deciding to go on this trip is to find Scotty and Marcos so, focus on that instead of some little thing about fictitious romance novels.

It's her outlet Matt, I mean, other than pestering you." Carla chuckled and decided to help them make a decision. She turned off the vehicle and climbed out. "Come on you two." She walked over to where Doug and Lilly still talked under the shadow of the restaurant. "Lilly, do you have rooms available?'

Doug and Lilly looked at each other then her. "Sure. Come on, I'll get you set up." Lilly smiled at Doug as the two women walked to the motel lobby.

Grudgingly, Carla was glad for the break. It was a better decision than what she previously thought by waiting until they were in Mexico. Besides, what were the chances Doug would run into a woman he fell in love with years ago from a one-night stand in a small desert town. "Two days and that's all." She told Doug.

"It wasn't necessary, Lilly understood."

"What? You told her why we were here?"

"No, she guessed that. Remember when she mentioned seeing you on TV.?"

"Yeah. That noticeable?"

"That's what she says."

◆ ◆ ◆

Carla, Doug, and Lilly sat in folding chairs outside of their rooms, smoking and drinking beer and watched the sun set into the desert. Matthew and Terri left to check out the town and talk. Carla finished the rest of her beer and put it in the trash can. "I think I'll turn in, check the route and watch some TV."

She stretched and reached over ruffling Doug's head. "I'll see you all in the morning." She gave a small wave to Lilly. "In case I didn't say it earlier, I'm glad to have met you. You have been a most gracious and wonderful hostess."

"Thank you, Carla." Lilly reached her hand out to shake Carla's. "Anything I can do to help, just let me know."

Carla grinned sheepishly and shook Lilly's hand. "Sure thing." She left them sitting and went into her room. She turned on the television and changed into a pair of lightweight pajamas. She didn't like the idea of being half dressed or naked if she ever had to leave her home in a hurry, or should the paramedics have to take her to the hospital. She had a friend once who fell getting out of the shower because of a rug on the floor. It slipped and when she fell, she broke her leg.

Fortunately, her brother was at home when the incident happened, and he managed to get her covered as much as possible. The really bad part about the whole thing was the friend knew both paramedics and they gave her a lot of good-natured teasing for some time.

She found the weather channel, a familiar and comforting noise. At home, Carla had the Weather Channel on most of the time as background noise when she was cooking or cleaning. "Thank God for satellites." She said as she propped up her pillows against the headboard of the bed and dug out her journal. She stared at the front of it. "*Scotty and Marcos Chronicles*" was printed in bold, black marker. She brought her legs up closer to her chest and opened the notebook.

"We decided to stay a couple of days in Gila Bend, Arizona. Doug has run into an "old friend" and Matthew and Terri need to reconnect. By Monday, we will have been away from home only a week. It seems like a month! I feel like we aren't making any head way sometimes, but maybe that's how it's going to go, maybe there is a reason for this delay. I need to find a way to convert to Mexican money too. It would be nice if that can be done before we reach the border. There is a tropical storm moving out into the ocean too. I wanted to mention that since I am documenting my "rescue mission."

Carla jumped when she heard what sounded like a vehicle crash outside her door. She got up from the bed and ran to the door opening it up to find the Jeep's grill on the right-side smashed in. "I'll be....." She gritted her teeth and took a deep breath. "I'll skin them both alive." She dug out a tee shirt exchanging it for the pajama top and ran outside. Matthew and Terri were embracing each other and Terri was crying.

"Is she okay?" Carla ran up to them. "Are you okay?"

"We're fine, but there's another dent on the Jeep."

"A dent is an understatement. Have you been drinking?"

"I had a couple, but I'm not drunk."

"I don't care if you drank a half a beer! You had no-"

Mathew held up his hand in front of Carla's face. "First of all, Terri was driving, she's sober, and we were parked. That car came from nowhere so don't get all wigged out about it." He snapped at her and pulled Terri closer to him. "You know she doesn't drink."

"Yeah, probably high." Carla mumbled as she stepped away from them and walked to the other vehicle to make sure they were okay and exchange insurance information. When she got to the driver's side there was no one in it. She heard no audible groans or other sounds of anyone in pain. Carla circled the vehicle and searched the shallow ditch on both sides of the road.

It was lit up well enough and revealed no one lying on the ground. She took out her flashlight and checked under both vehicles and thankfully, no one was there. The police came and took down information and hauled away the sedan. They ran the license plates of the abandoned vehicle and came back as stolen. The officer told her it happened all the time, people crossing the border, some fool has left their car keys in the ignition and that's probably what had happened with this incident as well.

Carla pulled the Jeep into a parking space near her room and brought out the camera to once again take pictures of damages she incurred. There wasn't anything more she could do tonight as far as contacts and repair estimates. It wasn't how she planned to spend the day but plans change. Matthew and Terri were already in their room. She knocked on the door.

"Look, I'm sorry about getting upset, but I'll have to pay for those repairs when I take the Jeep back and it's going to cost a lot. "

"That car came out of nowhere. What a terrible end to a wonderful night! I'm so sorry Carla, I am." Matthew hugged her.

"I know, I know. It's just weird that in less than two days we've been involved in two accidents." Carla said. "I'll have to get an estimate tomorrow and make phone calls first thing I guess." She started for the door. "You guys don't worry about it."

"We'll help out with the damage costs when we get back." Teri came over to where Carla stood in the doorway and hugged her. "This isn't going how you planned it is it Carla?"

She laughed and hugged her back. "It's okay, really. It's not been a complete disaster."

"It's going to be alright from here on out." Matthew gave her another squeeze across her shoulders.

"Let's hope so." Carla pulled the door open, feeling the hot outside air woosh inside the room. "I'm going to go to bed. Good night." She stepped outside and closed the door.

Carla felt antsy when she woke up. She had planned to stay two extra days; she had spent most of the previous day with the insurance adjuster on the phone. He had a hard time believing her and why she had two accidents within a week. She called the car dealership she rented the Jeep from, this time he wasn't so happy and forgiving. She promised to pay for the damages and that seemed to satisfy him. Then she had to find a mechanic. Fortunately, Lilly knew someone and he was kind enough to come to the motel to check things out on the Jeep just to be sure nothing else was wrong with it. Fortune smiled on Carla again when the mechanic told her everything was solid and in good shape.

But the second morning she couldn't wait to leave Gila Bend. She didn't have a good feeling about the mysterious crash from the night before. She wondered if Juan knew she was looking for him and her grandchildren and was trying to get rid of her. That was it. Carla decided they had wasted too much time in Gila Bend so Doug could reminisce with a one-night stand. It wasn't that she disliked Lilly. She had been a gracious hostess and gave them some tips on driving on Mexican roads on the Baja. She felt refreshed and anxious, and everyone else seemed a little more at ease. Hopefully, Carla prayed, hopefully, without incident, they would be in Mexico before noon.

◆ ◆ ◆

They drove through ancient volcano lava fields and miles of sand. Carla thought the desert was beautiful. Yucca plants and Cacti bloomed adding stark color to the desert. She liked that she could see for miles, but didn't care for how deceiving places in the distance were much further than she believed them to be.

The thing that amazed her the most was how they could farm the arid soil. They drove through endless stretches of the desert; everything looking the same. They would top a hill or come around a corner and there would be fields supporting lush, green vegetation. She'd read about the possibility of bringing the desert to life by bringing more irrigation to arid regions of the world. If enough water could be pumped, stored, and distributed to crops grown in desert soil it could very well end world hunger.

They drove through the small town of Dateland, known for growing palms which bear the date fruit. Carla didn't care much for the taste of dates, and hadn't eaten one since she was ten. Every Christmas, she remembered her great grandmother made date bread and Christmas Stolen, a fruit and nut bread and, both very tasty when toasted in the oven and covered with homemade butter. To simply eat the dates like her father ate them was another matter. They were sweet and very sticky. The outer covering was crunchy from the process and the taste foreign. It was not something she could eat on a day-to-day basis.

They drove past several places that must have been grand in their time, now they were nothing but outer shells of adobe baked white from years in the sun. Life in the desert could be harsh, and like the people who live in extreme regions, it was a survival game every day. They passed through Yuma and the fields of vegetables, and fruit trees. The town sprung up around the Colorado river which flowed through and helped to create the acres of green vegetation. She was surprised to find she liked Yuma, the people were friendly and glad to answer questions. Most of them smiled despite the desert heat.

Even though the mechanic told her everything was intact, Carla hoped the accident to the front of the vehicle wouldn't cause radiator problems, and so far, no overheating or leaking of fluids. They continued through Yuma, a bustling city of twenty thousand. They crossed the Colorado, peering over the girders of the bridge to see the great and mighty river of the west. "Not much of a river here." Carla spoke out loud.

"It looks like most of it runs into irrigation ditches for the farms."

"I thought the mural on the water tower was really pretty. I liked how they mixed the cool colors with the desert terrain." Carla said.

"What are you an art critic?" Doug glanced at her sideways. It was the first he had spoken since they left Gila Bend.

"Yeah, that's what I am, Casanova."

"I find that so odd, that even though the ground around here is sandy, they can grow so much from it." Matthew said as he stared out the window.

"Remember the lava fields? There is a lot of rich fertile soil. I saw on the Discovery Channel once about how researchers were looking for better ways to bring water into this part of Arizona. They are worried with all of the years of drought the Colorado won't be enough to support the farms and are looking for ways to recycle water that doesn't actually go into the fields." Carla said, shaking her head. "It's amazing what is being done now days."

"They have been digging irrigation ditches for over a hundred years." Doug added. "I read this book in American Lit in high school called "Centennial" by James A. Michner."

"I thought you hated that class." Matthew said as he dug into a bag and produced a package of fig newton cookies.

"I did, but this book was really interesting. It talked a lot about the German immigrants moving west and using the rivers to help grow their crops. They were pioneers in the irrigation canals that are all over the place out here. Did you know that they used to grow beets and made sugar from them? Back in late eighteen hundred and into early nineteen hundred they started harvesting sugar cane." Doug informed her. "I know beet sugar is also used in treating roads when it snows in some places."

"Now I've heard everything. So, is it purply-red like you see in the jars at the store?" Carla said. She imagined ice and snow stained beet juice purple.

Doug shook his head. "That I don't know."

They crossed a large section of the Colorado near Araz Junction. "Not too far from here if you were to float down this river, is the Mexican border." Doug told them. "We could cross at Los Algadones." He told Carla.

She nodded her head in agreement. "I did consider that but I found a better way and no back tracking."

They drove in silence until they came to the small town of Felicity, California. They noticed a sign proclaiming it was at the center of the world. "This is too interesting to not stop and check out." Carla said. "Let's go see what makes them think this is the center of the world. Besides, I want to know what that huge building is on top of that hill."

"Your wish is my command. But that big building is a church. There is also a memorial to French Aviators during World War Two."

"Why?"

"I don't know, but we can check it out." Doug slowed the Jeep down and turned off the interstate.

"Is this even a town?" Matthew asked.

"Not really, I think at one time, somebody had an idea for one, but other than the memorial and the church, there isn't much else here." Doug pulled up to the entrance and they walked into the open area.

"Wow, this is cool, here, this tells all about the center of the world. It's the location of the longitude and latitude. It says the sundial is a bronze piece made in New England and taken from Michelangelo's "Arm of God" painting on the ceiling of the Sistine Chapel. Here's something I didn't know, sun dials are only accurate once a year, and they set this one at noon on Christmas Day. It also says the arm points to the Hill of Prayer." Carla paused to stare at the direction in which the arm pointed. "Let's go check it out."

"It's hot and look at all of those friggin' stairs!" Terri shaded her eyes against the sun and stared at the steep incline.

"It says here that it took over one hundred and fifty thousand tons of earth to make the Hill of Prayer." Matthew shook his head. "That's a lot of dirt."

"Hey," Doug called out to them where he stood on the base of a stair way. "it says that these stairs were part of the Eiffel Tower at one time. How about that? This section was bought at an auction a few years back. Now I don't have to go to Paris to say I've touched the Eiffel Tower."

"You could win a few bets that way." Carla said as she stood next to him. They all stood at the base of the stairs, the sun beating down on the backs of their necks. Carla once more shaded her eyes and stared up the stairs. "Terri's right, that's a lot of stairs and we've got road to burn."

Doug turned toward them. "You should at least touch a step."

They each stepped up one stair then returned to the Jeep.

Before long the landscape began to change, and soon they came up on huge mounds of sand dunes. "Whoa, check out the people riding dune buggies!" Matthew pointed at several of the cars roaring across the face of huge piles of sand. Tire tracks crisscrossed each other from years of riders.

"I wouldn't think the sand would be stable enough to ride on them, but I guess they can!" Carla watched the buggies jump small mounds of sand and drive on near vertical faces of some of the larger dunes. A short time later they pulled into Holtville, California to fuel up and stretch their legs. Matthew came back from the gas station and told them this was carrot capitol of the world. Anything and everything a person wanted to know about carrots or how to prepare carrots in various ways could find the answer here during the annual carrot festival. Carla and Doug looked at each other. "I like carrots, but how did...?"

Matt waved a pamphlet at them. "All the facts are right here." He handed Carla the paper. It was bright orange and did claim Holtville as Carrot Capitol. She handed it back to him and watched as he stuffed the pamphlet into his back pocket.

He caught her looking at him. "I like carrots. I might want to come check it out one day." He shrugged his shoulders and climbed into the Jeep.

They drove a short distance before Doug pointed to a fence, "That's the border."

"It's so strange that there is another country on the other side." Matthew spoke in a whisper.

Carla swallowed, her heart beating hard in her chest. She knew without a shadow of a doubt they were alive and she would find them. "Scotty and Marcos are on the other side of that fence somewhere."

CHAPTER FIFTEEN

Carla couldn't take her eyes off of the structure.

"There are places where there isn't a fence; they just have border patrol driving back and forth." Terri said, "I've seen Mexicans running across when border patrol drives by into the desert."

"I saw some pictures on an online magazine once; not that long ago as a matter of fact, where many immigrants cross into the U.S. and left a trail of trash as far as you can see covering the ground. To think people can just throw away their things like that with no regard to the land." Carla felt herself getting tense. "Trash was piled so high in one place, there was a border patrol officer standing next to it and he was dwarfed by the pile. The article said that the place is heavily guarded anymore. Of course, people will always find a way to get through. I feel for those who want to have a better life, but it shouldn't give them the right to use the land as a dumping ground."

They passed through El Centro, California, with its fertile grounds then back into the desert landscape with its rocky out croppings. Carla wondered how many rattle snakes and other desert creatures were holed up from the baking sun. They wound their way through the high desert and passed a sign that said "Devil's Canyon". At one point they spotted several big horn sheep standing on top of a large pile of rocks. The light of the day and its surroundings made it hard to spot them unless they moved. Carla took several photos of them wondering if they ever went into towns for water. More than once she watched deer standing on the banks of the many small creeks flowing through Green Valley after a rain.

They wound through the mountains and valleys, every now and then they would spot a big horn sheep standing on a pile of rocks. Did they ever walk on stable ground? Carla speculated how she would look if she had to climb the rocky terrain. A large structure rose from the desert floor, they speculated on what it was and soon found that it was a tower people could climb if they wanted to see the desert vista. Carla wanted to push on. Seven miles past the Jacumba turn off they finally came to highway 94 that would take them to Tecate, Mexico.

Carla barely paid attention to the landscape as she drove through the winding hills of desert terrain. Her mind was on her grandsons. *Hold on babies*, she thought as a shiver of either excitement or fear, she wasn't sure which ran down her spine; *I'm on my way.*

They finally came to the town of Tecate and crossed into Mexico without incident. Carla and Terri went into a small grocery store, Tecate Mart on the U.S. side to find out about motels in the area and exchange some of the cash into Mexican currency. The woman at the counter thankfully spoke English well but Carla was glad to have Terri with her. Until she knew her sister-in-law had mental health issues, Carla could hardly stand to be around her. They also lived next door to Terri's mother. She was quick to start arguments between Terri and Matthew then call the cops and complain about the yelling. Now that they were spending so much time together Carla thought she may have misjudged Terri all of these years. She didn't know if it was the medication but she was sure it helped keep Terri calm.

"I think that went quite well." Carla put her arm around Terri. "Open that brochure up and let's see what Hacienda Santa Veronica has to offer." They walked to the jeep and got inside. "This may be where we will stay tonight, so we need to get going. We'll need to get on El Hongo; a toll road, and it's about twenty-four miles in from there."

Terri opened the brochure. "Oooh, look at that swimming pool!"

"What's it say?"

"Hacienda Santa Veronica is a place where time appears to have stopped, situated just 55 miles from the city of Tijuana." Teri commented as she scanned the colorful brochure. "A calm environment is what you need to charge up and escape your routine.'" She turned the brochure over. "They have a restaurant, bar, swimming pool, outdoor grills, paint ball, all sorts of stuff."

Matthew reached over to get a better look. "I don't know, it looks kinda expensive." He took the brochure from Terri and checked the back of it.

"There are no rates listed. There's a phone number though."

"I haven't tried using my cell phone out here." Carla pulled it out and opened the top. "Well, look at that. I have reception, isn't technology wonderful?" She had Matthew repeat the number and waited for the number to start ringing.

"Buenos Dias, Hacienda Santa Veronica." A woman's voice sang into Carla's ear.

"Uh se habla English?"

"Oh si, yes ma'am. How may I help you?"

Carla let out a relieved sigh. "Do you have any vacancies? I'm in Tecate on vacation, sort of a live by the seat kind of thing. I don't have reservations."

"Well, normally, we require that you make them. Where are you from?"

"Arkansas. My family and I wanted to do something big together and so, here we are, roaming the country, or countries, I should say." Carla chuckled.

"Well, as I said, it's not regular policy to do so, but most of our places are empty. People can't afford to get away these days."

Carla nodded her head. "I can understand that. We've been saving up for this for about a year or so. Actually, I've never been to Mexico and now I can say I have." She laughed again.

"Well, Miss, uh?"

Carla hesitated. Should she use her real name? "It's Carla Simpson."

"Okay Miss Simpson, we have a cabin with three bedrooms for two-hundred fifty U.S. dollars a night. It's the closest to the pool and has a lovely view from practically all sides. The restaurant and bar are close too."

"Wow, that's a little steep, what else do you have? Two bedrooms?"

"There is one, it's further back on the property so it's more private. One hundred dollars a night."

Carla winced. "Can I call you back?"

"No problem, Miss Simpson."

Carla hung up and looked at the rest of them. "You are right, it is expensive. But we can stay in one cabin, every one pitch in and it won't be too bad."

"Another thing Carla is it's kind of out of the way, let's drive a little further in and see what there is. I'm sure there has to be something closer." Doug reasoned. "I didn't bring a whole lot of cash, and I've been buying the gas."

Carla sighed. "It is out of the way. Maybe when we come back through."

Doug nodded his head and grinned. "We will do that. It could be a plan for another time too."

"Okay, I'd rather get further away from Tecate anyway. So, let's drive."

They made good time despite the stop in Felicity. The curvy roads made Carla a little homesick. She found herself wishing for oak, pine and maple trees. Trees leafy and green, tall; not stunted like the long stretches of scrub brush, cactus and Joshua trees. Soon they came to El Chale, a small town south of Tecate.

"How about that place?" Carla pointed towards a motel a short distance from them. As they drew closer, she could tell the area around it was clean and landscaped well. "Looks like a nice place and they have a pool."

"Looks good to me. I'm tired and ready to stretch out. Look, not only do they have a pool, there's a bar, or a cantina I should say." Doug nodded to an open area where crystal blue water sparkled in a kidney shaped pool.

"When we get checked in, I think I'll take a swim." Matthew wiped his forehead. "I don't know if it's a change in humidity or what, but it feels hotter."

"It might be that woman laying by the pool, babe." Terri scoffed at him.

"I did not see her. But now that you mentioned it-"

"Just keep going." Terri pushed him into the entrance of the motel office.

They registered for rooms and got their luggage from the Jeep. Carla hadn't realized she was exhausted until she sat down on her bed. The walls were decorated with pictures of the desert, and one small window overlooking Tecate, she found her room small but tasteful. She contemplated taking a swim. The cool blue water of the swimming pool did appeal to her frazzled senses. I'll just lie her for a few minutes and relax then go for a swim. She stretched out on the bed and within minutes was sound asleep.

It was still daylight when Carla woke up. At first, she was disoriented. She looked at her watch; nearly seven o'clock. She could hear splashing coming from the pool area and then heard Terri's unmistakable squeals and laughs. Carla fixed her hair a bit then opened the door. Sure enough, Matthew, Terri and Doug were lounging around the pool, Doug and Matthew both had a beer and were sitting at a covered table. What the heck, she decided to join the party and dug out her swimsuit.

Carla stepped outside her room and could hear a Mexican ballad was playing on a radio coming from the Cantina. Ceiling fans from open trellises spun lazily in the air. The only lighting inside came from a juke box and a Tecate Cervesa sign behind the bar. There were several people sitting at some of the other tables scattered around the patio.

Doug and Matthew first spotted her coming out wearing her towel wrapped around her waist. Before they could get to her, Carla beat them to the punch by jumping into the pool. The cold water shocked her fully awake. She came up out of the water laughing. "Wow, that is the way to wake up!" She swam for a few minutes then grabbed her towel and sat at the table with her brothers who were still laughing at her. Terri sipped on some kind of pink drink that had a maraschino cherry and an orange slice floating in it. "I knew you two were going to try to knock me in."

"I never gave it a thought." Doug grinned and took a drink from his beer. "You want one?" He lifted his empty bottle towards her.

"What are you drinking Terri?"

"Something with Kalua in it. I forget the name, but it's pretty good." She offered her drink.

"No, I think I'll just have a beer."

"Coming up." Doug stood up and left.

"This place is nice. I'm glad we didn't go to that other place now." Carla said as she opted for one of the lounge chairs next to Terri. "I must have been dead to the world. I didn't hear a thing."

"We've been out here since we got here, making the best of it. You've got to try their enchiladas, mui yummy!" Matthew rubbed his stomach. "I ate three of them, they stuff 'em full of meat with lots of cheese and con carne sauce."

"I am pretty hungry, where's a menu?"

She looked over the menu, of course it was written in Spanish. She recognized enough of it to decide on a plate of quesadillas and stuffed jalapeño peppers. While she waited for her food, Carla drank her beer and watched the people inside the bar. She guessed most of them were tourists, like her, but unlike her they probably were not looking for kidnapped grandsons. She wondered if the boys were getting enough to eat, and if they missed their home. She wondered for the hundredth time if she had made the right decision to leave home to find them. What if they came home and she wasn't there? What if they never left Arkansas? She tried to shake off the feeling by ordering another beer which arrived the same time as her food. She was too far into it now to turn back. Besides, if that were the case, Richard knew how to reach her.

She could hear someone in the bar singing "Hit Me with your Best Shot", a Pat Benatar hit from the eighties. The singer was doing a decent job with the song. Then she realized it was a karaoke machine and the woman who was lounging by the pool when they came in was the one singing it. The audience shouted and cheered for her, shouting "Lolita! Lolita!" Carla assumed that was her name. Then the woman began singing Copacabana. "Her name was Lola; she was a show girl!" Carla groaned; she hated that song. When she was in her teens Copacabana was overplayed on the radio she would turn the dial when it came on. She tuned out the din while she ate her supper. They still had a long way to go, the Baja California Sur Peninsula was over a thousand miles long.

She wasn't sure about how to go about asking questions. Her and her brothers Spanish speaking skills were lacking and Terri's were mediocre. She thought it might be in her best interest to find someone she could trust to help her out. She hadn't given it much thought, but it occurred to Carla Juan's name could pose a problem. How many men in Mexico had the same name? One thing that made any sense is to be specific of the region where Juan could be. Refer to family members she thought, which meant looking up provinces. That also meant finding out which existing family members were around. Another thought nagging Carla, was Juan Gonzales Pedraza his real name? The search was going to be a difficult one unless she found help.

The food was very good, Carla thought as she wiped her mouth and drained her second bottle of beer. She had to laugh when Terri stood up and sat back down in her chair. One drink and the woman was tipsy. "How about another one?" Carla asked as she rose up from the table.

"Woohoo! Oh yeah, I want another one, wait, I wanna try a tequila sunrise." Terri struggled to pull herself up from the lounge chair. Carla helped to pull her sister-in-law up from the chair, nearly sending them both into the pool. They wrapped their arms around each other's shoulders and headed to the bar. There were more people inside, sitting at tables with candle light. Several strings of Christmas lights ran around the outer rafters, giving it a festive mood. Carla ordered their drinks and turned to say something to Terri when she heard what was supposed to be singing but sounded like sandpaper on a blue jay's butt. It was Terri with the microphone singing "Taking Care of Business" by Bachman, Turner, Overdrive. Terri wasn't really singing it, more like shouting it. Carla found that everybody was enjoying this silly, drunk, white woman making an ass out of herself. There was Matt clapping and encouraging his wife.

"You get up every morning from the alarm clock's warning, take the eight fifteen into the city, there's a whistle up above us, people pushin, people shoving' and the girls are trying to look pretty!" Terri raised a fist in the air. "Wooohooo! Yeah!" The crowd answered her by raising their fists in the air. Carla never laughed so hard in her life. She was amazed Terri got the crowd singing with her. Terri shuffled her feet across the stage and shimmied her body; her voice out of tune and cracking.

Good thing she never tried to be a rock star Carla thought as she laughed and shook her head. She tried to get her sister-in-law down from the stage when Terri caught her arm.

"Come on, sis!" Terri tugged at Carla's arm, "come sing with me!" the crowd started clapping.

"No!" Carla hissed, "I can't sing and neither can you!" Carla tried to step off the stage. Terri was stronger than she looked. "Come on!" She pulled her back up onto it. "Left a good job in the city...."

Matthew and Doug were both in the front shouting at Carla to sing. Tears streamed down their faces they waved their hands for her to stay up on stage. Terri was behind her trying to be Tina Turner, walking across the stage and leaning into the audience. "Working for the man every night and day...." Terri stuck the microphone in front of Carla's face and took off leaving her there standing in front of the crowd waiting for her to sing, the chorus began to light up on the screen.

"Big wheel keeps on turnin'" Carla laughed nervously and searched for Terri who was chugging around the stage like a train. "Proud Mary keep on burnin' Rollin', rollin', rollin' on the river." Her voice sounded foreign. She remembered hearing how she sounded when she recorded her first message on an answering machine. When she listened back to the message, she thought she sounded like someone who had stuffed cotton balls in her mouth and imitating a hillbilly from the back woods. Yet. never in her life would she have given thought to singing in front of a live audience for the second time in a few days. The song picked up tempo as the second round of the chorus went by, Carla was getting into it now, shaking her hips and throwing her head back. What the heck, she thought, no one knows me here except my family. She threw her cares to the wind and sang.

She was getting into the next song and had the crowd clapping their hands. She looked out and saw everyone had smiles on their faces and clapping. There were more people coming into the bar and the night was just getting started. "I got that green light baby, I got to keep movin' on. I got that green light baby, I got to keep movin' on. Well, I might go out to California, might come down to Mexico, I don't know!" The crowd sang with her and cheered for her. Carla found herself having a good time.

She stopped after the second song with the crowd clapping and whistling. She stepped down from the stage and decided she needed another beer. Adrenaline pumped through her and she felt like she was on top of the world, a star is born. "Ha, not likely!" Carla laughed and sat down out by the pool. The air was much cooler and it was less noisy or it was until Terri and Matthew jumped into the pool, laughing and splashing each other. She noticed the bar tender heading her way with another beer. "I didn't order that."

He bowed "Por la patilla." On the house. Carla thanked him and set it on the table. Doug came and sat down next to her.

"I didn't know you were a singer."

"I'm not." She chuckled. "Oh, Terri's got a payback coming, she's not off the hook!"

"Oh, come on, admit it, you were having fun."

"Well, yeah it was fun, but she embarrassed me and then left me standing up there."

Doug took a drink from his bottle. "Seems you had it under control. Anyway, you were having fun and I think you did all right."

"Thanks." She clinked her bottle with his and drank. "We need to leave by no later than noon tomorrow, some parts of the highway will be going through rough territory and I'm told some of it isn't paved."

"I heard that too. Oh, by the way. The woman who was singing earlier, oh, I guess she's singing now. She knows of some Pedraza's in La Paz. She said they are an old family and number into the hundreds there and throughout the southern tip of the Baja. She said we need to be careful, some of them are in bad businesses involving drug smuggling."

"Why is it you have to keep telling people what we are doing here, Doug?"

"I didn't, I thought you said something."

Carla looked at him and took a drink. "No, I haven't talked to anyone except to the waiter and bartender."

"May I sit with you?"

Carla looked away from Doug and noticed the woman who had recently been singing standing next to her holding out her hand.

Carla reached out and shook the woman's hand. "Sure, have a seat." Carla motioned the empty chair across from her.

"My name is Rosa; I own the motel and bar."

"You have a nice place and everyone is very friendly."

"Gracias. I do pretty well for a single Mexican woman. I do not want to be nosy, but I am told you are going to La Paz?"

"Thinking about it. We are just driving in no place particular." Carla took a long drink and drained her fourth bottle of beer. She wondered how Rosa knew her.

"I am from there, it's a beautiful place, right on the gulf. I haven't been back home in many years. I am sort of an outcast. I didn't want a husband or live there selling fish and homemade baskets to tourists."

"I suppose I can understand that." Carla stared at the woman. She was pretty, but her eyes held an intelligence Carla hadn't seen in many people; her sister, Abbey had the same characteristic. "Even in today's world women are still not held in high regard."

Rosa smiled. "Yes, but your Hillary Clinton, she made history for women in the States. I would vote for her if I was an American."

"Well, I'm sure she would be happy to know that Rosa."

"I know why you are here."

"Oh?" Carla made a note to talk to Terri about telling strangers their mission.

"You are looking for your grandsons. Be careful is my advice."

"I'm on vacation. I'm a tourist, just like the rest of those people." Carla nodded to the knot of brightly colored shirts and dresses spinning around the dance floor.

"If you say so." Rosa pulled out a slip of paper and handed it to Carla. "This is my uncle Ramón. If you need any help, go to him. He and some of the Pedrazas have been friendly business rivals for a long time. They have respect for each other, but there are some of the Pedraza family who play dirty. Juan and his thugs have tried to put my uncle's business under once many years ago. Uncle Ramón has worked hard to make sure he keeps his customers happy and that they will come back to his resort every time. He's a very nice man and even if you say you are just on vacation, he can accommodate you nicely. It's a lovely place right on the Sea of Cortez, the Gulf of California. I wrote the name of the place and his phone number."

Carla unfolded the paper and stared at the information. "Thank you. I appreciate your help." Carla shook Rosa's hand. "Can I buy you a drink?"

Rosa shook her head, her long black hair swayed gently and her gold dangling earrings made a soft, tinkling, musical sound. "No thank you. I have to keep an alert mind. Most of the time I have no trouble in my bar, but then you get some of those who cannot hold liquor well and cause problems. I try not to let that happen. But thank you for offering the drink." She stood up and smiled at her, then walked away.

"Why is it Hispanic people have the whitest teeth?"

"Habaneros." Doug down the rest of his beer. "Keeps bacteria away."

"Very funny." Carla took a drink and then tapped Doug's shoulder. "Uh oh, look who's back up on the stage." Matthew and Terri were singing into the microphone together a song that was not made for duets.

"Desperado, why don't you come to your senses, you've been out riding fences for so long now…"

"Good God, I'm going to bed." Doug rose up from the table.

"Hey, I'm not wanting to pry, but you haven't said much about Lilly."

"There's not much to say." He kissed the top of Carla's head. "Night."

"…Desperado, oh you ain't gettin' no younger, your pain and your hunger is driving you home...."

Carla watched as her younger brother strolled toward his room, wondering what really happened. It wasn't any of her business, but she was concerned. He was never one for talking about his feelings or emotions even when he was a kid. He didn't show too many emotions and generally kept to himself. But if he did have a problem, he came to her.

"It may be raining, but there's a rainbow above you. You better let somebody love you...'

"Let somebody loooove you!" Terri screeched.

"Before it's tooooo, laaaaaate." They closed the song singing the last line together and horribly out of tune. Matthew and Terri stepped down from the stage and saw Carla. "Sis! You hear us?" Terri shouted and stumbled towards Carla.

"Oh yes, I could hear you just fine."

She grabbed Carla's shoulders for support. "Oh my!" Terri laughed and struggled to gain her footing

"I hope she doesn't get sick. She had two more of those tequila sunrises and now she thinks she can soar like an eagle." Matthew struggled to hold up his wife's body.

"An' sing like a birdie!" Terri slurred then hiccupped.

"More like a turkey or a screech owl." Carla said as she helped Matthew get his wife into their room. They hugged her and told her good night. She shook her head and opened the door then walked into warm evening air. She glanced back into the room as she closed the door, Terri was splayed out across the bed; her arms thrown back over her head and her feet hanging off its edge.

CHAPTER SIXTEEN

They stopped briefly at Feo Roco, or Ugly Rocks. "They have to be the ugliest rocks I've ever seen." Carla said. "This must be some kind of old lava field. Remember the ones in Arizona?"

"From what I read about them, " Doug spoke, shading his eyes as he scanned the alien landscape. "It's a series of lava flows back when the volcanoes here were active, and the lava thicker. It said the volcanoes erupted all of the time and each time the lava was just cooling; another eruption happened and pushed the cooling lava over on itself." The shapes were eerie and resembled large intestines.

They stood there staring at the rock formations for a few minutes longer before climbing into the jeep and heading south.

They drove through the winding roads of the mountains. Carla was happy to see trees, Mexican Pinions, oaks and other species of pines in the upper elevations of the mountain range. She was amazed by the bright pink and purple colors of the bushy muhly grasses dotted throughout the desert landscape.

They climbed back into the mountains and into wine country. The climate and soil make up were perfect for grapes and wine making. They passed a sign that said Guadeloupe Valley. There were rows upon rows of different varieties of grapes for wines such as, Cabernets and Merlot.

Near one winery both sides of the highway were lined with what appeared to be a variety of poplar trees. The tall wispy branches reminded Carla of their grandmother's house in Nebraska where a row of them grew alongside the driveway leading up to her two-story home. She heard Terri groan in the backseat.

"Glad to see you are back in the land of the living." Carla turned in her seat to look at her. Terri's short red hair was pushed up on one side of her head.

"Yeah, I feel rough. How much of an ass did I make of myself? I remember getting thrown in the pool more than once and singing."

"You thought you were Tina Turner." Everyone including Terri laughed.

"Well, I probably won't see any of those people again so it doesn't matter."

"We saw you and it's not going away any time soon. Hoot, hoot, hoot, hoot, rollin', rollin' on the river!" Matthew mocked his wife. She punched him in the arm.

"Besides I have a bone to pick with you about pulling me up on that stupid stage and then leaving me up there."

"I did that?" Terri asked, her eyes wide.

"Yeah, but it's okay, Matt said you threw up about a dozen times."

"I figured that, it's the main reason I don't drink." Terri rummaged around until she found some moist towelettes and washed her face off. "Ugh, I look horrible and my mouth feels like I ate cardboard or sand. Babe, what is in the cooler to drink?"

Matthew opened the cooler. "Two diet sodas, a mountain dew, water, and a couple of iced teas."

Terri chose water and nearly drank the whole bottle.

They wound through small towns, people sat in front of their houses staring or waving at them as they drove by. Children lined up along the roadside and waved. Carla couldn't help but search the faces of the children, hoping Scotty and Marcos would be among them.

On the other side of Guadalupe, they noticed two huge holes in the ground.

"Wonder what those were at one time?" Carla wondered.

"Back in the olden days, the Spaniards used the natives to mine for silver. These could be old silver mines." Doug offered.

"Wow Doug, did you study Mexican history?" Carla glanced over at him and grinned.

Focusing on the road Doug told her they studied about Mexico in school, so he had some familiarity with the region.

They drove passed Rancho Santa Maria; another winery situated right on the edge of the highway. It's bright terra cotta borders and golden yellow fronts brought out a loud splash of color against the dry, brown desert hillsides. They drove a little further down the road when Doug, who had been silent most of the day said he was beginning to get hungry. They all agreed that since no one ate breakfast, it was time to find a place to stop and eat. Several miles further they came to Restaurant Mustafa. "Looks like they must do a good business, look at all the cars." Terri pointed to a parking lot.

"We could drive further, but I can smell food and now I'm really hungry!" Doug said smacking his lips. "Carla, pull in here."

They went inside where the air was cooler. Several patrons looked up from their meals then resumed eating. The foursome was seated in a corner table with a splendid view of the mountains they had just drove through and a spreading valley floor filled with vineyards and olive groves. Carla spotted several fields with bright yellow flowers wondering if they were sunflowers. The waiter brought them menus and nothing was in English. "Okay Terri, you are the more fluent in the language what's it say?"

"This is an almuerzo, pronounced, ahl-mooehr-soh, it means lunch. Everything here is served with tortillas, frejoles and rice. There's fajitas, made with shredded beef, more likely the tongue. The torta means sandwich in a bun served with beef or chicken. Gazpacho, it's a cold soup made from different vegetables, that's usually kind of like an appetizer. There is molleja, chicken gizzards.

"Por favor? Estan listos para ordenar?"

"What did he say?" Doug asked Terri, who was engrossed in the menu.

"He wants to know if we are ready to order. Do you guys all want a salad?"

Everyone thought that sounded good. "Una ensalada mixta."

"Mui bien. ?Quieren algo para beber?"

Terri told the waiter they all wanted iced tea. "Pollo frito y con elates frescos, y Calabasas entomatodas, por favor." Fried chicken with zucchini in a tomato sauce.

They ate in silence, until the food was almost gone. "This is almost better than American food."

Matthew commented, smacking his lips and taking a long drink of tea. "I don't know what was in the tomato zucchini sauce, but it's pretty spicy stuff, good, but very spicy."

"The sauces they use here are called mole." Terri wiped her mouth. "Most of the time they are served hot with meat, such as chicken and beef. What we had is called mole Amarillo made with almonds and raisins. It goes really well with chicken. The green stuff you see is called mole verde or green mole, it's usually much spicier than what we had. The really hot stuff is called mole Colorado, or red mole, made with hot chilies."

They left the restaurant, full and satisfied. Carla glanced around the country side. It was warm and sunny, birds twittered and soared across the desert sky. She wondered what Scotty and Marcos were doing right then. She thought about Richard and decided she would call him tonight when they checked into the next motel.

She lit a cigarette and leaned against the jeep. "We shouldn't be too far from the coast. I can almost smell the ocean."

"I caught glimpses of it when we were coming into the valley, so we probably aren't far at all." Terri shaded her eyes from the sun. "I could go ask."

"Nah, let's just go, it'll be more adventurous that way."

Within a matter of minutes, they were driving into the outlying area of Ensenada and the Pacific Ocean spread out from the town in all its majesty. "Looks like Beverly Hills with all the yachts and landscaping and palms lining the highway." Doug commented. "But it's much cleaner, I think."

"I wouldn't mind living here." Matthew said as they drove past an art museum. "I bet I could sell my paintings around here."

"Didn't know you were still doing anything like that." Doug turned from the window and patted Matthew on the back. "Proud of ya, bro."

Carla wondered why anyone would want to leave a country so beautiful and full of happy people just to come to the U.S. It was an easy answer. Money of course. Most of the attractive hotels and well-kept buildings were for show to the tourists. She knew that many of them probably didn't want to leave but had to because poverty was so high and wages earned in Mexico were far less than in the states.

Even working in lettuce fields of California migrant workers could make better wages. In a way it made her sad for those who had to leave. She didn't think she would want to have to pull up stakes from a place she was familiar with and go to work somewhere else. The irony was not lost on the fact she now had a sense of how some immigrants must feel entering into a strange country, unfamiliar with the language, and knowing nobody.

They cruised along Mexican Highway One, Centra Rodolfo Sanchez Taboda Ensenada, ooohing and awwing over the white sands and huge ships in the harbor. There was even a large cruise ship which seemed to dominate the landscape with its blazing white outer surface, against the azure blue of the Pacific.

Carla was so engrossed with the scenery; she almost missed the turn to continue on the highway that would take them to La Paz. The way the highway was designed reminded Carla of 412 highway which ran through Springdale, Arkansas. Until she traveled the route several times, she never failed to miss the turn because of the way it zigzagged through the city with sharp turns and abrupt lane changes with little notice of junctions. This was the case in Ensenada.

She was actually paying attention when the second odd switch of the route came up, but she passed the turn off before she knew it. They had to find a place to turn around which wasn't too hard and were soon back on track. "We need to remember that when we come back." Carla said, hoping they would all have the privilege to do so.

CHAPTER SEVENTEEN

They drove past cactus fields near San Vicinte into long stretches of desert flat lands and curving winding roads in the mountains. The day was growing long and they were trying to decide on where to stay for the evening. It was unanimous that a hotel on the beach was what they wanted so Carla had Terri and Matthew searching the map and hotel brochures.

Carla never got tired of the vistas of the sweeping desert. It was so beautiful, yet for miles there was nothing but desert sand, scrub brush and cactus. Perhaps it was the fact she was no longer in Arkansas, the adventure if she looked at it that way, was still exciting and new.

Right away the thought turned her mood somber. That was the real reason; to find her grandchildren. With Doug's persistence to avenge the deaths of her daughter and sister how could she even think about beauty when there was so much ugliness in the world? Because that was the nature of things. In nature life revolves around death. It was a fact. It was a fact she took upon herself. It was a fact she could have left well enough alone and let the authorities take care of it. It was a fact the possibility of Scotty and Marcos would be found soon were slim to none if she sat back and did nothing. It was a fact she would continue the search and as long as she had what she came to do firmly centered in her heart; there would be nothing to stop her but death itself. To that she surmised, there was nothing wrong with enjoying beauty of the desert and sea.

Driving through Punta Gorda, a small village near the Pacific, she noticed a dry alluvial bed and a large sign boasting the cirregimiento or district was proud to host part of the Baja 1000, a race which takes place through the rugged terrain of the Baja. Carla had heard about the races a few years ago on the news when officials contemplated stopping the race altogether because buggies and the track in areas were being sabotaged and officials didn't want lives at stake. The problem must have been resolved because it looked as if they still had them. There was a large banner on the front of a store front wishing the participants of the upcoming Baja race good luck.

They came into the town of San Quentin, a quaint village. There were clusters of children who ran along the tops of dunes, their black hair shining in the sun. Nearly all of the children were barefoot. Carla loved walking barefooted, even as a child, she was the only one of her siblings who could walk across rocks not hurt her feet. There were many people dotting the beaches, the tourists were obvious, dressed in bright colored shirts and wide brimmed hats to shade the sun, and cameras strapped about their necks. Many of them lounged under umbrellas and relaxed in chaise lounge chairs, reading or watching their own children as they played near the ocean's edge.

Carla saw a couple playing in the waves, splashing water on each other, another couple ran toward the waves by following the outgoing water then running back onto the beach when the next wave came rushing in. She was glad that the water's surface looked calm, she hoped it would stay that way. She hadn't heard the latest weather report that day, but the large cluster of storms that came off Central America were now in the waters of the Pacific. Forecasters were now confident those storms would form a tropical depression, but now the sky was a bright, happy blue, and the Mexican sun strong.

It was decided on a hotel near the beach called "Preciosa El Tucan", which meant gorgeous or lovely toucan, a tropical bird. "I wonder if they serve fruit loops here?" Matthew asked when he wanted to know what it meant and Terri told him, as they climbed out of the vehicle. It had been a long drive with little stopping time. They walked into the lobby of the hotel; Carla immediately loved the three-tiered water fountain that was the center of the lobby.

The room appeared larger than it looked by tall glass French doors leading to a patio. Inside the lobby were sweeping spiral staircases leading up to balconies draped with flowering bougainvillea vines and weeping figs that reached the domed ceiling. Terri and Carla walked up to the counter while Mattew and Doug tried to read several signs posted on the walls.

"Beunos tardes." Carla said. "Habla English?"

The clerk smiled and answered," Mui poquteo", very little. "You need rooms si?"

"Yes," Carla held up three fingers, "tres, por favor."

"Con banos?"

Carla looked at Terri, who whispered that she was asking if they wanted ones with bathrooms. "Oh, si."

"?Le gusta hacia la calle o hacia el patio?"

"She wants to know if we prefer patio views or street views, tell her patio view. You also need to find out if they have both hot and cold water.

"Prefiero el patio, por favor. Uh, do the rooms uh, con, con auga caliente?"

"Si, all do. Las del patio son muy tranquilas. Las habitaciones hacia el patio cuestan una cente cuarenta peso, sin desayuno."

Carla turned toward Terri, "I got lost after Las de patio, although I think she said something about it being quiet."

"You're picking up the language quick Carla!" Teri beamed. "She did say they are much quieter than street side. They cost one hundred and forty pesos and that's without breakfast." Terri turned to the receptionist. "Las habitaciones hacia el patio, en el primer piso?"

"No," replied the receptionist. "Las del Segundo piso. Las del primero son a una cente cincuenta pesos."

Terri turned back to Carla. "The first-floor rooms cost one hundred and fifty pesos, without breakfast."

"I guess we'll take second floor rooms then, we'll have better views from them."

Terri turned back to the receptionist to tell her of their preferences. "She wants to know how many days we plan to spend here."

"Just for the one night and tell her to have someone wake us up at six a.m." Carla wanted to get an early start. With luck, they would be in La Paz the following day.

◆ ◆ ◆

"I don't know about the rest of you, but I'm ready to go find a place to eat." Terri replied when they agreed to meet in front of the hotel after settling into their rooms. "I can go ask about restaurants or we can go walk around."

"Carla, what do you think? Take a walk sound good?"

She thought the walk would do them all some good, she also thought it would help relieve some building anxiety. Cooped up in the jeep with the three of them and as much as she loved them, there were times she wanted to open the door and push them out. Besides a little exercise couldn't hurt. "Let's take a walk."

They strolled along the well-tended street; the air filled with sounds of the town. The inhabitants went about their daily lives. There were many booths along the strip, some selling produce such as oranges, pineapples, limes and lemons. Another one sold handmade serapes and woven blankets in the bold colors of the Mexican people, another one she liked was the handmade jewelry from sea shells, rocks and handmade baskets. It seemed to Carla everyone smiled a lot. She couldn't help but wonder why the Mexican people always smiled. They were drawn to a cantina where music was pouring out from it. The door stood open and several young men were sitting outside drinking and watching the passing traffic. "Hola." One of them said as they walked by.

"Hola, que paso?" Doug replied. "Bueno cervesa?"

The men laughed, "Si" the one who greeted them first answered. "Come in, mucho frio cerveases."

"Maybe later." Carla responded. This could be a good place to start asking questions. "Where is a good place to eat?"

"La Favorita, keep going, you will see it."

"Gracias."

They continued down the strip, stopping occasionally to look at window fronts of stores selling clothing and other goods. It was getting close to sunset when they walked into the La Favorita, "Bienvenidos y buen provecho"

Terri asked the waiter if they served soda, to which he said they had Coca cola and Pepsi, auga de frutas; a diluted fruit juice, wine and beer. He took the drink orders while they munched on appetizers of stuffed jalapeños and tortilla chips and salsa.

They were seated near a large window that had a grand view of the Pacific and the setting sun. Carla couldn't help but stare at the beautiful display of turquoise sky and wisps of feathery clouds that caught the sun's last rays setting them on fire. They ordered several types of tacos and quesadillas and barbacona or Mexican barbeque.

"Buen provecho!" The waiter said as he set their dishes in front of them along with extra helpings of beans, corn tortillas, guacamole, and Pico de Gallo.

"Gracias" Carla smiled at him then helped herself to Barbacona.

They made their way back toward the hotel; full from supper. "That's one thing about Mexican food that I like, they don't skimp, and I haven't eaten anything yet that hasn't tasted good." Doug commented between picking his teeth with a toothpick. They walked past the cantina where Doug had spoken to the men sitting outside earlier. "Any of you want to go in and have a beer?" Doug asked.

"Not me." Carla said. "I'm going to make a couple of phone calls and take a shower before I turn in. You guys go ahead, but just remember; we leave early in the morning."

She watched them as they entered the cantina then walked back to her room. The night was pleasant, a soft breeze came in from the ocean and a full moon was cresting on the horizon. She strolled along the strip. Most of the little stands that were opened earlier had closed up for the evening, but there were plenty of people walking about, most of them were couples or groups and a few families.

Suddenly she felt alone, far from home and very aware of the people walking arm in arm or holding hands; laughing and staring into each other's eyes. She had been alone for so long; she didn't think she could have any more feelings of loneliness that were raw as an open wound. She missed her daughter Katie, but felt joy knowing her other children waited for her return. This whole thing was for Katie, Carla thought as she unlocked the door to her room.

She picked up her cell phone, hoping there would be service then smirked. She had one that could get service to Antarctica if she were there. She highlighted Richard's number and pressed select. It took a couple of seconds for the connection but then she heard the phone ringing and Richard answered it on the second ring.

"I am so glad to hear your voice." Carla wanted to cry and felt tears forming in her eyes. "I've been watching happy people all day and I needed to hear a familiar voice."

"What? Where's everyone else?"

"Oh, they're around, but I wanted to hear your voice."

"I've missed yours too. I'm glad you called."

"I kind of wished you were here."

"Where's here at Carla?"

"I'm in San Quentin."

"That's a prison in California." His voice was mildly surprised.

"I'm talking about on the Baja."

"Carla..."

"I decided to take a turn south is all. Nothing other than sightseeing, you know that."

"We don't have to talk in circles. I'm coming down there. You are going to end up in a lot of trouble lady."

"I won't be here by morning."

"Carla please, wait for me. I didn't' think you were actually going through with trying to find Juan, there is no telling where he is-"

"I've done some investigating and have an ally. Her uncle owns a resort in La Paz and his family and the Pedrazas are sort of like the Mexican version of the Hatfields and McCoys."

"Carla, I've been doing some checking too. Most of the Pedrazas in that area are bad news and are mixed in with the Mexican Mafia, or have family in California who are in the gang. Do one thing for me, if you see anyone that has a black palm print, the number thirteen, EME, or MM tattooed on them, do not go near them. I mean it, they are very dangerous and won't hesitate to toss your body in the desert for the buzzards. There is another thing you need to watch out for too. It's called Mexican Justice. It's a practice used on usually the rich white people who are on vacation and get framed for crimes committed by locals."

"Well, if I were rich, I'd be concerned."

She could hear Richard sigh. "You guys shouldn't even be trying to take this on. Have you talked to a consulate?"

"What's that?" Carla flopped onto the bed, wishing she hadn't told him her location.

"It's legal representation. Find out where the nearest one is and ask them what to do."

"I'll do that first thing." She hated lying to him, but she had very little faith in Mexican law and those who are supposed to represent citizens from other countries. She had given it some thought and knew she should probably get legal help of some kind, but all she wanted was to get her grandsons and get back home, no matter what it took. If it came to her having no other options then she would talk to the Consulate.

"If you get into trouble down there, it's a whole lot harder for a person from a foreign country to get justice."

Carla sighed. He was right as much as she hated to admit it. "Is there anything you can do from your end? We are far into the country now, what could I do from here?"

"I'll see what can be done."

She could hear him moving about as he continued talking.

"There's one other thing. That cluster of storms that came off of Central America? It's turned into a tropical storm named Nadia and is about seven hundred and fifty miles from Cabo San Lucas, according to the weather channel. They are talking that it's possible it is going to turn east and head toward the peninsula."

Carla groaned. She reached for the remote and searched for a station that would have some sort of information pertaining to the weather. As luck would have it, there was a weather channel but it was broadcasted in Spanish, but she didn't need to hear what the meteorologist was saying.

"I turned on the weather channel, dear God in heaven. That thing is huge!" She watched the buzz saw shaped sphere rotating slowly on the satellite image, a graphic popped up showing the pressure was down to 1098 millibars. The latest projections didn't look promising either. The Baja was going to get hit.

"Carla? Are you still with me?" Richard's voice broke her thoughts.

"Yes."

"I'll be waiting for you in La Paz."

"No, I want you to stay out of this Richard. I shouldn't have told you anything."

"I would have found out sooner or later anyway. I want to make sure you stay safe."

"Richard-"

"It's not going to do you any good to persuade me to stay here now."

"Please don't, what about your daughter?"

"She can stay with a friend for a little while, she's a good kid. Like it or not, I'm coming."

"I won't have room for you."

"I've seen the Jeep, there's plenty of room. Stop arguing with me. If I didn't love you-"

"What? Wait a minute-"

"See you in La Paz." Carla heard Richard kiss the phone then he hung up.

"This isn't how it's supposed to turn out." She hissed and tossed the phone onto the nightstand. She rummaged through her luggage for something to sleep in, tossing them onto the bed then stepped outside on the balcony to smoke. Although it wasn't necessary, no smoking bans weren't in effect as much as they were in the states. She did it mainly from habit. How was she going to add another person's belongings and another person as well to the already cramped confines of the jeep?

She was sure Matthew, Doug and especially Terri would not be thrilled to have a cop riding with them. Terri and Matthew were actually doing well without smoking pot. Nothing had been mentioned about it since entering Mexico. She stood on the balcony watching several people swim in the hotel's swimming pool. Suddenly, she was angry, angry at the fact that she wasn't on vacation and living it up, carefree and happy. She was using money saved for her own children and now she had two problems; coming one from the north and one from the south. She finished her smoke and went inside the room.

◆ ◆ ◆

Carla woke with a start, her book lying beside her, the television still on. She thought she heard knocking on her door. She jumped when the door banged again, this time she heard Terri's frantic voice through the door, yelling for her to wake up. It was almost midnight.

Carla pulled her into the room. "Don't you know what time it is?"

"Matt and Doug are in jail."

CHAPTER EIGHTEEN

Carla was furious. She thought about driving, but by the time she would have took getting to the vehicle and finding the police station, she could be there quicker by walking.

According to the arresting officer, her brothers were caught red handed with a bag of marijuana and were smoking a joint behind the cantina. There was no way they would get released tonight and it would take a day or two for a representative to get here from Mexico City. Carla and Terri walked outside the station. Terri's eyes were puffy from crying. "It's all my fault, I'm so sorry!"

"Why is it your fault Terri?" Carla asked, her teeth clenched tight she lit a cigarette. "I told you all not to have any of that when we came here. I assumed you took my word of advice, but now I see I was wrong."

"No, you weren't, we didn't have any, the last of it was smoked in Gila Bend, honest." Terri threw up her hands. "We were drinking and having a great time. Then one of the guys who was sitting outside when we walked past wanted to know if we wanted to buy a little bit. We went behind the bar to make the transaction; he had a small baggie and when he saw the cop, he took off! I didn't know it at the time, but he shoved the bag in Doug's hand. Matthew tried to tell the cop the pot wasn't Doug's and he was arrested too."

"Why didn't you go to jail too? You just said you were there."

"I was walking over to where they were. I told Matt I would catch up because I had to use the bathroom and when I came around the corner Doug and Matt were getting hauled away, I followed the car to the station and that's how I found out what happened."

"That makes it your fault how?"

"I was the one who wanted to smoke and talked Matt into pitching in on the bag."

Carla wanted to strangle Terri, but she couldn't, she needed her. "Let's go find the...." She took a deep breath. "We have to find that man. He's gonna have to help us get them out."

"How? He's probably long gone by now." She trotted beside Carla. "I don't see how he's going to be any help."

Carla came to the cantina, her heart racing. For a split second she almost thought about not going in. The way things were working out she thought, and sure as the world is round, she would go in there and he'd be gone. She walked inside, surprised at how many people were still in the cantina she guessed most of them were locals. "Do you remember what the guy looked like?" Carla asked Terri who was trying to fix her hair. "About five ten I'd say, black hair to his shoulders and dark eyes. There are so many people in here, it's hard to tell if he is around.

Carla thought it could be any one of the younger men in the bar.

Terri shouted so Carla could hear her. "Maybe we should stick together. It was getting rowdy when all that was going on and it looks like it's gotten crazier."

Carla thought about it and looked around the bar. She's right. Carla thought. The place was hopping, wall to wall people dancing, shouting above the band's music. They were constantly getting bumped into by people and there had already been a small skirmish within the time they walked in. "If you see him point him out!" She shouted back. They pushed their way further into the cantina, until they were on the far side of the exit. One end of the place opened up to the outside where still more people were gathered in and around a large covered patio with Christmas lights hanging from its ceiling, out here it was much quieter.

"Carla, there he is." Teri whispered.

"Where?"

"Over there in the corner by those two big guys."

"Oh no."

"What's wrong?"

"Terri, you see the tattoos on their necks?"

"13 and MM" Terri stared at the tattoos then covered her mouth. "DVI."

"DVI? What are you talking about? They are members of the Mexican Mafia." Carla said.

Terri nodded her head in agreement. "I know, but the Mexican Mafia were originally called Duel Vocational Institute, they used to kill off anyone who threatened Hispanic inmates, I don't know if that's the case now days, but apparently you know something about them."

"No, only what Richard told me tonight. I called him and let it slip where I was at. He's supposed to be in La Paz sometime in the next couple of days."

"Richard who? How did that happen?"

"I'll talk about that after we get this mess cleaned up." Carla walked up to the group of men sitting at a table playing cards.

"Excuse me."

One of the men looked Carla up and down then returned to his card game. "I need to speak with that man right there. Tengo que hablar con ese hombre." She pointed to the man Terri said was the one who sold them the marijuana. The whole table ignored Carla and that was the wrong thing to do. "I'll say this one more time." her voice flat. "I need to speak with you, amigo."

One of the men with the MM tattoo looked at Carla. "Can't you see we are busy? You can talk to him later; he owes me money and needs to finish the game."

"He got my brothers thrown in jail tonight, I speak with him now."

"Not my problem puta, now go."

"I go when I say so."

The man pushed back his chair from the card game and stood up. "What did you say?"

Carla never took her eyes off the man. He was broad shouldered and heavily tattooed. He had a large flat nose with one nostril pierced with a small gold hoop. His eyes were dark and bored right through Carla. She thought if she tried to run off it wouldn't end well. It was too late to do anything but face the giant man. "I said, I'm not leaving. Your friend there got my brothers into trouble."

His lips curled over his teeth. "I don't know what you are talking about, he's been here losing his ass all night. Perhaps you are mistaken."

"No," Terri replied. "He's the one who smoked mota with us, and took fifty dollars from me for a bag of weed. Then he tried to make a pass at me."

"You are bonita, chica. It would be hard not to try to steal a kiss." He tried to grab Terri about her waist but she slapped him across his face. He stood full 6'5" height, towering over the two women. "You are interrupting business, leave." His eyes glittered hard; boring into hers. Carla noticed his jaw clenching and his nostrils flaring.

"Please," she interjected. "I'm in dire straits and need help. We are only passing through to find my grandchildren who were kidnapped. This is an unfortunate incident and the sooner we solve our problem the sooner we can be on our way."

The man glared at them. "I kill perras like you."

Carla didn't back down "I'm searching for my grandchildren; their father is a monster." She tossed out the name. At first it looked as if the man had been hit on the head with a shovel. All of the people who were nearby and at the poker table stopped talking, and stared at her. She explained that her daughter was also killed by the same man. She told of her suspicions about who murdered her sister as well.

She noticed that the man they needed to talk to was slipping out into the night by the patio and started to run at him when the man grabbed her arm. "Chica, it is your lucky day." He grinned down at her, so close that she could smell beer on his breath. "My name is Jorge; I know who can help you out." He nodded to another man standing near the poker table and he slipped out onto the patio, disappearing around the corner. Jorge turned back towards Carla and Terri. "You don't need Paco; he's a coward and you were set up."

"How do you know that?"

"Paco said that a man came up to him and told him that your brothers like weed and were looking for some. Why the police showed up, I don't know, but I have a feeling whoever talked to Paco is the one who put your brothers in jail."

Since Tuscon, Carla had the feeling they were being watched and the only one she could think of had to be Juan. She was sure he had eyes everywhere. They followed Jorge a few blocks behind the main street to a flat roofed concrete building. As they walked, Jorge told them about the long-standing feud between him and Juan. They were school mates in La Paz and at first, they got along fine. As they grew older, Jorge explained that Juan started running drugs across the border for an uncle and pulled him into the "business".

Money flowed freely, women were at their service, there was nothing to stop them. Then the day came when the U.S. Feds found out about the tunnel used to smuggle drugs and people. Both Juan and Jorge ended up in prison, but it was Jorge who lost out because Juan turned against him, pointing the finger at him as the ring leader when it was Juan's family who held the reins.

Juan spent six months on probation while Jorge spent eight years in prison. "To this day," Jorge vowed. "I will avenge the wrong done against me."

"Aren't you with the Mexican Mafia?" Carla asked.

"Yes, but Juan, he's a snake, he disappears for a while when the heat is on him." He stopped a few feet from the Police station. "Thanks to you, maybe this time I will find him and give him what he deserves."

"A bullet between the eyes?"

Jorge's laugh made Carla cringe because of the rage seething beneath the surface. She knew how he felt. "No, that would be too good, too merciful. When I catch him, he will die slow."

"If you catch him first, I want to be there."

"No, you don't Chica."

CHAPTER NINETEEN

It took two days before Matthew and Doug were released from the San Quentin jail. Carla and Terri both talked to the judge, telling the reason they were in Mexico, doing research for a book, which of course was a lie. Carla had no intention of letting anyone in the town, aside from her new friend, Jorge, know the truth. In the end, she had to post most of the bail money, six hundred pesos, with Terri only pitching in a third. Carla was a little chaffed about it, but to gripe about it would make things worse, and they needed to leave. The once tropical storm Nadia was now a category two hurricane, and less than five hundred miles from Cabo San Lucas. She glanced worriedly at the sky, laden with some of the first outer bands sliding across the desert sky, their shadows dotting the landscape like hundreds of ink blotted Bingo game cards.

The group remained silent for some time, each lost in their thoughts. Carla was not happy about the whole jail issue, but thankful she didn't leave San Quentin empty handed. They now had two solid allies Jorge and Rosa, involved in searching for Scotty and Marcos. For the first time since leaving her home, she could feel victory in her grasp. The silence lasted about ten miles before anyone spoke up.

"I'm sorry about what happened back there." Matthew lifted his head from Terri's shoulder. "I don't think anyone would believe me if I said I did time in San Quentin." He chuckled lightly. Terri pinched the underside of his arm. "Hey! What's that for?"

Carla held her tongue. It was a major flaw in her character to fly off the handle when the other side didn't have a chance to speak or defend themselves. She was working hard at controlling her spontaneity and was proud she was doing well.

"Never saw that coming." Doug admitted, turning towards Carla and flashing her a grin. When she didn't return with a smile, he fixed his eyes back to the road.

◆ ◆ ◆

Hugh Simpson woke to the sound of running water and a massive hangover. The last thing he remembered was confronting a weasley looking man and paying him a hefty sum of two-thousand pesos to throw a wrench into his ex-wife's plan so he could finish what he came to do. Kill her. Hugh swung his legs over the bed and went to the bathroom where a woman showered. He had no clue what her name was or who she was for that matter. He flung the shower curtain aside causing the woman to jump.

She stood there for a moment with water pouring over her body. "Hola Senoir." She smiled at him. She held out her hand, "You want shower? I will soap you good, come in, I show you." She picked up the bar of soap and began swirling it over herself. "Get you nice and clean."

Hugh stood watching the woman continue to work the soap into a lather on her body, her long, black hair slicked back from her face. He watched her moan with pleasure until he couldn't stand it no longer and pushed her. The woman lost her balance and fell against the tiled wall. "What'd you do that for!?"

"Get out."

"What? You don't like it? Huh? Bendjo! You did last night!"

"I said get out." Hugh raised his arm and slugged her in the mouth with his fist. She screamed and grabbed the shower curtain attempting to hide behind it. He snatched the flimsy plastic away from her, grabbed a handful of her hair and drug her out of the bathroom. "You have ten seconds." Hugh stood over the woman who shrank away, holding her leg where a large, purple knot stuck out below the knee. "Starting now."

◆ ◆ ◆

Hugh wasn't concerned about losing track of his ex-wife because the Baja's limited highway system. He threw his suitcase into the trunk of his car and left San Quentin in the dust. Hugh believed that Carla's meddling cost him the respect of his children. Those stupid journals she'd given them; when he read the first one his rage seethed, burned deep like a three-day campfire stoked around the clock. By the time he was into the third one, he kicked and stomped the remaining journals into every corner of his apartment living room. At first Hugh tried to play off the writings, he told the kids that their mother had suffered a mental breakdown, that it ran in her family. Most of what she'd written was nonsense; only ammunition to make them go running to her and make him look like a slug.

Through the years, Hugh pointed the finger at Carla. Hadn't he been the one to raise them? Hadn't he been the one to clothe, feed and send them to school? Take them to doctor and dentist appointments? Hadn't he been the one to go to ball games and plays? Where had she been all this time? The rouse seemed to satisfy them until they came over three nights earlier and told him they met with Carla and she'd given them the journals.

He should have expected it he guessed, and should have taken care of her long ago. His story of her threatening the children when they were little and putting a hit on his head held no merit now. Hindsight told him he should have killed her and dumped her body in a ravine filled with feral Razorback hogs.

Now, his children hated him and now he hated Carla with a rage that would only become sated when he ripped her to shreds and tossed her bones into the Pacific. The thought of her crying and begging gave him immense pleasure. If he had his hands on her throat right then as he sped down the highway, he mused, he wouldn't let up until her eyes popped from their sockets and her tongue turned black.

◆ ◆ ◆

Crawling to a stop, Hugh groaned as a short line of cars waited at a road block. He craned his neck, to see if he could spot the maroon Jeep. Disappointed that Carla wasn't ahead of him, he sat back in the seat and watched as the traffic crawled. As he waited, he thought about the next step he wanted to take, relishing at the possibilities that existed. He stared at the landscape, thinking about his ex-wife when the traffic began moving a little faster. The line of cars inched through the road block as heat waves from the asphalt and exhaust shimmered in in the air like doors to another dimension. Finally, he pulled up to the roadblock and rolled his window down.

"Buenos Dias, where are you going?" The officer queried.

"Cabo San Lucas."

"Oh, you will have to take a detour, señor." The officer pointed toward the west facing road. "You can take this, follow the signs, easy road."

"Is there something wrong?"

"Yes, a bad wreck. That route is closed. I assure you señor, this will take you there no problem, just follow the sign."

"That's odd. You let other cars through."

"They are local people who do not live far. Santa Maria is very close and the wreck is another ten miles past it. You are welcome to drive to Santa Maria if you wish, but it will be a long wait."

Hugh decided to take the alternate route; he had no idea of when Carla and her brothers had left San Quentin. Yet, it was possible they could be close. Turning the vehicle onto the road, he punched the accelerator to the floor, thankful for the straight stretch of highway. He lost two hours sitting in the car, roasting like a turkey in the oven since the air compressor quit working in Tecate. The air flowing through the open windows cooled him down some, but it was still hot. The thought of Carla maybe driving the same road spurned him on.

The night fell in beside Hugh as he raced on, unaware he was in the middle of the desert where there were no towns until he ran out of gas.

◆ ◆ ◆

A half a mile from his car Hugh came to an intersection. A sigh of relief blew between his lips when he spotted a gas station and several buildings. It was hard to see into the night, but the dim light from the stars told him the buildings were old. Some of them leaned enough if a strong wind fell on them, they would crumble into jumbled piles of lumber. Still, Hugh reasoned there could be someone living in one of the buildings and maybe help him out.

He walked up to the window of the gas station, the pumps were antiques, rusted numbers stuck in between the sight glass and no hoses on either one. Cupping his hands around his eyes he peered into the building; the shelves were bare and a pile of tables and chairs took up part of the floor. There could still be someone living in one of the other buildings Hugh thought and decided to check. He rounded the corner of the building and ran into two men holding rifles at him. He backed away from the men.

"I am lost." He held up his hands.

"No, you aren't lost." One man motioned with his rifle for Hugh to get on his knees.

"I'm not doing that!" Hugh shouted at him.

"Yeah," the man answered him as he hit him on the side of his face with the butt of the rifle. "you are."

He motioned once again for Hugh to get to his knees.

Hugh, not wanting to cause any more problems than what was facing him for the moment complied with the man's command. He stared up at the two men. "I don't understand. I don't have any money, but I'll give you what I have." He started to pull his wallet from his back pocket.

"I don't want your money. I want justice." With that the man sneered at him then squeezed the trigger. When Hugh's body tumbled onto the ground the man stepped over him and spit on his chest.

CHAPTER TWENTY

Toward the south huge billowing clouds filled the sky. Carla determined they were probably more of the far outer bands of the hurricane. Menacing but beautiful; towering high into the atmosphere where the sun bathed the tops in fiery oranges, pinks, and salmon hues. Looking to the Pacific she could see the bottoms of the giant sentinels were flat, heavy and dark. Where the clouds broke and the sun shone on the surface of the ocean in piercing shafts of light as though the god Zeus were searching for dinner.

They were as close to the Pacific Ocean as they would get before swinging back inland and Terri wanted to stop to take a few pictures of the salt flats near Guerro Negro. Carla kept silent for most of the time since leaving San Quentin.

"Carla, I really need to pee."

There was a small grocery store near the highway and Carla pulled in. They piled out of the vehicle and walked around while waiting for Terri. The air was saturated with sea brine and a stiff breeze blew in from the south. It was beautiful and scary at the same time. How insignificant a human being was compared to the power of the ocean, weather and mother nature herself she mused. She pulled her hair into a pony tail to keep it from flying in her face then leaned against the jeep. Matthew and Doug had walked some distance looking toward the ocean. Carla loved her brothers and glad they were with her, but another setback and they'd be on the first plane back home. No. She reigned in her emotions. It wasn't their fault. She was looking for a scapegoat.

Terri walked up to her husband where they stood talking. Carla continued to watch them for a few moments before calling out she was ready to get back on the road. She drew a couple more puffs from her cigarette then ground out the butt and started toward them. "You guys ready?"

"Oh, just a couple more minutes, okay?" Terri had her camera out taking snapshots of the salt flats.

"We need to go."

"Ease up sis." Matthew patted Carla on the back and put his arm around her shoulders.

Carla shrugged him off and opened the door and began throwing out luggage.

"Wait! Carla!"

"You all want to play tourists?" She fought the tears wanting to spill over and swallowed the huge lump rising in her throat. "Well then, be the tourist."

"Carla, wait-"

"I do not and will not have or take time for you anymore. Understand?" She started toward the driver side door. "You're either going or staying, and you have about three seconds to decide."

They sped down the Santa Rosalia Ensenada, into the mountains. Carla at the wheel and her mind churning on the odd incidents since Tucson, two flat tires, the fender bender in Gila Bend, Doug and Matt's incarceration, and the strange man. She couldn't help but wonder if there was a connection. She didn't think it was Juan, because her gut told her they'd all be dead by now.

Although the marine greens and aqua blues of the Pacific soothed Carla's frazzled nerves it was certainly easy to be said the opposite of the dusty browns and gray greenery of the Baja desert. Maybe it was the sameness of it, so many miles of desert and little variance of topography; so far away from home.

"That's weird how the sides of the road are painted white." Doug glanced over at Carla.

She felt bad about the blow up, but she couldn't help it. She would apologize when she was able to make sense of the whole situation. That, she surmised may not happen anyway. "Yep, it is." She concentrated on the highway. They were climbing into the mountains. The highway curved in between the rocky terrain with an occasional peek of the ocean now far into the distance. At least the cactus and sagebrush were greener and more of it. She made a stab at smoothing the hurt feelings. "I guess it's because of the erosion. Look." She pointed at Doug's window. Both sides of the highway supported erosion barriers painted white.

"Yeah, I guess that makes sense." He chuckled and took a drink from the soda he bought at the store. "It sure makes you pay attention huh? You know, the road's black," He nodded at the painted embankment. "they're white."

"Hey," Terri spoke from the back seat. "Check out the volcanoes!"

"Where?" They all craned their necks to get a glance. The hillsides fell away and they were in a wide shallow valley. The desert tones traded for a barren landscape covered old lava fields and dormant cones.

"Wow." They all said at once.

"It's like we went to another planet!" Carla pulled over to the side of the road. "Terri, you have the camera loaded?"

"Yep!" She was already out of the door, snapping pictures.

They all got out of the vehicle surveying the scene, void of life from their perspective from the top of the valley rim.

Doug and Carla stood side by side the wind tossing their hair about as if giant hands dropped from the sky and gave them both a tousle.

"You ready?" Doug asked her.

Carla shrugged. "I don't think a couple of minutes will really matter." She looked over at her younger brother. I'm sorry. I know I'm being too pushy." She felt her face grow hot; tears filled her eyes. "I just want my Scotty and Marcos back."

Doug reached for his sister and held her. "You don't need to apologize. We should have been more cautious. He hugged her tighter then pulled back from her. "Don't worry so much. Okay? I mean, yeah, we have to be careful. We have a hurricane to deal with, and the possibility of getting shot is magnified a hundred times, but understand I am with you. You always were one to fly off the handle."

"I know." She looked at Doug. She could see the fine lines of crow's feet crinkling the corner of his eyes. His skin leathery from years of being in the sun.

Doug squeezed her shoulder. "I'm sure they are safe."

She nodded in agreement. She knew Juan was a good father to his sons. She didn't think he'd be so hardened to harm his children, but what action would he take if he knew she was looking for them?

CHAPTER TWENTY-ONE

They were starving. Many miles had passed and they hadn't seen a gas station. Carla was beginning to get nervous; the gas gage read out edged closer to empty. Every so often, she'd lean over to check it, holding her breath, praying for a highway sign to the nearest town.

Minutes later, her prayer was answered by a sign informing her they had 10 km before Jesus Marie.

"Don't worry sis." Doug told her. "We'll make it." He shifted a little in his seat. "This thing gets great gas mileage for the horsepower."

Carla grinned uncertainly at him, hoping he was right. And he was. By noon they arrived at the small town of Jesus Marie and pulled into what looked to be the only filling station. Doug climbed behind the wheel of the vehicle and told them the manager suggested a small café on the other side of the town if they were hungry. It had been a silent leg of the trip inside the car and all agreed that lunch was a good idea. They opted for a booth facing the mountain vista and blooming cacti spreading out across the desert sand like living jewels.

The food was delicious, but Carla poked at her meal. She felt bad she kept nagging about time slipping away. Not only for Scotty and Marcos, but for them too. She knew they understood the severity of the situation. However, now it was becoming an ever increasing necessity to find the boys because crawling up the South American coast in the Pacific Ocean Hurricane Nadia churned over the warm waters; feeding the storm.

"That was probably one of the better meals I've eaten since Dallas." Doug patted his stomach then belched.

"Good food for a good price." Matthew added. "I'll warn you though, I might get a little gassy."

"Then I guess you'll be hanging your butt out the window." Carla said. They all laughed when Matthew volunteered to tie himself on top of the Jeep.

◆ ◆ ◆

"Well, I've got bad news." Doug peered over the raised hood of the Jeep. "Someone cut the spark plug wires."

Carla threw open the passenger side door and ran to stand beside her brother.

"What? You're kidding me!" She stared down at the mangled mess. "Some of them are gone."

"Yeah, I found them, and one other thing, Carla." She turned around where Matthew held out tattered remnants of the fan belt.

◆ ◆ ◆

"Señor, it will take at least two days to fix your car. The man shrugged his shoulders and grinned which faded when Carla shoved her brother aside and slammed a fist on the counter.

"I don't have two days!" She felt her chest tighten, her voice she knew was veering toward a panicked state. "Isn't there someone you can call nearby?"

"Si. Pero le costará." But it will cost you. The rotund Hispanic man grinned a wide smile and spread his arms. "This is a beautiful place. You would like it here; it is a wonderful place for vacation.

Carla took in a deep breath and closed her eyes. "Señor, we need to get to our destination."

The man stared at her for a few seconds and shrugged again. "My friend is very expensive."

"Get him."

CHAPTER TWENTY-TWO

At a quarter to one that afternoon they came to the outskirts of La Paz. Carla for one, was glad that international signs were easy to read, how can one mistake an airplane for anything else other than an airport? She was nervous. When she had to stay the extra days in San Quentin, she called Richard to let him know. When he asked why, she lied to him again and said she had a lead to check out. He told her he loved her. Did he really? Carla chewed over the thought. She hadn't felt love like that in a long time. Could it be possible for her to love a man and he return that love? She wouldn't know the answers, and until this ordeal was over, she couldn't even think of pursuing a relationship.

Matthew spotted the airport sign and turned into the lane leading to it. "The thatched roofs are a nice touch." He remarked as they pulled up to the terminal.

Before now, Carla hadn't mentioned Richard to her brothers because she felt it unnecessary. Her news of Richard arriving caused a great ribbing with Matthew and Doug. He was merely a friend, she had told them, an acquaintance, someone she knew. Yet inside her heart he made her gush, swoon like a schoolgirl with a crush on a teacher. She told them to shut up or they'd walk to the airport.

Her breath was stolen from her when he walked up from the waiting area. My he's tall. His smile, I've forgotten how beautiful it is. At first, she stood rooted to the spot, watching him drag his small luggage bag through the crowd of people. Surreal in motion, time slowed to a crawl. He drew close, she couldn't help but notice how nice his jeans fit him and the way his shirt tail fell over his hips. He could have been a model she thought. Richard stood in front of her and smiled.

"Hello beautiful lady."

The strain of the trip, the hammering of her heart, the setbacks, and the hurricane fell away. She realized how much she missed him; how much she wanted to be with him. She threw her arms around Richard's neck and kissed him.

"That's one of the best welcomes I've ever had." Richard stared into Carla's eyes and smiled softly. He brushed a strand of her hair from her lips and kissed them again.

She looked up at him, "I've never been so glad to see someone I didn't want to see."

Richard laughed and pulled her in closer to his body. She could feel the warmth of his skin through his shirt and hugged him tighter. She hated to admit it, but she was glad he showed up.

"The Mexican government is urging tourists and locals alike to leave the area. Hurricane Nadia is supposed to be one of the worst storms to hit the Baja in a long time. Fortunately for me, I found a pilot who was coming here to get his family out and so here I am."

"Ahem."

"Oh!" Carla looked over her shoulder at her brothers and Terri standing a short distance away with huge grins on their faces. "I guess I should introduce you, but we can do that on the way out of here."

Richard picked up his travel bag. "This is all I have."

Matthew opened the back of the Jeep and found a spot for it. "All right, let's get a move on. Time's a-wasting." He grinned at Richard and hopped into the driver's seat. In the back seat, Carla wedged herself between Doug and Richard. It was a little cramped but she didn't mind. With the introductions out of the way, Richard explained to the group that Chief Bristol was transporting a prisoner to Little Rock, and he ran into an old college buddy. As it turned out, the old friend was with the U.S. Marshall's office and knew about the abductions.

"Bristol gave him what information he had on the case."

Carla gripped Richard's leg hard. "You know where they are?" She felt the tears beginning to brim over.

"Supposedly in Cabo San Lucas. Juan has family living there."

Carla's hand covered her mouth.

"The old college buddy told Bristol the Feds are after Juan Pedraza and his gang." Richard stared out the window. "I think it might be a good idea to go to the local precinct in Cabo and tell them. I don't think you should be chasing this guy."

"Uh-oh." Matthew muttered.

Carla glared at Richard. "I'm doing no such thing."

"They are extremely dangerous; they will stop at nothing to get what they want."

"I'm not stopping until I get what I want, and I want by grandbabies."

Richard took one of her hands and squeezed it. "I know this is hard...."

She pulled her hand away. "I'm not going to the cops."

"Carla."

"No."

"Look at me."

"Matt, stop the car."

"They will kill you."

"Matt."

"Yeah, yeah, okay!" Matthew grumbled as he pulled alongside the curb.

Carla reached over Richard and pulled on the door handle. "Richard, I'm glad to see you and thank you for caring, but I'm not giving up. If you want to leave, then go." She pushed the door open.

"I'm not saying we can't look for them but, the hurricane is coming fast. If we leave now, we can make it to Mexico City and wait it out."

Her mouth dropped open. "I can't believe you just said that."

"You are risking your life and theirs." Richard grasped her hand. "Carla, there are people looking for your grandchildren, it's their job. We need to leave."

"What? And let them just ride out the storm?" She shook her head. "No."

"We have seventy-two hours before Nadia makes landfall. That pilot is leaving in three hours"

"Matt, get out, you too Richard."

"What'd I do?" Matt retorted.

"Nothing, I'm driving, you drive like an old lady."

She nudged her brother out of the driver's seat and slid behind the steering wheel.

"You will get killed Carla. If not by the storm, by Pedraza."

She adjusted the seat and mirrors to her satisfaction. "I'll take my chances."

"Carla-"

"Scoot over man! She'll leave me behind if I stand out here too long."

Richard stared at Carla. She grinned at him and stomped on the gas.

"Is she always this stubborn?" Richard asked Doug.

Doug grinned at him. "Oh, you haven't seen anything yet. That was mild."

The closer they got to Cabo San Lucas, the more Carla thought about how to search for Scotty and Marcos. She knew Richard was right, if Juan knew how close she was, he'd certainly send her a welcome gift. She just couldn't justify or forgive herself if she gave in and left the boys now. Yet if she died and if Juan was caught where would the boys go? She was glad she gave Charli a copy of her will. She hated to think about it, but an important issue. The boys would be taken care of should it come to that.

Although most of the sky was cloudy, she could see the fiery orange and yellow rays of the sun kissing the tips of the low-lying clouds that were beginning to thicken as the hurricane drew closer. Hurricane or not, she would get her grandchildren back. And if Juan decided she would die, then she'd make sure he went with her.

CHAPTER TWENTY-THREE

Carla hadn't realized how large Cabo San Lucas was and spread out far into the desert. It was a pretty city, she thought. For the most part many of the cities and villages they drove through were beautiful in their own way. She stared out the window watching the buildings and landscaped terrain pass by them.

Night came early due to the heavy cloud cover. By the time they drove through the city, the streets were nearly deserted. What few people were out, stared at them, making Carla nervous. One of them could be Juan's lookout and were on their way to tell him she had been spotted. She fought the nagging doubt back inside then rubbed her eyes.

"We should find someplace to rest for a short while Carla." Teri offered.

Carla looked away from the street view and nodded. "I guess you're right. I am pretty tired and I haven't thought about eating until now. Maybe we can ask around and show the picture I have of the boys."

Teri nodded in agreement. "Yeah, ok after we've had showers and rested a bit we can scout around the area." She glanced in the rearview mirror. "It appears that our men folk are getting along nicely."

Carla turned to see what Teri meant and had to stifle a laugh. All three men were asleep and Matt rested his head on Richard's shoulder. Richard's head lolled from side to side, his mouth open.

"Not very dignified now, is he?" Carla replied.

"Honestly, I don't think it would matter if he was drooling, he'd still look good. I've never seen Officer Yummy, I mean, Richard in nothing but a cop's uniform."

Carla blushed; her smiled widened.

"Oh, don't tell me," Teri whispered. "you've slept with him!"

"Sssh!" Carla's thought that if her face and neck were as red as she felt hot, she might burst into flames. She rolled the window down for fresh air. Her hands shook when she tried to open her bottle of water. "I don't want to talk about it. Especially with Richard and my brothers in the back seat."

"Okay! Okay!" Teri whispered then giggled. "You promise to tell me later then."

"I doubt it."

"You need someone to tell these things to. I'm here and so are you. Come talk to me later." Teri briefly rubbed Carla's shoulder and smiled.

"There's a Best Western ahead." Carla nodded at the windshield. "Let's get a couple hours of sleep then back on the search."

"Hopefully they still have rooms or haven't closed down." Teri craned her neck to read the sign on the side of the building as they came closer to it. "Ah, lights are on, and cars in the parking lot is a good sign!"

A bolt of lightning slammed the water's surface. The immediate snap, crack of thunder caused Carla to sit straight up in the bed. Another flash of light; but this time the thunder was less intense. She sat on the edge of the bed and rubbed her eyes with the palms of her hands. She glanced at the digital clock on the night stand. Less than three hours had passed since she laid her head down on the pillow. Unable to sleep, she got up and rummaged through her suitcase. Finding the Baja Journal, she opened it up and began to write.

Charli called me before I fell asleep with the news that her father, Hugh is hasn't been seen in a week. No one knew of his whereabouts. She filed a missing person's report but, it was as though he'd disappeared into a void or a black hole. I hope I convinced her that he's probably gone somewhere to sort out things his way. Should I feel bad?

Because of Hugh, I lived in a bubble of sarcasm and self-loathing; not worthy of having a happy life. But all that has passed; I've moved on and forward, I have survived, I have faith, and I am strong.

Should I be worried? Would Hugh be that determined to find me? It makes sense in an odd way I suppose. If the situation were different and my whole world had fallen into a crevasse, would I track whoever did it to the depths of Hell and back? There's no probably to it.

I came from the bottom, I'm climbing my way up and out, and I'm better for it. So, if he's following me and we meet? I'll claw his eyes out, make him feel all the years of pain he's given me. He gets what he deserves. I couldn't kill him, that's murder and I'd be no better of a person than he is. But I'd like to make sure he spends the rest of his life in misery.

Closing the journal Carla decided she needed to tell Richard her suspicions about Hugh. Another flash of lightning hit close accompanied by the instant crack of thunder made her jump. Time was running out to find the children. What if Juan took them elsewhere, away from the hurricane? What if they were already gone? Would he take them someplace safe? The thoughts swirled inside her head trying its best to break her down; made her want to get in the bed, crawl under the covers, and cry. Instead, she stood up and wiped away a tear rolling down her cheek. She grabbed a change of clothes and decided to take a shower and get underway.

The shower did little to ease fatigue, what she needed was caffeine and food. Carla slipped her journal back into the suitcase and closed it up. She was about to pick up the key card to her room when she heard a soft knock at the door. She put her eye to the peep hole and saw Richard standing there holding two cups of coffee and a small paper bag.

"You must have read my mind." Carla took the bag from him and pulled out a chocolate covered factura. She offered him a chair.

"They had fresh coffee in the lobby. Even in a hurricane you can't go wrong with that." Richard smiled and raised his cup. "To Hurricane Nadia."

Carla raised hers and tapped Richard's cup.

"Did you get any rest?" He asked.

"A little bit." She sipped on the beverage. "Did you?"

"I'm too wound up to sleep."

"So am I. Time is running out." Carla set her coffee on the nightstand. "Look, Richard. I-"

"Carla, it's okay."

"No, I'm sorry. I don't know what I was thinking." She stared out the window of the room.

"What are you talking about?" He walked over and stood next to her.

A tear rolled down her cheek. "They could be anywhere."

"And we'll find them. I just want you to see this realistically. It's a huge, dangerous task." He put his arm around her shoulder. "Hey."

She turned to face Richard. Her emotions were torn apart and tossed to the four winds. God, she was tired and angry. Happy and scared. It was as though she was caught in a whirlpool and it was trying to suck her down into a deep dark depression that she didn't know if she would be able to crawl out of it or really wanted to try. She felt Richard hug her tighter and, at that moment, she was grateful for him. She put her arms around him and felt the tears rolling down her cheeks; unable to stop them she let them go.

"Go ahead, cry your eyes out." He pulled her closer.

"I'm in an emotional taffy pull. I'm so tired but I can't sleep. I won't until I have those kids in my arms."

Richard kissed the top of her head. "I know." He pulled her away from his body. "I'm with you, but just so you know, we keep looking for the boys, we may hit a lot of dead ends."

Carla flopped down on the bed and Richard sat next to her. She felt so small and lost. "I feel like crap."

He laughed and stood up pulling her up with him. "Since you mentioned it, you don't look bright and perky."

"That just makes it much better."

Richard laughed again and bent down to kiss her. "I promise you Carla, we will get Scotty and Marcos. But we need to think about that hurricane. We may have to find shelter; go look for them after the storm passes. Hopefully Nadia is a glancing blow." A flash of lightning lit up Richard's face making him wince against the harsh light. "Call it what you want but, we shouldn't just go in and take them."

"Yes, we should!" Carla stepped back from him and pointed out into the warm tropical night. In the distance lightning flashed across the horizon. "He took them from me, I'll take them back."

"Okay, look." He once again stood in front of her. "We need a plan." He sat down on the bed and pulled up a map of Cabo San Lucas. He looked up from his phone and stared at her. "I want you to know I wouldn't do this for anyone else. I love you, Carla."

"I-" She struggled with a dark blue windbreaker she'd brought. "I can't do this now. Not yet Richard." Carla saw his genuine concern for her welfare and happiness in his beautiful blue eyes. She also noticed a light in them she'd never seen before. Did he really love her? She didn't want to think about anything but her grandsons, a relationship was not what she wanted to concentrate on. Not yet. She struggled to find the arm to her jacket.

He helped her with the garment. "Okay, let's do this; we keep looking and we find where they are at, then we'll call the Police." He turned her around and kissed her on the mouth. "We do that, then you don't have to tell me you love me."

"Well, I mean-"

Richard chuckled "It's okay, we take our time. As of now, we are partners, not potential lovers."

"Richard!" Carla blushed at the thought of his body near hers. On top, underneath, it didn't matter to her. She didn't want to admit she had feelings for Richard too and found it may be useless to tuck away those feelings if she let them linger too long.

They ran across the road to the café and ordered a quick meal of tortas and more coffee. Compared to fifteen minutes earlier, the night air was warm and the winds calmed down. Carla waited for Richard outside so she could smoke. She looked into the dark sky and saw stars.

"We're getting a break in the weather according to the manager back there." Richard nodded at the café where the little man quickly locked it up and ran to his car. "The newscaster said Hurricane Nadia slowed down some. It gives us maybe another twenty-four hours max before landfall."

For the first time since leaving Dallas, Carla was rejuvenated, it was a good sign. Thank you, Jesus! She thought as they began walking down the quiet streets of Cabo San Lucas.

By ten p.m., Matthew, Doug and Teri were back were in their rooms to grab some sleep while Carla and Richard drove around showing Scotty and Marcos' photo to anyone who would stop. What few people they did encounter knew nothing of her grandchildren's whereabouts.   They decided to call it quits and try to figure out where to look for them when the last person they asked, an old man recognized Juan from a photo Carla pulled up on her phone through an online search engine. He'd known the family well at one time, and told them what extended family there was in Cabo no longer spoke to Juan because of his ties to drugs and gang activity. His parents had died several years earlier, leaving an aunt and uncle still living in La Paz.

They walked to the jeep. "Do you think that woman in La Paz lied to the college buddy informant?" Carla asked as she climbed in the passenger seat.

"Who knows maybe she was told to say that? It could be Juan meant to throw anyone off his trail if anyone were to ask." Richard said as he started up the vehicle.

Carla snapped the seat belt into place. "Well, it worked."

CHAPTER TWENTY-FOUR

Since they had another hour before waking up her brothers and Teri, Carla decided she would try to take a short nap herself. She stretched out on the bed and instantly fell asleep.

"Scotty! Marcos! Time for supper, come in and wash your hands and face!"

"Katie?"

"Oh, mom! Why did I have little boys?" Katie threw up her hands then laughed.

"Is that you Katie?" Carla reached out to touch her. Katie smiled softly at her and turned around and disappeared.

Carla's eyes flew open, searching the room. She blinked several more times then looked over at the clock. A half hour had passed which surprised her because it felt like a minute to her. She sat up and swung her legs onto the floor, sitting on the edge of the bed. She started to turn on the lamp on the bedside table when a shadow filled in the small crack at the bottom of the door of her room into the main hallway.

At first it appeared as though the owner of the shadow was merely walking down the hall then stopped in front of her room. She saw the shadow move as it left something in front of the door and then knocked. By the time she opened the door the hall was empty except for a small box. She started to pick it up when she felt the hairs on her arms rise and an uncanny feeling of being watched. Leaving the box, she went to Richard's room and knocked on the door. When he opened his door, she pointed to the little white box.

"Now we call the cops Carla." he said, grabbing her arm and pulling her into his room.

They both stood rooted to the spot when a ball of flame filled the evening sky in front of the hotel. He slammed the door to his room. "Stay here!" He told her as he cautiously cracked open the door again before stepping out. "It's where we parked."

"My jeep!" She rose from the chair.

"No. You stay right here. I'll go see what's up." He closed the door and ran down the hall. Not heeding Richard's order, Carla opened the door and ran to Teri and Matthew's room. She raised her hand to knock on Matthew's door when it flew open. "Teri!"

"What?"

Matthew raced past Carla. Carla's breath hitched. "No." When they reached the parking lot, the Jeep was engulfed in flames and Teri lay on the ground; her clothing and hair smoldering and Richard dragging her back away from the flames.

Matthew reached them first. Gently he scooped his wife into his arms and sat down in the grass away from the heat of the fire.

"Matt she's-."

"Don't say it."

In the distance the wail of a lone siren began then several more joined in. More emergency vehicles, fire trucks and police sirens chimed in until the night was saturated with tragedy.

◆ ◆ ◆

Matthew climbed into the front seat of the coroner's vehicle; his face pale, jaw firm, eyes blinking furiously to hold back the flood of tears Carla knew he wanted to spill. Matthew had a soft heart and had been an emotional sort of kid. She remembered when he accidently stepped on a lizard and cried because it lay in the dirt twitching.

The first time he found out he was going to become a father he would come over to Carla and voice his concerns. They had many talks during that time. Then when he found out they were going to have another child he seemed more at ease and the talks became less frequent. Those two girls were his world. He and Teri doted most of their time on them. Carla fought the large lump threatening to close her throat because Matthew would not have an easy time telling his daughters about their mother.

Carla and Richard stared after them and watched the ambulance race down the road. An hour later Matthew called her with the news the coroner said the explosion probably killed her immediately and judging the extent of the burns on Teri's body she probably would not have survived anyway. There would be an autopsy, but until the hurricane had passed over, her body would remain in the morgue. He didn't know how long he and his deceased wife would remain in Mexico, but he would stay until he could take her home for a proper burial.

He assured Carla he blamed no one. Teri had forgotten her make-up bag in the Jeep and since he had been the last one to drive it, still had the key. Carla promised to check back with him as soon as she could. But they now had a bigger problem. Now they were without a vehicle, but Carla knew someone who could get her one.

◆ ◆ ◆

An hour later, a couple of heavy muscled, rough looking men with tattoos pulled up in two vehicles leaving a sand-colored SUV at the opposite side of the hotel near the street now clogged with emergency vehicles and police. Neither man spoke when the driver walked up to Carla and handed her the key. He turned back toward the waiting vehicle and left her standing in front of her hotel room. She opened the driver's side and climbed in. She had to park further down from their rooms because of the crime scene and felt uneasy about leaving it unguarded.

"How did you do that?" Richard asked.

She grinned at him. "I made a phone call to a friend who said to call if I needed help." She swept an arm towards the vehicle. "Ta-da."

Richard shook his head and opened the door to the hallway of the hotel. "So, what's the plan then? The Constable said not to leave Cabo."

"I know, I heard him." Carla knocked on the door a second time before Doug opened it. He opened it wider and motioned for the pair to come into the room.

Doug fanned his hand in front of his nose "No offense, but, you two stink!

"Yeah, that happens when...."

The loud rapping on Doug's door caused them all to jump. Richard, being next to it checked the peep hole first. "It's the Constable." He opened the door and let the man inside the room.

"The box outside of your room was not an explosive, it was a tactic to get you distracted."

Richard nodded in agreement.

The Constable studied Carla. "I am curious, Senora Simpson, is someone after you? I mean, it's not every day a visitor to our beautiful country has their vehicle planted with a bomb. The proprietor is nervous about you staying here as well."

Carla turned to Richard then back to the Constable. "Perhaps it is a mistake, maybe whoever it was thought we were someone else."

The man nodded in agreement. "Yes, it could be, but is it coincidental you also have a decoy, a fake bomb as it were, in front of your room?"

"I think my ex-husband has been following me." Carla briefly explained the reason she thought would suit him.

"Well, just the same, you need to stay close. We have a touchy situation here and I don't want any of you leaving the area within the next day or so."

"What about the hurricane?"

The Constable thought about it for a few minutes. "I need to make some phone calls. I will speak to the motel owner and see if he will let you stay."

He walked to the door and Richard followed him out. A few minutes later, he came back into the room. "I thought you were going to tell him about Juan and the boys."

Carla looked at him for a moment. "I started to, but I felt like I shouldn't. Richard, what if he already knows? What if he's associated with Juan? I didn't lie."

"What's this about the ex? What's his name?"

"Hugh." She sighed. "I was going to tell you earlier, but...." she swept her arm toward the parking lot. "Anyway, Charli called me and said Hugh hasn't been seen in over a week. None of his friends have seen him either. She filed a missing person report. I think he could be the one doing all of the sabotage to the jeep, and getting Matt and Doug arrested."

"What?" Richard shot a look at Doug. "What happened?"

Carla gave him a short version of the incident in San Quentin and how she met Jorge. He gaped at her as she told him how she stood up to the hulking bulk of Mexican rage. "My God woman, he could have killed you!"

"Yes, he could have, but he didn't. He told me I had the biggest balls he'd ever seen, bigger than any of his boys."

Richard laughed, "I can't say he's too far off the mark." His face clouded over. "Still, you need to be careful with this man. My instincts say not to get in debt with this guy. One wrong move and he can make you and us disappear."

"I trust him, even if he is a gang leader." Carla shrugged her shoulders and stared at Richard. "I have to take a chance. I can't sit around waiting for paperwork and red tape before something is done. Who knows where they could be in a week, a month, a year?"

Richard sighed and glanced about the room. "You don't know if your new friends will really help. Do you?"

"He helped us out with a vehicle. So, he can't be all that bad. I have to trust them, Richard. They are the only leads. Jorge wants Juan and isn't going to stop looking for him! Rosa gave me names of relatives who may help us. She wants justice from him too."

Doug opened the door carrying more coffee. "Here, we are going to need these."

"How did you leave without us seeing you?" Carla took the top off the cup and blew into the dark brown liquid.

"I simply walked out the door. Nothing to it." He sat down in one of the room's chairs. "They've taken the Jeep and we have to give the Police another statement."

"But we did that already."

"Not with an American Ambassador Representative present. Technically, they can't do that."

"Why?"

Richard took a sip of his beverage and grimaced. "Needs sugar." He picked up a packet and tore off the top. "Carla, remember, we aren't in the United States. There's been a crime committed on Mexican soil and we're involved. Now is the time to tell the authorities, remember what you said? We are in this far too deep to not tell someone. I'm not too sure I won't get into trouble for letting you continue on as it is, even though it's not in my jurisdiction-"

"Or country." Doug interjected.

Richard glanced at him. "Or country, yes. Look," he sat down on the bed next to Carla. "We've gone as far as we can alone. We tell the American Consulate what happened; let them take care of this."

Carla knew he was right. But it didn't mean she would stop looking. She couldn't help waffling back and forth on what to do. She knew the odds; her chances weren't good. But, her heart told her to find the boys. If something were to happen at least someone besides Carla, Doug and Richard knew the story. Perhaps the authorities in both countries would intensify the search. Plus, depending on the aftermath of Hurricane Nadia all agencies would undoubtedly focus on rescue and recovery efforts.

An hour later, they sat in the American Ambassador's plush office while he read the statements and listened to Carla's story. And as she knew would happen, it was suggested they go home while they still could leave and let the officials take care of finding the boys. Carla learned Juan was being tracked, but it was unknown if the children were with him. Juan had not shown up in Cabo San Lucas.

"This man is dangerous and will stop at nothing to kill you." He stared at the trio.

"I've been trying to get her out of here for the past twenty-four hours, sir. She's very stubborn." Richard replied.

Unsmiling, the Ambassador stared at Carla. "That stubbornness will get you killed Mrs. Simpson. Go home."

The motel owner did not want them at his establishment. Carla understood his reasoning and paid for her room. They packed the new SUV with their belongings. Richard was quiet until they walked out from the motel to climb into the SUV. They headed north out of the city

"Are we headed to the airport?" Richard asked.

"No."

"Carla, you told that man, Mr.-"

"Ferguson? Yes, I did."

"Ah, but not on a plane, just leaving Cabo San Lucas."

"Correct."

CHAPTER TWENTY-FIVE

The three were silent as they drove to La Paz. Carla's thoughts were centered on the explosions at the hotel. Teri's death rattled her to the core. They had grown closer and Carla wanted to keep the bond together once they were back home. Although they choose to come with her, she felt an obligation to Matthew. She would have to be there for him if only in support. He was a resilient person and would eventually move on, but his tender heart would stay broken for a long time. Despite the arguments and fighting, Matthew and Teri did love each other. They stuck it through good and bad for twenty years. Carla had a lot of respect for his dedication to his wife. She didn't think many couples could have endured the hurdles they had encountered through their marriage.

She turned her thoughts to the grandchildren. How much higher would the stakes go for her? Could they find them before Hurricane Nadia hit La Paz? Should they just go? Let the authorities find her grandsons? I can't. Carla could not simply walk away. No was not an option for her, she had to find them. She had to keep the doubts at bay and trudge on, no more hum-hawing around.

She leaned her head back against the headrest. She closed her eyes for a short time letting the rhythm of the vehicle lull her to sleep. It was dreamless and short, but Carla felt better when she woke up. She glanced over at Richard.

He glanced over at her and grinned. "Glad to see you awake. Feel better?"

Carla smiled at him and nodded. "Yes. I'm not one to fall asleep in a moving vehicle."

"I'm sure you're exhausted. So, any sleep is better than none."

They drove in silence as they made their way up the highway. They decided to stop in El Pescaderos to fuel the vehicle and themselves. The humidity was higher due to the oncoming storm; Carla wiped trickles of sweat from her forehead and around her neck. Even though she spent many years of living in southern climates one thing she didn't miss was the humidity. She heard the waves crashing onto the beach and noted the low hanging clouds looming in the distance. The Sierra de la Laguna range rose to the east of them.

The wind was brisk; cooling the back of Carla's neck as she leaned against the SUV and lit a cigarette. It was hard to think straight; so many obstacles had blocked their way. Was she being selfish? She wondered. It wasn't her idea, but she had definitely taken ahold of the reigns and went with it. She took a drag from the cigarette and closed her eyes. She could feel the energy from the air swirling around her, ruffling her shirt, shuffling her hair about like a tossed salad.

There were few people in the streets. This close to the Pacific Ocean the townspeople knew that even if Nadia dropped to a tropical storm, it would still do major damage and many were taking no chances. They saw several business owners boarding up their stores while some bought supplies and piled them into vehicles full of family members moving out of the area until the hurricane passed.

"You okay?" Richard put his arms around her. Together they stood watching the wind blow across the desert landscape.

"I'm doing all right. Been a long day already."

"I can drive a bit longer; only been an hour since we left Cabo."

"I'm sure you're just as tired as I am." Carla dropped the cigarette to the ground and quickly smashed it with her foot so the wind didn't whisk it into the desert.

He gave her a quick hug and a peck on the cheek. "I'm fine."

Doug walked up to the SUV and handed them each a paper cup of coffee. "The hurricane slowed down a little from what the radio announcer just said. But bad news is that it's changed its course a little and will make landfall at Todos Santos. Not too far from here. That makes it closer to La Paz."

"Did you show anyone Scotty and Marcos' picture?" Hope against hope.

"No one in there saw them." Doug climbed in the back seat and closed the door.

◆ ◆ ◆

Just before Todos Santos they took the bypass to avoid the small town. Carla noticed there was a lot of traffic; most of it going to La Paz or other smaller towns along the route. She winced as a flash of lightning lit up the sky sending a deluge of rain onto the road. They slowed down so the windshield wipers could keep up with the torrent, many travelers pulled to the side of the highway which Carla was grateful. The rain might slow them down some but at least they wouldn't get caught in a traffic jam and be stuck for who knew how long.

Before too long, the traffic and rain thinned out and Richard made good time. They soon saw signs of town life, gas stations, hotels, and houses. Although there were places boarding up their businesses and homes people still went about their lives; a man swept the sidewalk in front of his small grocery store, two young girls were staring into a boutique window showcasing dresses, schoolchildren chased each other in a play area. The sun was shining, but dark clouds scuttled over the city. In the distance they could see shreds of clouds as rain fell on the hill tops.

They continued through the boroughs swallowed up by La Paz; Carla soaking up the scene, watching, wondering, hoping she may catch a glimpse of Scotty and Marcos. "It's a huge place!" She shook her head. "I didn't pay too much attention the first time through; all my thoughts were on Cabo San Lucas. I don't have any idea where to start looking for them now!"

"We just keep asking around, like we've been doing Carla." Doug reached over the seat and squeezed her shoulder. "Someone is bound to recognize them."

She patted his hand. "I know, it tries to overwhelm my emotions."

Richard slowed the vehicle to enter into the parking lot of a Pex Mex convenience store. "I need to stretch my legs, take a bathroom break."

"While we're here, might as well ask the clerk." Doug climbed out of the SUV and went inside. Moments later he came back out waving at Carla.

"The girl at the counter has seen Scotty and Marcos." He grabbed her by the arm and pulled her into the store. "She said both boys came in the store yesterday morning with her boss. He introduced them as his family from America."

Finally. Carla stood there unable to believe what she just heard with her own ears. They were here, in La Paz and somewhere nearby. She collected herself and walked up to the counter. "Excuse me."

The young woman smiled at her and nodded at Doug. "I know who you are."

"Can you help me find them? My grandsons?"

"All I know is what I told him." She pointed at Doug. "But, I overheard my boss, Mr. Pedraza, two days ago talking to his wife, Maria, about two young American children their nephew dropped off at his house." The clerk looked toward the back of the store. "They were in here yesterday with Mr. Pedraza, but not for long. I know it was them. They didn't act like local people. They kept staring around and pointing. They seemed to be having fun."

Carla felt some of the huge weight lift from her shoulders. They were in good health and seemingly happy. "Will Mr. Pedraza come in today? Is he here already?" Carla dared to ask. She felt like she was on very thin ice.

"He left about an hour ago, but will be back soon."

Carla thanked the girl and went back outside to where Richard and Doug were waiting by the SUV. "The man who owns this store has Scotty and Marcos and we are going to wait for him." She pulled out her phone. "I have to make a call."

A few minutes later Caral disconnected the phone call. "I called Rosa's uncle Ramon. Remember that woman who sang karaoke?" Carla asked Doug.

He nodded his head. "Yeah, beautiful woman; she sang good too."

Carla filled Richard in on how she met Rosa. "Anyway, I called him and yes, Juan's uncle does own this store. He said his niece had called him the day we left El Chale, and has been waiting for me to call him. He also knows Jorge and vouches for him too."

Richard lifted an eyebrow. "Let me guess, he's a relative?"

Carla ignored the remark, but gave him a smirk then turned away from him. "Uncle Ramon says I can trust Gorge as long as I don't rat him out to the police or screw him over. I assured him I had no intentions of doing anything of the sort." She turned back to Richard. "And no, they aren't related. Jorge's father and Ramon are old friends. He's known Jorge all of his life."

Richard took a drink of bottled water and looked at the sky. "How will we spot this guy Carla?"

She walked to the passenger side of the vehicle and pulled out her pack of cigarettes. "We don't, but my guess is he knows who we are. The clerk said he was talking to his wife on the phone about the children. She couldn't understand everything he said, but he seemed pre-occupied this morning when he came in and then left, told her he'd be back within the hour and that time is almost up."

Doug nodded toward a small gray pick-up pulling up in front of the store. When the man got out, he glanced their way and quickly went inside the store.

"I bet that's him." Doug said. "He seems worried."

They went back inside the store and the clerk nodded in the direction toward the back where a door was closed. "Mr. Pedraza is in there. Good luck reuniting with your grandchildren." She smiled at them and turned to wait on a customer.

Carla walked up to the door and knocked. The man she saw outside the store opened it up and smiled at her. "Si?"

She handed him the photo of the boys. "Where are they?"

The man handed back the picture. "Please." He whispered. "I will meet you outside." He nodded at her and closed the door.

"I guess we have no choice."

Back outside, Carla lit the cigarette she started to smoke earlier. A few tense and unsure moments later the man came out and stood near the wall. "I am taking a great risk being seen out here. Juan knows you are here. If he sees me talking to you it will be bad."

"I am sorry and I thank you for talking to me Mr. Pedraza." Carla held her breath for a second. "Is Scotty and Marcos all right?"

Staring at Carla he flashed a quick grin. "Oh Si. They are fine. Maria, my wife, takes good care of them. They like her and they like me too."

She couldn't take it anymore. "Please, can I see them?" He started to shake his head no. "Senor, they are my life. I have come a long way to find them. I promise I will not cause you any trouble."

"It is a great risk Senora."

"Is Juan close?" Carla was trying to form a plan.

"I don't know. He was supposed to come get the boys tonight but I told him that they should stay with my wife and I until the hurricane passes, we have a strong home. It is not far from here."

"I have money, I will pay you." Carla knew she sounded desperate, that's because she was.

"Oh no, Senora, I cannot take your money. Juan, he is evil, a bad man and so are the people he is associated with. They will not think twice about killing anyone who interferes. That includes family. My brother, Juan's father, didn't want to even associate with him. Juan didn't come to either one of their funerals."

Carla was not going to walk away, there had to be some way she could talk the older man into letting her see Scotty and Marcos. "Sir, I will make sure you or your wife are not harmed. We can come later tonight."

"But the hurricane, it is very close."

"I know, and that's why there is not much time. Please Senor, we will not make problems for your family. We can take you to a safe place if you want. I have to get my grandchildren and take them home. There isn't much time, please if you love your children and grandchildren, would you not do the same for them?"

"Senora-" The man looked from Carla to Richard and Doug standing next to the SUV.

Carla got as close as she could without stepping on the man's feet. She wanted him to see her plight; the desperation; see the pain in her eyes. "There are people looking for him, he will be locked up and you can breathe easier. If you let me get my grandchildren, I will make sure you have safe haven. I know someone who will take care of you until Juan and his people are gone." She tried not to let tears fill her eyes, but they did anyway. "I have so much pain and sorrow, my daughter is gone because of Juan. He took my grandchildren without consent; kidnapping is what it is called. You and your wife could be seen as an accessory to the crime. I don't want to see that happen to you."

The man looked away from Carla and sighed. "All right, I will help you, but we have to be careful." He took out a small memo pad and pen from inside his jacket pocket. He scratched out an address. "Here, meet me here at this place at five o'clock. I will take you to them. I will have to talk to Maria so she knows what is going on and can have everything ready."

Carla started to put the paper in the pocket of her jeans.

"Wait. Give me your phone number. If I don't think it is safe, I will text you."

"Do I have a choice?"

"If you want to see them, then no." He turned and walked back inside the store.

Richard stood by the SUV watching the older man walk into the store. "It's only one o'clock, we could go get something to eat and relax, get some rest. It sounds like we're going to need it."

"We could just go over to the Bahia Dorada, right across the street." Carla said.

Richard laughed. "You want to keep an eye on him. I bet you'd be a great detective."

Carla climbed in the car and smirked. "Nope, that's all you." She slammed the door and buckled up. "I do want to keep an eye on him. Hopefully we can get one of the rooms facing the street."

"You mean all of us in one room?" Doug asked.

"Sure, why not? That way someone can watch while the others sleep, we won't be here long as it is and no sense spending money for each one of us to have a room for a few hours."

No one argued. They drove to the hotel and managed to get a room with double beds. They were told however, that there could be a mandatory evacuation from the hotel should the storm create a hazardous situation. The desk clerk told them Nadia was less than two-hundred miles from the coast and would cross the Sierra de la Laguna range then continue to La Paz. It was good news for them, it meant the hurricane would slow down some as it crossed over the mountain range and hopefully weaken before it hit them. For Carla, she hoped it bought them time to rescue Scotty and Marcos.

They opened the door to the room; it was small, but suited their needs. Doug announced he was taking a shower and left Richard and Carla looking out the window. "You don't trust him?" Richard asked.

"Not sure what to make of him. He seems genuine and scared."

"I can't blame him." He turned Carla around so she faced him. "How are we going to find these people safe haven? What did you mean by that anyway?"

"Jorge will get them to safety. He won't hurt them."

"Carla, this is serious stuff going on here. We aren't a rescue team like S.W.A.T. You promised that man he would be safe, where are we going to put them? I know you trust this Jorge and I admit, he's been more than gracious, but don't you think you might be pushing the envelope?"

"If I step out of bounds, Jorge will let me know it. He will help them."

Richard sighed. "All right, I'm just along for the ride, but Carla, if Juan gets wind of what you are doing, we all die. I mean, he probably already knows we are here. You may have put that man and your grandsons in jeopardy."

"Richard, if I don't do this now....." She went to one of the beds and flopped down. "I don't think I could live with myself, not after coming this far, and getting this close."

He turned away from the window and sat down on the edge of the bed. "Sit up."

She did as he asked and he massaged her shoulders. "We'll get through this. Okay? No matter what, we will do all we can to get the boys. But you have to put yourself in that man's position. He's probably known Juan all his life, he knows Juan is a fugitive, but he's also family. It's a situation I would not want to be in. Just give him a chance, if he doesn't come back, we go to the police and tell them where Scotty and Marcos are at, at least tell them about the uncle."

She let her chin drop to her chest letting Richard's hands knead her shoulders and back. "Thank you." That was all she remembered before sleep took over.

CHAPTER TWENTY-SIX

Hurricane Nadia churned up the coast of the Baja Peninsula; winds gusted to 110 miles an hour whipping the ocean water into foaming frothy waves that washed ashore. The tide was high sending deadly surges of water, seaweed and marine life miles past the tiny villages nestled on the coastline. At times, the wind howled like some horror filled monster, growling, churning, eating up the miles; eating up farmland and houses alike.

Carla woke to the sound of rain battering against the windows of their motel room. Both Doug and Richard were nowhere in the room. She glanced at the clock sitting on the tiny table situated between the two beds. It was almost four-thirty; close to the time they were to meet Juan's uncle. She prayed he wouldn't back out; she had promised safety to the old man and his wife. That made her realize she needed to talk to Jorge. She located his number in her phone and waited for Jorge to answer. When he answered Caral updated him on the recent events plus another favor.

"Chica, you ask for a lot, you know?" Jorge told her when she explained to him about the elderly couple caring for Scotty and Marcos.

"I know and I am truly grateful. I'm just wanting my grandsons, and see Juan fall hard." She hesitated to let her statement sink in. "You want him too."

Jorge laughed into the phone. "You are a hard-ass lady. I could use someone like you in my organization."

She didn't know what to say. "I think I'd be too much of a pain in the ass for you Jorge. But I am forever in your debt. I won't forget."

After she hung up, Carla went into the bathroom to freshen up. She felt grimy and really wanted a long, hot shower but that would have to wait. After washing her face and fixing her hair, she looked outside and saw the rain was falling nearly sideways. It was raining so hard she barely made out the Pex Mex neon sign in the window across the street. Carla wondered how close the hurricane had come since they arrived in La Paz. She heard the door click and turned around. Richard and Doug came in with sandwiches and drinks setting the items on a small dresser. "Where did you get this stuff?" She asked as she tore open one of the brown waxed paper wrapped sandwiches and bit into it.

"There's a little kiosk in the lobby." Doug replied as he sat down next to Carla. "It's the only place nearby that was open." He bit down on the sandwich and nodded. "Not bad." He turned on the bed and faced his sister. "The rain is pounding the daylights out of the street and that wind....whew! I don't want to try walking in it."

"I saw it from the window." She nodded her head toward the large bay window and the rainy scene. "I also don't want to be in here when that breaks from flying debris."

"We also heard Hurricane Nadia made landfall about fifteen minutes ago." Richard opened his sandwich added a packet of mayonnaise to the contents and took a bite. "You're right Doug, it's not that bad."

They sat in silence eating. When they were done, they packed their belongings and checked out of the motel. The rain band that assaulted the area was gone and thankfully the wind let up. Yet, there were occasional gusts which threatened to topple Carla to the ground. They sat in the SUV waiting for Mr. Pedraza to show up. Carla tried not to get impatient, tried not to get anxious, tried not to get her hopes up. She couldn't sit in the vehicle any longer and grabbed a cigarette then stepped out to smoke.

Richard rolled down his window and smiled at her. "You okay?"

"Can't wait in the car." She looked up at the sky and watched the clouds swirling above her. How much longer? She thought. Soon the rain started again and she had no choice but to get back inside the SUV. The three of them sat in silence. Waiting. The clock on the dashboard read ten minutes after five. Carla could feel her heart beating in her chest much too fast, a hot, hard lump threatened to fill her throat making her swallow hard. She wiped away the tears that filled her eyes. The uncle was not going to show up after all. But just as she made that assumption, the little grey pickup truck pulled into the parking lot, but did not slow down as it passed them. Carla didn't realize she was holding her breath until she went to take a deep sigh of relief.

Richard put the vehicle into drive and followed the pickup down to a

174

seedy looking area containing warehouses. The truck pulled into a warehouse parking lot and waited for them to pull up next to him. He rolled his window down and motioned them to follow him. They traveled several blocks, finally coming to a neighborhood with narrow streets and yards littered with car parts and kid's toys. Finally, they pulled up to a nice little bungalow with beautiful roses lining the porch and lights blazing through the windows.

By now, the rain was falling in great torrents and the wind was screaming into the early evening. Carla tried not to think of it as an ominous warning they may not be alive for long. They pulled in to the carport next to Pedraza's vehicle then waited.

When Mr. Pedraza stepped out of his truck, his wife came to the door and stared at the SUV. She twisted her apron with her hands, and kept glancing over at the vehicle. Richard turned to Carla. "They seem nervous, jittery. I hope he hasn't set us up."

"Well, I would feel much better if I had Gina with me." Doug said as he climbed out of the SUV. "I have a weird feeling about this whole situation myself."

"Keep your eyes open and watch him." Richard told him as they made their way up to the door.

The woman kept wringing her hands, but smiled at the trio as they came into the living room. Carla thought it was a nice, cozy little home making her anxious to see her grandchildren.

"I thank you both for helping me, I mean us. I told your husband I will make sure you have safe haven and have made arrangements. All I have to do is call my friend."

The woman looked to her husband who translated Carla's comments. Carla noticed for the first time how small she was compared to her husband. Her gray hair was wrapped up onto her head in a tight bun, but her dark brown eyes sparkled. She thought the small, older woman was beautiful and wondered how many young men waited to court her when she was younger. Now that Carla was able to see Mr. Pedraza in better lighting, she could see the family resemblance and that was enough to give her the push to ask about the boys.

The man and woman looked at each other, then she quietly turned away from him and motioned to Carla and the others to follow her. This was it. Carla kept swallowing back the tears as they made their way down the hall. The woman came to a door and opened it letting Carla step through first.

There were her grandsons sitting on a bed playing a game. When they saw her, both boys screamed "Amma!" Their game forgotten they bowled over Carla. All she lost, all she had struggled for; all the setbacks, and tragedy fell away. She kissed their smiling faces over and over, whispering each of their names. She had her grandbabies! She held both boys tight, they would never get away from her sight again.

◆ ◆ ◆

She felt Richard touch her shoulder; bringing her back to the urgent issue they now faced. They had to leave. Carla nodded at him. She managed to calm down the children. "I have something to tell you. You must listen to me very carefully. It's important to understand what I am going to say." She starred into each one's searching eyes. They wanted to know. Scotty and Marcos nodded their heads in unison.

"Yes Amma."

"We have to leave here right now. The things we can take are already packed. I'm sorry boys but we don't have much room. Maybe later I can see if these kind people will send them to you."

Maria stood in the doorway. Her hands fumbling with the hem of her apron. "I like these boys. They are polite. They help me and my husband with things around here." She looked at the children. "They have been raised well and are loved. They asked about you and when they were going home." Maria smiled once more at them and left the room.

Carla faced the boys toward her. "We are going to be in the rain and thunder. We will have to find another place to hide so your father can't find you."

"Why Amma we have to hide from Poppy? Is he mad at you?" Scotty asked.

She tried not to laugh too loud, *oh from the mouth of babes.* "Yes, I'm sure he is. But I am not very happy he took you two from me."

Marcos said. "He told us we were going on a vacation. I was surprised to see you Amma!"

"We got new clothes too Amma!" Scotty piped up.

"That's great Scotty! But listen boys. You might see some scary things, but you have to be brave for your mom. Your Poppy is not a nice man. He has hurt many people. I came here to bring you both home. So, you know there is bad weather outside, right?"

They nodded their heads. Scotty got up from the bed and went to the tiny closet in the room. He pulled out a pair of rubber boots and a yellow rain coat. They were in rough shape but fit him.

Carla went to the closet and found another coat but no boots. It would have to do. "Okay Marcos, put this on."

Richard came to the doorway. "Are you ready?"

"Yes, Doug can grab that suitcase-"

Two rounds of bullets broke the lull.

"What's going on back here esse? I don't think I know you."

Carla gasped and grabbed the boys. Her eyes widened when Richard came into the room with Juan holding a pistol to his head.

"Now these two. I know." Juan grinned at Carla. "What up C Madre'?"

Scotty and Marcos began to whimper. She held the boys tighter and whispered to them. "Don't cry. Be brave for your momma."

Carla stood up and faced Juan. "You took them without consent Juan."

Juan grinned at her and motioned for the children to come to him. They were hesitant. "Now!" He shouted making everyone in the little room jump. He motioned for Richard to kneel down. "Now you Doug." Juan leaned into the hallway. In Spanish he shouted to a man a few feet from him. "Hey, Jaco, get in here and tie them up. Blindfolds too." He kept the handgun at the back of Richard's head. Come on Scotty, Marcos."

"Where's Aunt Maria?" Marcos asked.

"She had to go to the store. Come on. We have to go. Hurry!" They stood their ground near Carla. He shouted at the boys. "I SAID NOW!"

Carla nodded to them. "Go. He won't hurt you." She scowled at Juan.

Juan moved next to Doug to let his partner blindfold and tie up Richard. After doing the same thing to Doug, Juan moved closer to Carla waving the pistol in her direction. "Let's go. Kneel down."

Doing what he said, Carla knelt down on the floor; facing the wall like Richard and Doug. She could hear her grandchildren protesting, crying; begging their father to not kill Carla. Tears raced down her cheeks. This was it. Today, they would die.

They faced the wall. Carla could feel her nose touching it. "I love you, Doug. I'm sorry I got you in this."

"Sshh."

"I love you too Richard."

"That's good to know, but please be quiet."

They stopped talking. Carla waited for the click of the pistol which would put bullets in each of their heads. She prayed to be first so she wouldn't have to hear the other two gunshots. As the seconds ticked by, she wondered what was happening. "I don't hear anything."

"I think I hear a car. Everybody quiet." Richard hissed.

Carla strained to hear it as well but all she heard was the wind rattling the window pane. Then a piece of sheet metal siding was torn from the house; it screeched as the twisting metal broke free and caught ahold of a lounge chair slamming it into the window.

She ducked as the glass shattered from the impact of the chair against the window. She felt hands grasp her arms and haul her up from the floor. She had been unaware of anyone coming into the room. She winced, waiting for the bullet.

When the blindfold was pulled from her eyes, she saw Richard leaning over her. "Hi." He quickly removed the flimsy thin rope from her wrists. Moving over to where Doug knelt, he cut the ropes from his wrists.

"How'd you do that?" Carla asked as they gathered themselves and started to move down the hallway.

"No time to explain. This house is getting torn apart." No sooner had Richard spoke then another loud clunk hit the roof. "They killed Mr. Pedraza." Richard pointed to the pair of shoe clad feet sticking out from behind the living room couch. "I don't know where his wife is, but I covered his face and put a note inside his coat pocket who killed him."

They quickly made their way to the front room and onto the porch. The wind blew against the house, bending the rose bushes into each other ripping off the beautiful blooms the Pedraza's worked so hard to nurture. They climbed into the SUV and Richard started it. When he switched on the headlights, they saw Maria's body near the little gray pickup truck. Without thinking, Carla got out of the SUV and ran to the older woman whose life spilled out onto the floor of the carport and pulled her windbreaker off covering the woman as best as she could. She took another look back before running to the vehicle, hoping the covering would stay put.

CHAPTER TWENTY-SEVEN

The wind buffeted against the vehicle making it rock back and forth as Richard navigated through the down pour. The windshield wipers worked furiously to keep up, but it did little to clear Richard's vision.

"I see taillights!" Carla shouted above the din of the storm.

"Yeah! I see them!" Richard punched the gas and raced down the street narrowly missing a tree as it crashed to the ground knocking out a power line. Electric arcs raced down the wire, igniting a small bush in its path before fizzing out.

Just as fast as the rain fell, it quit. The wind died down and blue sky peeked from scuttling clouds. "That was weird." Doug said.

Eyes darting back and forth Richard watched for downed live wires.

"How did we not die? Blindfolded, handcuffed, and facing the wall?" Carla mused.

"I guess he thought the hurricane could do it for him. Clean hands." Doug offered.

"Clean hands in Juan's case is a moot point." Carla scoffed.

"I don't know, but I'm not sorry." Richard spoke as he navigated the narrow streets, keeping a close tail on Juan's vehicle.

"Maybe he wants us to follow him." Carla said.

"He's still counting on the hurricane to get us." Doug said as Richard turned a sharp left when a huge tree slammed to the ground, barely missing the SUV. All three let out a sigh of relief.

"Look down that way, is that them?" Doug pointed through the windshield where two men were pulling on a small tree from the road.

"It looks like it. Kinda hard to tell with that tree in front of it." Without another word, he threw the SUV into drive and sped down the road. "Shit!" He ducked down as a bullet pinged off the hood of the vehicle. He took his foot from the gas and braked hard. "I guess that question is answered."

He put the vehicle into reverse and backed up. They watched the men as they drug the tree off the road and into the ditch. The men glanced up the street then one climbed into the back seat and the other stayed behind as the car took off. He stood in the middle of the street with his firearm aimed at them.

"That's not good." Doug said as they stared down the street.

Once again, another band of rain and wind pummeled the man as the standoff continued. He stood in the down pour a few seconds later before running into a house. "He was to keep us from catching up to them." Richard surmised as he sped past the run-down shack.

"I saw them go down this street." Carla said pointing to the left.

In the distance, they could see the tail lights once more then suddenly brighten as it came to a stop as another tree fell onto the road. It was small enough to drive over, but it slowed the car's progress down considerably and soon Richard had caught up to them again. However, he kept his distance. "Just in case they feel the need to shoot at us again." He told them while focusing on Juan's vehicle.

Carla and Doug both agreed. She saw bright lights glaring into the night not far from where they were watching the car in front of them. "What's that on the right?"

It was hard to see through the new band of heavy rain, but the area was lit up. The rest of the area did not have power so the lights blared against the rain burdened sky made a bizarre setting. Carla thought maybe they were solar powered. In the distance, Carla noticed flags moving up and down. The closer they got she understood what she was seeing; mast from boats still in their slips. "It looks like we're getting close to a marina!"

"They're turning that way too." Richard sped up a little more.

They followed the car as it twisted and turned through the narrow streets, finally they came to the parking lot of the marina. Juan, the boys and the man who was shooting at them ran toward the docks. Carla held her breath as she watched the boys running on the wet wooden surface. The rough surf caused the docks to buckle and warp. The curtain of rain turned Juan and the others into vague shapes the farther away they went down the dock's walkway.

Tearing her away from the image, Richard slammed the SUV into park and opened the door and ran after Juan. Carla and Doug quickly followed. She couldn't see well as they ran down the docks; and in the pouring rain, she was soaked in a matter of minutes.

Without hesitation Richard ran onto the bobbing walkway but Carla froze. The waves sloshed up on the wooden surface; they flipped and flopped threatening to tear apart at any minute. Doug didn't give her much more time because he pushed her on. "Go on! Just don't stop and don't think about what's happening!"

They ran toward the boat, but as they got closer Carla could see it wasn't just a small boat. It was a yacht; a big one. She could also see the running lights were on and pulling away from its slip. As big as the yacht was, it still pitched and rolled in the large swells. Then Carla slipped and fell into the water.

"Carla!" Doug shouted above the wind and knelt down to pull her up. Fortunately, she managed to pull herself up on the dock before completely submersing into the water. Just as Doug helped her to her feet, the wind ceased, but rain continued to pour from the dark sky. "Go!" Doug grabbed her arm and they caught up with Richard as he stood where the yacht was recently moored and watched it pull away from the marina. He turned to Carla and Doug.

"What happened?" He held her, checking for cuts and abrasions.

"I lost my footing. I'm okay. Just a little shaken." She watched the yacht pull out further into the sea. "Now what are we going to do?! We don't have any way to follow them!" There was no way for her to know where Juan would go, there were many small islands and she was definitely in unfamiliar territory.

"Hey, your phone's ringing Carla." Doug said

Astonished, surprised she answered it. She couldn't remember even grabbing it when they left the SUV. "Hello?"

"Chica! You see the flashing light?"

She looked around and further down the marina there was someone flashing a light in their direction. She pointed at it so Richard and Doug saw it to. "Yes, we do."

"Follow it and hurry up. We don't have much time!"

She took off with Richard and Doug following her. Soon they came to the boat, it too was a huge yacht, she wasn't sure if it was bigger than the one Juan had, but it didn't matter. They climbed aboard the boat and was led to the bridge where Jorge LaNaya and the captain of the yacht stood looking out the huge window.

"How did you know Juan would come here?" Carla asked, suddenly chilled to the bone from her wet clothes. She tried not to let her teeth chatter. She was grateful when someone put a blanket over her shoulders.

"When we were younger, Juan and I used to go to El Mogote. It's a sand barrier but on it is Paraiso del Mar, a golf resort. We both worked there, that was our cover for smuggling drugs. Anyway, there are many places on that island but I think I know which place he will go and hide out until the storm has passed." Jorge stared at Richard and Doug. "So, you are the brothers who were in jail in San Quentin?"

"I am." Doug spoke up. "And I thank you for helping me." He stepped over to shake Jorge's hand.

Jorge shook hands with Doug then stared at Richard. "And you Esse? You the other brother?"

For a second, Carla held her breath, she hadn't thought of this scenario. She glanced at the man who dropped everything in his life to help her. Would he know Richard was a cop?

"No, I'm a family friend. I came to help Carla."

Jorge stared at Richard a moment longer then reached out his hand toward him. "Ah. I'm sure she is grateful." He smiled at Richard. "Well then, we need to go." Jorge turned back to the captain as the boat backed out of its slip and headed out to sea. "The sea will be rough; I suggest you find something to hang onto. And if you get sick, go outside and try not to fall overboard."

CHAPTER TWENTY-EIGHT

Hurricane Nadia continued to churn onto the peninsula, leaving the town of Todos Santos in shambles as it slammed into the Sierra de la Lunga Mountain range. There were news crews in the area showing clips of the storm chewing up buildings, cars and anything that was unfortunate enough to be caught in Nadia's path. One on site Meteorologist faced the camera as he stood in knee high water. The wind buffeted against him while he told those who watched him Nadia was one of the worst storms to hit the Baja Sur Peninsula in many years. "Fortunately, the storm is down to a category one hurricane, but no one's out of the woods yet! We've been told there are reports of mud slides and some of the smaller towns are blocked off."

The camera operator panned the view from the ocean where thick purple-black, bruised clouds hung over the water in the distance. Then he aimed the camera at the sky above them where blue skies prevailed for the moment.

"Right now, we are in the eye of the hurricane and from the look of the clouds rolling in now, my crew and I better get back to our shelter."

Jorge stood at the helm next to the captain as he steered the yacht into the deeper waters of the sea. The boat as large as it was had its share of difficulty navigating through the choppy water and riding waves as they drove on. Jorge turned to Carla.

"That's El Mogote!" He pointed at the large land mass on the opposite shore from La Paz. It was raining harder than it been at any point of the storm. Carla knew it didn't take a genius to see they may have a rough time getting to the shore if they didn't go faster. The waves hitting the yacht flopped Carla around on the bench she and the others sat hanging on as tight as they could. She nodded at Jorge.

"That's where Juan is going!" He shouted over the roar of thunder. "We'll be there in about five minutes. I can see where he landed!"

Carla stood up; her legs unsteady as she crossed the floor of the bridge to stand next to Jorge. She clung onto one of the supports and peered out the window into the night. She couldn't see the water except when lightning arced across the sky. Then when the boat crested a wave, she barley caught tail and headlights before the boat dipped back down into another wave. She was grateful so far no one was sick. She didn't know if she would be able to keep her stomach calm if she were to witness that. Instead, she focused on the nearing shore. For each wave that brought them out of the water she had a clear shot of the vehicle which was still sitting on the road.

Carla was instructed to sit down because they were nearing the shore and it would be rough getting the yacht to dock. She sat down next to Richard and let him wrap his arms around her. It felt good to have him holding her close. For a few brief moments she was safe, she wasn't in the middle of a hellish storm; she hadn't teamed up with a gang leader and wasn't hunting down a killer. Then reality came back in as they slammed into the dock sending Carla, Richard and Doug to the floor.

Jorge motioned them to follow him as he ran to the lower deck of the boat. He jumped onto the dock shouting at them to hurry. Carla tried not to think of missing a step as she jumped down and followed the men as they ran to the club house of the resort. Concerned for the captain of the yacht she turned to see the boat lift from the water and wedge itself onto the shore from the ten-foot waves crashing against the land. She hoped he was unhurt.

They stood under the large overhang that sheltered them from the blinding rain. "Stay here, I need to get a car." Jorge told them as he opened a side door into the resort. Quickly, Jorge and one of the men from the ship which Carla recognized as one of the men from the bar the night her brothers were put in jail in San Quentin slipped inside. They stood there as the storm lashed and clawed the area. Where on this place would there be a safe spot for the boys? From what she could see, there wasn't much vegetation on the island; there were a few trees, but she couldn't see anything past the huge elaborate club house and the small hill it sat on. Had they not been in the middle of a hurricane and risking their lives, it could have been a beautiful place.

Within a few minutes, Carla saw a black Hummer pull up. The passenger side window rolled down and a brown, tattooed arm waving for them to come. Once more she took a deep breath and ran behind Richard with Doug behind her, each one quickly jumping into the vehicle. Before Doug could get the door fully closed, the Hummer pulled away from the resort and sped down a narrow strip of road. Doug swore under his breath as he slammed the door shut.

Out in the open the wind pounded against the multi-ton vehicle; rocking it back and forth with each gust. A bolt of lightning slammed the ground off to the right of them sending a shower of tree bark and branches flying through the air, some of the debris hit the Hummer as it shot past the tree now in flames. Carla was impressed at Jorge's driving as he dodged a large branch that snapped off one of the trees lining the road. Moments later they came to another building which Jorge told them was a maintenance shed. It was bigger than she thought initially and seemed a little fancy for a shed. When they pulled up to the front of the building, Doug started to open the door when the man in the passenger side held up his hand. "Wait."

Jorge and his man ran to the overhang scanning the entrance, Carla noticed they had rifles, she didn't know what kind or where they got them. The trio watched as Jorge and his man swept the area checking the small nooks and darkened areas of the building. Jorge waved for them to get out of the vehicle.

"Okay, this is what we do. You stay with me." He nodded to his man who ran back to the vehicle and returned with two AK47 rifles. He handed those to Richard and Doug. "You know how to use these? They are powerful and will knock you on your ass if you're not careful."

"I'm familiar with them." Richard whispered as he inspected the firearm.

"Me too; have one of these at home. I shoot rabbits and squirrels with it." Doug said as he inspected his rifle.

Jorge stared at Doug for a few seconds and watched the two men familiarize themselves with the guns. "I guess I don't have to worry about you getting shot then." He started toward a small side door and slid inside where his partner waited. The noise of the hurricane was not cushioned by the interior of the building as they walked along the far wall. With no light inside, it was difficult to make out anything but large lumps of covered golf carts. Thankful

186

for the lightning it allowed little more detail of the interior with each flash. They continued against the wall all eyes peering into the darkness. If they had been able to hear the gunfire, they would have seen one of Juan's men hiding between a row of golf carts when he stood up. Instead, they watched Jorge's man fall to the ground holding his leg.

"Son of a bitch! Owww!" He rolled over onto his back cussing in rapid fire Spanish. Jorge, Richard, Doug and Carla knelt next to the man. "Be quite!" Jorge hissed at him. Richard found some discarded rags and with Carla's help they managed to wrap the leg and get him propped up under one of the tarps covering a large tool box.

Richard ran to one of the covered golf carts and peeked over the top aimed his rifle and fired off several rounds. They watched one of Juan's men fall to the ground as he knocked over a pile of paint cans which sent them scattering across the floor. He ran back to the group as they ducked in the corner.

"You know how to handle an AK47 esse?" He nodded at Richard.

"Learned how at the Academy."

"I had the feeling you were a cop. You carry yourself like one."

Richard grinned at Jorge, "And you are the leader of a gang, but I'm not here to call you out. Not my jurisdiction."

They ducked as a volley of bullets came from a far corner of the building. "Yes, we are Vatos right now." He stood up and sent a spray of bullets into the corner where the gun fire came from. They listened for movement from the dark corner but nothing moved. Another bolt of lightning crashed to the ground just outside the building where moments ago someone was shooting at them. The two large paned windows shattered as a large tree smashed through the roof and onto the floor. Glass, metal framework and tree limbs littered the floor as water pummeled down onto rakes, shovels and other lawn tools thrown about the area. They watched for signs of anyone trying to break free from the damage but, did not see movement or hear anyone cry out.

At the further most point in the building was an enclosed space which ran the back length of the entire wall. Jorge nodded in that direction. "That would be the most likely place to go. Part of it is the office for the Foreman, but there is an underground garage for working on lawn mowers and golf carts. There is another way to get in too, but it is down below. We would have to go outside to get in that way."

Richard peered into the darkened room and saw the outline of the enclosed area. "Let's get back to Carla and Doug." They duck walked back to the corner where Jorge's man lay stretched out.

"He fainted and fell out from under the tarp. I've got his leg elevated and wrapped more rags around the wound. Carla found some water and gave him some to drink. It's about all that can be done for now." Doug whipped his head around to the far end of the building. From where they were situated, Doug had a good visual on the office area and told everyone to hold still. He wedged in between fifty-gallon barrels of oil and discarded refuse.

Carla was the closest to him. She leaned in close to enough to whisper. "What's going on Doug?"

He turned back to her, "I saw movement in the window, in the corner."

They heard scuffling as if someone were running. Doug rose up and fired a shot hitting Juan's other man.

They ducked back behind the rows of barrels and waited for a response but none followed. Doug whispered to Richard and Jorge. "I'll go make sure he's dead." He crept back between the barrels and made it to where the man lay sprawled on the floor. Doug scanned the area to make sure no one else was in hiding then hunched over the fallen man and put two fingers on his neck. He tried to pull his arm back when the man grabbed it and pulled him to the ground.

Carla and the others heard shouts of surprise then grunts of pain as the two men wrestled each other in the dirt and grease knocking over more discarded cans and trash piled against the wall of the office area. Doug waved to them; motioning to move on.

"We have to go Carla; he's got that man distracted!" Jorge shouted as he ran past her and headed for the door of the enclosed space. Richard and Carla followed him inside the room. It was dark, she couldn't see her hand in front of her face, but could hear fighting on the other side of the thin wall. A shot rang out above the din of the storm, Carla prayed her brother was okay.

"Lucky for you I know this place." Jorge remarked as they stood in the room. He took out a pocket flashlight but pointed it downward to keep the room from lighting up. It was just enough light to make out a row of lockers and more lawn equipment lined up against the wall. They were next to the outside of the office area and had to navigate through the room to get to the farthest point where a solid steel door lead to the underground garage. The three crept toward the door and reached it in a matter of minutes.

It opened with a slight suction of air. The only thing visible was the top three stairs. No light came from below.

"Well, this is new. Good. We don't have to go outside. You two stay here." Jorge started to turn and Richard caught his arm.

"I'll go with you. Carla, stay here. Don't move."

She started to protest but Richard put his index finger to her lips. "This is too dangerous. I don't know what's down here, but you stay right here. I will be back." He felt a nudge at his elbow.

"Give her this. It's loaded all she has to do is point and shoot." Jorge told Richard and handed him a .38 pistol and a tiny pocket-sized flashlight.

"You ever fired a gun?" Richard whispered as he handed her the gun.

She nodded yes and stuffed the light in the front pocket of her jeans. "It's been a while. When I was younger, my grandfather would take us to the firing range. He taught us kids how to shoot."

"Good. You know where the safety is on here?"

Carla nodded her head yes. She felt for the tiny button. "Is it on safety Jorge?"

"Yes."

"Good." Richard stepped through the threshold. "Now, don't shoot it unless you have to. If something happens up here and you need help, shoot it. I'll be back here before you can say Huckleberry Hound."

Had it been any other situation besides trying not to get killed, Carla would have laughed at the statement. Instead, she only nodded and took the pistol. Richard kissed her then turned and followed Jorge into the dark.

Carla sat on the floor and focused on massive storm outside mauling the resort island; uprooting trees, picking up small boulders and slamming them into buildings and vehicles. The wind was at banshee force; it screamed and wailed against the Maintenance building. She could hear pieces of metal screeching as it tore away from the damaged end left open to the elements.

The rain hit the metal roofing like someone poured buckets of nails down on top of it. She had never heard a sound like it in her whole life. It was LOUD. She wouldn't know if there was someone coming up on her because she couldn't hear, but she could see the area from the faint light coming through the small window since the storm opened up one end of the building.

As her eyes adjusted to the darkness, she took note of her surroundings as best as she could. She tried to remember what she saw in Jorge's subdued lighting and peered into the dark where the Foreman's office was located. Dark shadows lay thick in the corners. She could make out the door they came through. Carla turned her focus on it. She hoped Doug would have joined them by now. She tried not to think about why he hadn't. Other than the lockers and equipment there seemed to be nothing else.

A few moments later Carla saw a tinge of light coming from the stairway of the underground area. Richard and Jorge came up.

"He's not down there."

CHAPTER TWENTY-NINE

"Where could they have gone?" Carla asked.

"I don't know Chica, he's a fool if he left here. There are no other places nearby."

"What about the office?" Richard asked.

"That's just as stupid as going outside, but we did not check it." Jorge whispered. "There are a lot of windows on the other side of the office. Chances are they will see damage." He doused the flashlight leaving the room in near darkness. Hurricane Nadia continued unleashing her fury on the island, threatening to pull the building apart and tossing the remnants into the sea.

They gingerly crossed the room until they came to the office door. It was locked. There were two windows situated on either side of the door. Carla noticed the windows from the other side silhouetted in the dark when a series of lightning bolts flashed across the night sky. When that happened, Carla thought she saw someone in the office. She ducked down below the window.

"Richard!" She whispered waving him closer to her. "I think I saw someone in there."

"Stay down." He told her and waved Jorge closer.

As he relayed the information, the rain and wind eased up some, making him think he was speaking too loudly. They crouched by the door.

"Hey, did you hear that?" Jorge whispered to Carla and Richard.

"No."

"Listen."

Carla put her ear to the door. Nothing. "I-" Then she heard it. A child's voice. Then a chair scraped against the floor and a man's voice seeming to scold someone.

"It's them!" She clutched Richard's sleeve. "I know that voice."

Jorge pulled Richard away from the door and instructed Carla to get as far as she could from it. She couldn't see them very well, but it didn't take a scholar to realize they were trying to break the door down. The second attempt was successful but then she heard a scream. Marcos!

When the door caved in, Jorge quickly shone the light in where it fell upon Juan holding Marcos in a chokehold with his pistol pointing at his youngest son's head.

"Poppy! Please let me go!" The boy screamed, pleading with his father. "Please don't kill me!"

Carla felt her stomach roll over and her head started swimming. "Juan! Let them go now!"

She could hear both boys crying; begging their father to release them.

"Yeah, C-madre, that's what you want. I just let them come to you and you be on your way. You think I'm stupid!?" Juan shouted a bit too loud.

"He's going for broke. Chances are he won't hesitate to kill those boys." Richard whispered to Carla and Jorge. He slowly stood up and tossed a chunk of metal into the room where it clanked to the floor. Inside the room they heard Juan fire the gun.

"No!" Carla shouted. Then all hell broke loose. Richard and Jorge stormed into the office where she could hear furniture breaking and shouting.

"Amma!" It was Scotty.

"I'm here baby! Follow my voice!" Carla called out to him. "Keep coming towards me." She yanked out the penlight and turned it on. The thin beam of light shot through the dark. "You see that light? Go to it!"

The boy was crying but he soon found Carla and she grabbed him and held him close. "Shhh, now. It's alright. I've got you." She held him tight and wiped his tears from his tiny face. "Are you okay? Did he hurt you?"

"N-no. Marcos he-" Scotty began to sob.

"It's okay, baby, it's okay. Just hold onto me."

"Amma! Scotty!" It was Marcos.

"Over here Marcos!" Carla shouted, her heart pounded harder than the rain falling outside and, felt like it could jump from her chest and onto the floor. She shined the penlight again and talked to him until she could see Marcos in the beam. She hugged the boys close to her. They were not in a safe place and she needed to find somewhere to keep the children from further harm.

Carla leaned in closer to the children. "Listen, we have to leave here. It is not safe for us to stay. I am going to take you where you will be okay until the storm is over." She slowly stood up, not wanting to leave Jorge and Richard. But she could not risk the children's lives and keep them in the line of fire. She heard another gunshot. It was unclear where it came from because of the incessant pounding of wind driven rain. "You both grab a hand and do not let go of me." She felt their tiny hands slip inside hers. As fast as she dared, she ran along the wall to the door of the underground garage. When she reached for the door, a loud crash came from the office. Just as Jorge predicted, the windows on the outside wall imploded as a large branch from the tree nearest to the building fell on the roof; crushing the outer wall.

"Come on!" She shouted to the children as she opened the door. She flicked on the penlight. The thin white beam permeated a tiny fraction of the darkness leading down a small flight of stairs. She urged them down the steps with the beam of light as a guide. At the bottom, she shut off the flashlight and put it in her back pocket. It looked like they were in some kind of hallway. She could see a faint light at the end where it opened into a large room with lawn mowers and golf carts. At the end of the room were two large doors that opened to the outside. They shook in the storm's fury but so far had not pull loose from the frame. They looked sturdy which reassured Carla, but not enough to place her life on it.

"Okay, we need to find a place away from those doors." Carla pulled the flashlight back out and turned it on. She scanned the room. It was almost the entire length of the building itself. The floor was concrete and machine parts everywhere stacked in organized sections and on rows of shelves. She chose the corner farthest away from the doors and wove her way through the machinery and clutter.

She found a couple of plastic crates and a tarp then told the boys to sit down. She took the tarp and covered them then crawled inside. Confident she could navigate her way back to the stairs she gave Scotty the flashlight. "I'm going to ask you two a very important question. I have to go back upstairs. Do you think you can stay here and wait until I come back to get you?"

"Yes, Amma." Scotty told her. "I can protect Marcos."

"I can protect Scotty too!"

She knew they were scared, their faces were ashen, their eyes wide and Marcos tried not to shake. "I know this is scary. But if you stay here, you will be all right." She hugged them close to her and kissed the tops of their head. "Okay, you have the flashlight, but don't turn it on unless you have to, okay?"

They nodded their heads.

"I need to pee." Scotty stood up and began to tip toe in tiny circles.

She hadn't given it much thought, poor kids! "Hang on." She pulled the tarp away from them and searched for a bucket. She spotted a large green container; thankful it was empty and took it to the boys. "You'll have to use this buddy." She set it down outside the tarp.

He got up and went to the bathroom then crawled back under the tarp.

"Okay, I'm going to leave. You two stay here, don't go out for any reason except to pee." She hugged them tightly. "I love you both! I will be right back."

Carla glanced back at them and blew them each a kiss then made her way back up the stairs to help Richard and Jorge. She worried about Doug; she hoped he was okay. She quietly opened the door and squatted down. Then two figures rolled out of the office and onto the main room's floor.

She stood up and shouted at them hoping it would be enough to distract whoever was fighting. She heard someone grunt and crash into the lockers. Then a figure stood up. It was Juan. He started walking to where she stood. She raised the pistol Jorge had given her and pulled the trigger.

Her shot was way off but it made Juan duck giving her the opportunity to open the door and back to the children. Adrenaline coursed through Carla as she fled down the stairs and through the hallway. The room seemed a bit lighter. She could see light coming from the garage doors. She was almost to the corner where the boys hid when she heard Juan shouting in the hall. She made it to the corner and under the tarp, and put the children behind her. She aimed the pistol in front of her.

"C-Madre. I know you are here."

Her hands trembled so hard she was afraid she would drop the weapon. She tried calming down the nerves by taking deep breaths as quietly as possible. She had precious lives at stake. She could hear Juan's slow, careful steps as he walked further into the garage.

"I loved Katie. She needed me. But you had to butt in, you and your busy body whore of a sister. I killed her, she deserved more than a bullet for calling ICE. Katie with that puto? Just not gonna happen so I killed her too."

Carla tried not to let the words sting her. He was evil. There was no doubt whatsoever that he would kill her and the boys.

"You want to know how I did it? Eh?"

She heard him turning over boxes and kicking them.

"I told my sister to call Katie, I left her a hundred dollars to give her. I acted like I left and hid until Katie drove up. She should never leave a car running. Told her a hundred times bad things can happen. When she got back in, I was there in the passenger side waiting."

Carla tried to swallow the thick knot in her throat. She prayed he wouldn't reveal more details and hoped the children didn't hear him.

"Your sister-in-law Terri? Stupid nosy bitch too."

Carla pressed her back into the boys. He was getting closer.

"Too bad it wasn't you instead of her though. She was a good-looking babe."

She could hear him breathing heavily. One of the boys started to whimper and the tarp came off. Juan towered over them. His silhouette blocked out the dim light. Carla pulled the trigger but nothing happened. It had jammed.

He stood tall and aimed his pistol at her. "Good-bye C-Madre."

She squeezed again and felt the recoil slam her into the wall.

The shot rang and bounced off the walls. This was the second time she waited for the end. She prayed for forgiveness and for the boys to go to heaven. Seconds passed when she realized she wasn't hit. She opened her eyes in time to see Juan fall to the floor.

◆ ◆ ◆

"Carla!"

It was Richard. "Over here!" She shouted. She stood up and saw three figures running toward her. She noticed one of the shop's garage doors was opened and day light spilled into the front of the shop. The storm was over.

Richard ran to Carla throwing boxes off to the side as he made his way to her. "Dear God! Are you okay? How are the boys?" He held her tight.

"I'm okay. Thought I would die but, not yet." She laughed nervously. She turned to the children. "Stay here for a minute, okay guys?"

They held each other but nodded their heads, she could see tears streaming down their faces.

She broke from Richard's embrace and knelt down and hugged her grandchildren. "I love you, you both were very brave!" She kissed each one on their cheek. "Your momma would be so proud of you."

"Here." Doug came over to her and handed her a couple of candy bars and a soda. "They're probably hungry."

Carla stared at him. She was never to happy and thankful to see her little brother than now.

"Vending machine. One time I can thank a tree for almost falling on me."

She smiled at her brother and hugged him then handed the food to Scotty.

They went to where Juan's body lay on the ground. His limbs in twisted positions and a blossoming bright red spot on his shirt.

"Who shot him?"

"Jorge." Richard said squatting over the body. "He's dead. No question."

Carla turned her gaze from Juan to find Jorge. "Jorge, if you hadn't shot him, I'd be dead, and maybe the boys."

Jorge stood in the garage door opening staring out into the growing daylight. "I missed intentionally, you hit him. He fell to the floor just as I pulled the trigger. It doesn't matter now. He got what he deserved. Forever in Hell."

"I owe you."

"You owe me nothing." He told her and went outside.

Carla walked back to where the boys sat eating the candy bars. Thankfully Doug found a tarp and covered Juan's body. Richard was squatted down by Marcos trying to get him to give him a piece of his candy bar and tickling him. Doug leaned up against the wall and closed his eyes.

"What happened to Juan's man?" Carla asked him.

"Got him hog tied and gagged. It wasn't easy, but I did it. That guy had a bullet hole in his shoulder and still managed to slug me a few times. When I hit him in the wounded shoulder that made him quit fighting."

"Where is Jorge?" Richard asked as he stood up.

"I don't know he went out that door." She pointed at the opening.

"I guess we can go the same way. Maybe he's waiting for us. I'll go tell him we are on our way." Doug pulled himself from the wall. He went out the door but after a few minutes he came back inside as Carla, Richard, and the children were about to walk out into the open.

"He's gone. But just to warn you, it's like World War Three hit."

They walked far enough out to see tree branches scattered everywhere, and only twisted stumps of former graceful giants remained. The building was caved in on the front from the large Oak, twisted strips of sheet metal laying on the ground and debris scattered everywhere. It was hard to tell where the road had been because of the damage from the hurricane. They could still see clouds scuttling across the sky, and the wind blew bits of paper across the ground. Carla looked up and saw a few birds flying off toward La Paz and wondered where they had hidden during the storm. Jorge was nowhere to be seen.

CHAPTER THIRTY

After a couple of weeks, Carla was allowed to take her grandchildren home. During that time, she and Richard gave their statements and listen to the children tell their story. It was determined that Juan had taken them unknowingly against their will. The Mexican authorities had been working with the FBI to find and capture Juan and his death it made things a little easier for everyone.

◆ ◆ ◆

Carla walked with Doug into the airport terminal. After the hurricane was over it was impossible to get a flight out of La Paz, but after a week of cleaning off debris from the heavily damaged runways, some flights were running. Doug purchased a ticket to San Diego, California from there he would take a small commuter plane to Tuscon. He and Carla went to the section where Doug's plane was scheduled to take off and sat down in large black chairs. "So, you're sure about this? I mean going to Gila Bend?" Carla asked him as she unscrewed the cap from a bottle of water.

"Yeah, I left Gina with Lilly and since I've got another week of vacation to blow, might as well drive back."

"I understand. I worry about you."

He looked at her. "Why is that?"

"You haven't really said much about the whole thing."

"There's not much to say sis. We came, we saw, we conquered."

They sat there in silence for a few moments longer. When the PA crackled announcing his flight, they stood up.

"I love you little brother." She said and hugged him careful not to squeeze his left arm too tight since it was in a sling. When the tree crashed into the office, a piece of metal cut his bicep. The doctor told him as he stitched him up, he'd have a helluva scar, and a great story to go with it. "I can't thank you enough for what you've done."

"Glad I was able to help. It's been an experience, no doubt about that." He chuckled.

Carla rolled her eyes and laughed. "Once in a lifetime."

She watched him until he went through the security gate and into the hall toward the plane. Then turned and walked to the entrance where Richard and her grandchildren were waiting for them in the SUV.

They were a hot news item when they landed in Little Rock. Carla's story was being told on the local news stations in her home state and several morning talk shows wanted an interview. All she wanted to do was get home and pick up the pieces.

It was close to a month since she'd left her home, and it tore her pieces emotionally. So many memories came flooding through when she opened the door she nearly broke down and cried. Katie, Abbey, and Teri. She ushered the boys in who were happy and excited to be back home.

"Hey! Here's my truck!" Scotty shouted from his bedroom.

"Here's my soccer ball!" Marcos bellowed.

I'll just have to make new memories. Carla thought as she walked to the bedroom and watched them as they rediscovered their belongings. She leaned against the door frame and smiled at them. They were safe and happy. The one thing that concerned her was the long term effect it would have on the boys. So far, they hadn't shown any signs of distraught, but now they were back where they belonged, she wondered if they would think about what had happened. It was possible she would have to find someone who could help them through the process and understand what they went through.

The telephone ringing snapped her out of her thought. She answered it before it went to voice recording. "Hello?"

"Hey, heard you were back in town."

"Hey Matt. How are you doing?"

"I'm good, girls are doing good all things considered. We had Teri's memorial service two weeks ago."

"I'm sorry I wasn't here."

"No need to be sorry." He told her. There was a pause, Carla thought he'd hung up or something was wrong with the phone line. It had an issue whenever it rained, making the phone line crackle. "Uncle Joe called me last week."

"Oh? I haven't talked to him since mom passed away, three years ago. I thought he was mad because she wanted cremation instead of a casket. He definitely was against it."

"I remember. Look, I wanted you to know that he's thinking about selling his property and I'm seriously thinking about buying it."

"That's nearly a stone's throw from the Louisiana border."

"Yeah, since I'm family he's making me a deal. I help keep up the land with him and he'll do a rent to own option. That way, it stays in the family. He's just too old to keep up with it by himself. So, I told him I'd think about it and give him a call in a day or two."

"Well, what about the girls? They've lived here all their lives."

"I talked to them about it after talking to Uncle Joe. They think it would be great living on a farm. I think it would be good for them too. They can learn how to milk cows and feed hogs."

"He's still doing that?" Carla was surprised. Uncle Joe was in his eighties but the last she remembered of him he was spry and clear headed. Maybe farm life would be good for Matt and his daughters.

"I'd miss you, but I understand. Hey, that means I can bring down the boys and stay for a week or so during the summer. They would get a kick out of that."

"That would be a great idea. Well, I wanted to throw out the thought to you and get your opinion."

"I think you should do it Matt."

A month later, Matt and his two daughters piled into a U-Haul moving van loaded down with their possessions, including their two-year-old Chihuahua, Pico. Carla watched from the driveway of her brother's former home as he pulled onto Highway 62 and toward Southern Arkansas; waving at them until the van disappeared over the hill.

◆ ◆ ◆

Katie's story appeared one last time on a documentary about domestic abuse and the heart wrenching death of Katie, and how Carla searched for her grandsons. Once more she talked about the pain and suffering people go through during a domestic violence crisis and hoped more would be done to kill this crippling disease. She cheered when Arkansas passed "Katie's Law" which would help those who needed to get away from an abusive relationship geared toward women and men alike when it involved children.

She sat watching the show when her cell phone rang. It showed the caller as Charli. "Hey sweetheart! How's law school?"

"Hi mom. It's grueling. I called because I have some bad news."
Carla drew in her breath. Not again. Not one of her kids.

"Dad's been found. He was in Mexico. He was shot several times behind an old building way off the highway."

"I'm sorry honey." Now she knew he'd been following her. It explained the odd circumstances after leaving her children in Dallas with the journals. She wasn't really surprised that it was him.

"I don't know what to do. I mean, I was upset with him lying to us all those years, but-"

"I know, I know. Does anyone know how it happened?" She felt sad for her kids. They were his children too and they did love him.

"No, I haven't heard anything. He's getting shipped back and should be here by Friday. I already made arrangements for the funeral home to pick him up. I requested closed casket because the officer who called me said he suggested that or cremation. I guess it was bad. He'd been dead for some time."

Carla sighed and wiped the tears from her eyes. At one time she had loved Hugh. She felt a sadness for him she didn't realize she had locked inside. "I'll be there Wednesday." Carla was not going to let them bury their father by themselves. When she hung up the phone Jorge came to her and she wondered if he had anything to do with it. She thought about calling him but she didn't think he would answer if she did. She picked up her phone and scrolled though the list of names. She let the phone ring several times and when the person answered the phone, they didn't know anyone named Jorge LaNaya.

◆ ◆ ◆

Carla's children stood by her as they watched the casket lower into the ground. She thought about bringing the boys, but this was not the time to introduce them to her aunt and uncles. They were more than happy to hang out with Richard and Haley for a few days.

Carla made plans to get together with her children for Thanksgiving and Christmas. They had their lives in Texas. Lawrence had met a girl and it looked like there could be a wedding to plan in the near future. Carla couldn't wait to meet her in November. Roger had been accepted into Texas A & M and was shooting for a degree in Chemical Engineering. There was no disagreement when she told them they would not ever be separated again. Anytime they wanted to come visit their mother, they could. Anytime they wanted to call her, all they had to do was call. When the backhoe operator started his machine to fill in the grave, they left.

Carla packed the last of her belongings into the back of her van. It was a Chrysler Pacifica, perfect for carrying two growing boys and their gear back and forth to games. A year had passed since Mexico. After a few sessions with a grievance counselor, they seemed to understand what had happened. They never did have nightmares. That one Carla didn't understand. There were times she woke up drenched in sweat, her heart racing because she thought she'd heard a noise. There were times she thought she'd seen Juan in a car, but she knew that was not so. He was dead. She'd seen the bullet hole.

The children were happy, and excited about the move and gaining a cousin. Plus, the town near Uncle Joe's farm, had a great school system and a soccer curriculum. The Principal was more than happy to have the children get into the program.

◆ ◆ ◆

When Richard proposed to Carla, they were at his house cooking hamburgers. Matt and the girls had come back to get more things from the storage unit. At least that was the reason her brother told her when he showed up. Doug, Wayne, and even Beth was there. She was especially surprised when her three children showed up. When everyone was seated at the table and munching on burgers, potato salad, and coleslaw, Richard stood up and pulled Carla up from the table. Everyone stopped talking and set their utensils down. She looked at her brothers. Something was up, they both had huge silly grins, and so did everyone else.

"Carla, when I first met you, it wasn't under the best of circumstances. But we got to know each other. I knew that if we were able to make it through Mexico, we could endure anything. I just know that I love you," Richard pulled out a small box from behind a potted plant and everyone laughed.

"If I'd have known that was there, I'd have re-hidden it!" Doug shouted. "Just kidding!"

Everyone laughed then Richard got down on one knee and asked Carla to marry him.

"Do it Amma!" Scotty shouted.

Carla cried when she said yes and let him place the ring on her finger.

Richard came from behind and hugged her. "You ready?"

She had never been more ready. She turned around and faced her husband. "Are you ready to be a farmer?"

He kissed her. "Never been more ready for anything in my life." He looked over Carla's head and watched Haley, Marcos, and Scotty chasing each other around the yard.

Carla climbed into the passenger seat of the van after making sure the kids were secured in their seats. She stared at the house she'd lived in for many years. There had been many wonderful times; Birthdays, holidays, but there had been too much sorrow in the now vacant home. She smiled when the young couple with two children were buying the home pulled into the driveway to see them off. He was Richard's replacement as the school resource officer, and his wife was a fifth-grade teacher. Carla hoped they would have many happy times living in their new home. She turned and waved to the young family then closed the door.

As they drove out of Green Valley, she turned back and watched the town disappear. She felt a pang of sorrow but then Carla remembered what Doug said before he boarded the plane in La Paz. "In order to make new memories sometimes you have to make a new road."

NOTE: In reference to "Katie's Law" it is fictious.

ABOUT THE AUTHOR

Connie Clark

Connie Clark started writing short stories when she was thirteen. She credits her father, who was also a writer, a love for the craft and a passion for reading. Throughout her school life she wrote short stories and poems several of which were published in school newsletters.

One thing she credits to her active imagination is her life experiences. Her family moved quite often, finally settling down in the Ozarks. After moving out on her own she continued to gain knowledge from life's ups and downs to which she puts into her writing.

She got an opportunity to write articles for her employer's complex newspaper until it dissolved in 2002. In October of 2020 she retired from her job of 35 years and in August of 2021 after living in the same home for 32 years, it was time to sell and move on.

Two years later she and her husband found their forever home in Northwest Arkansas on Bull Shoals Lake.

Currently Connie has several novel projects in the works with plans to publish them in the near future. She also has several short stories she plans to publish as a collection of short stories she's written throughout the years.

REFERENCES

https://hernorm.com/obsessive-ex-syndrome/http://www.lilaclane.com/
oex/

https://www.tdcaa.com/journal

2019 Annual Report on International Child Abduction

https://travel.state.gov

https://www.americanimmigrationcouncil.orghttps:/https://
    www.migrationpolicy.org/pubs/287g-divergence.pdf

news/releases/ice-announces

    https://www.cato.org

    https://www.justice.gov/jm/jm-9-15000

ACKNOWLEDGEMENT

FOR MORE INFORMATION ABOUT DOMESTIC VIOLENCE AND SPOUSAL ABUSE THERE ARE WEB SITES AND PHONE NUMBERS LISTED BELOW.

National Domestic Violence Hotline

PO Box 90249

Austin, Texas 78709

Administrative Line: 737-225-3150

https://www.thehotline.org

https://www.domesticpeace.com   (Arkansas)

https://www.verywellmind.com

How to Prevent Domestic Violence & Child Abuse - Child Abuse 2022 | US Legal Forms

https://www.helpguide.org/articles/abuse/domestic-violence-and-abuse.htm

https://ncadv.org/learn-more

Made in the USA
Columbia, SC
05 March 2023

13350451R10120